LORD BENNETT OF ASHWOOD HALL

Heal Thyself

M. A. Grant

Heal Thyself

M. A. Grant

Copyright by M.A Grant and associates, 2025

First edition June 2025

ISBN: 979-8-9910972-4-6 [Paperback]

Illustrations and design by M. A. Grant

This is a work of fiction. Resemblances to specific people, places, or organisations are purely coincidental.

ALL RIGHTS RESERVED. For more information, reach out to gma.mb.co@gmail.com

FOREWORD

Mrs. Alma (Webb) Bennett co-authored her memoir with her associate Grant Abernathy, under the pseudonym M. A. Grant.

Mrs. Bennett is a most peculiar figure both in life and fiction, and Grant Abernathy's attempts to sanitise her character do not go unnoticed. Her personal accounts, while potentially entertaining, should not be considered an example of upright moral standing and poise; they are almost too indecent for polite society. She is perhaps influenced by the lax and dissolute younger generations, a common hazard for those in her position. We have found many of her sentiments to be unwomanly, unpatriotic, and potentially inciting rebellion, and at such a tumultuous time in our history. Abernathy's foray into anti-war journalism may have influenced her, and though she is entitled to her beliefs, we caution the reader to take her message with a grain of salt.

*For Michael A. G. Bennett; for my children;
for you, dearest reader; for myself.*

My dear reader,

I am Alma T. Bennett. You surely know me as the meek and elusive Alma Webb, from Grant Abernathy's book *Lord Bennett Of Ashwood Hall*. It is with great joy and bittersweet gratitude that I might share my life with you, as a woman, a nurse, a mother, and a wife.

I would also address the strange rumours about Grant Abernathy and me, a fire which will undoubtedly be stoked by our shared pseudonym. For some reason, it has been circulating that he and I are involved in a more than friendly way; in the first place, what a flippant thing to suggest! Secondly, there is nothing illicit between the two of us. We are as dear as friends can be, and that is the end of it. Michael called him his brother, and I consider him mine. That aside, Grant and I both have no desire to remarry. His amorous— nearly scandalous descriptions of me are from my husband's writing, and had already been considerably distilled to be palatable for all readers. It could not be helped that Michael found me irresistible from the start.

It was Autumn who begged Grant to write about her father. His book is derived from Michael Bennett's extensive journals, which he acquired with my permission, but not before I pulled out the entries that I considered too personal for anyone else's eyes. It is a mostly accurate account of his life, but many liberties have been taken. I cannot fault him for that, as the goal of an author is to spin a compelling narrative, and of course, there are some details he had to fabricate when he was unsure. I have read every draft, and he sought my approval every step of the way. Truthfully, Grant, Michael, and I all three authored the book. That being said, if I feel that something must be cleared up or addressed, I will do so to the best of my knowledge. And if you are not familiar with any of these names, then I shall be more than happy to tell you all about them, though I cannot recommend the original material enough! I say, you should read *Lord Bennett Of Ashwood Hall*, take a few days to digest it, and come back.

Reading Grant's book was something of a spiritual pilgrimage for me. First, let me say that it is an honour to have been portrayed by him. I saw myself plain as day in his writing, and reflected upon my youth. Figures of my past had been brought back to life. Moreover, I saw myself through Michael's eyes— and Grant's pen, of course.

I will try to explain everything in chronological order, though my mind wanders these days.

OF THE WEBBS AND THE CONNORS

I was born into an ordinary country life, to a
small middle class family, in 1869. There is just
my brother and me. I was the last, because Mama
could not have any more children after me.
Sometimes, I wondered if she was mad at me for
this. She always said she wanted three or four, but
also, "one of each is good enough for me."

The life of a common rural labourer is not easy,
but simple:

Women marry, make puddings, and keep having
babies until we die. Men sire our children and toil
away in the fields until their bodies break down,
and then the children take our place. We submit
to the Sisyphusian doldrums of life until death
finally takes us. And I was fine with living that
way.

The details of my parents are much softer in
Grant's book. He was only writing what he could
see, and Michael did not know them as I did.

For the most part, he saw them as very pleasant
and hard-working people, and indeed, they were.
There was also far more than that.

My mama, Ellen Beatrice Connor, was born in
London to Irish immigrants, in 1843. My `
grandmother Helen was fifteen when she ran

away with my grandfather Elisha Connor, who
was eighteen years her senior. Elisha was her
father's hired man, and he took her to England
without her parents' knowledge. Their first child,
my aunt Eliana, was born right before they
married, and they lived in one room. The others
are Ellen, Erinn, Elisabeth, Eileen, and Diana—
yes, there were six, not five, and two stillbirths.
Diana drowned before she was a year old.

Mama told me about it ever since I was three, any
time I was near the smallest body of water. Diana
climbed into the wash tub when Helen had passed
out from exhaustion while washing. She fell and
could not right herself, and drowned quickly and
quietly with linens on her face, before anyone
noticed. Eliana shook and screamed Helen awake,
and the hysterics spread to the rest of the inmates.
When Elisha came home, he beat and berated the
lot of them for not keeping an eye on the baby he
didn't even want, including little Eileen, who was
only four.

I never met Elisha, but nobody had anything good
to say about him, except Eliana. He was always
drunk and could not keep a job for very long,
which he blamed on his Irish background, and
took this feeling of injustice out on his girls. He
frequently held Helen's face over a hot stove
when she incurred his wrath, and forced her to
keep having babies in the hopes of producing a
son, but complained about the many mouths to

feed. After Diana's birth, he swore that the next girl presented to him would be thrown into the Thames. Eliana was his favourite, being the firstborn. That favour gradually diminished down the line, and likely would have continued to decrease until he obtained his prized male heir.

Fate checked him before that happened. It was found out that he had an intact marriage in Ireland, and was arrested for bigamy, on top of the debts that he'd fled to England in an attempt to escape. He died in prison before my mother became an adult.

Helen was almost equally unpleasant. I never saw much of her, because she wanted little to do with me, and she was always quarrelling with her daughters— sometimes escalating to violence. I suppose the strain she was under drove her mad. We knew it, and we pitied her… from a distance.

She had neglected to teach her girls many things about grooming and hygiene. They taught themselves how to brush their hair, and all had to learn about their bodies through their own experiences, which is how Erinn was surprised with my cousin Sarah. Nobody but God knows who her father is.

Still, Helen worked several jobs in order to keep the children in school until they were at least twelve. By the time my mother was fourteen,

Helen remarried, to a banker named Benjamin
Howard, a widower with two sons. He was
friendly to Helen's daughters, and actually took
more interest in the grandchildren than she did.
Sarah was Helen's favourite grandchild, possibly
even the only one she liked— after all, with no
man claiming paternity, there was no outside
force to interfere in her clan.

In her adolescence, my mother was a tomboy
who was quick with her fists, but she loved fine
clothes, which she had very little of while
growing up. She avidly collected fashion plates
for most of her life, some of which decorated the
walls of her home for decades to come. I was told
that she'd taken apart and remade the same dress
seven times in ten years.

When she turned nineteen, she took up work as a
seamstress, and began to attend a girl's college,
paying for her tuition one stitch at a time. She
was the first lady in my family to go to college,
but she was not there for long, because then she
met my father.

Henry Titus Webb was the youngest of four
children, born in 1838, to fairly wealthy farmers
in Yorkshire. The oldest is Sophia, an aunt who is
doting, but puts on airs. His father was Ronald
Ernest Webb, a minister, and Margaret Marie
Baker-Webb was the perfect housewife, or at least
made sure everyone saw her that way. My father

began preaching in his hometown, yet saw medicine as his calling. Against Margaret's wishes, but with Ronald's blessing, he went to London and studied day and night to become a physician at twenty-one, then joined the military to work as a surgeon for three years.

He had many wondrous stories to tell about his travels, but truthfully, he was deeply ashamed of his military service, believing he was manipulated. In his opinion, Britain's wars were unChristian, and not nearly as noble as they were painted to entice men to enlist. They planted him in India, and some high-ranking officers forbid him to treat them with the same tools he'd used on a native.

While he was there, he met and befriended Samuel Bennett, a very young officer of noble birth, and the eventual father of Michael Bennett. This would be his only contribution to society. More on that later.

The disillusioned Henry Webb returned to London at twenty-five and met my mother, who was of course twenty. They married in his parents' house within only two months of meeting, and remained in London until shortly before I was born.

Some of his relatives disapproved of the union, due in part to my mother's Irish background.

They viewed the Connors as brash, proudly uneducated drunkards who had too many children. I'm sorry to say that some of them did not disappoint. I suppose when you are told that you are one specific thing all of your life, you either defy it for all you're worth, or begin to believe it yourself.

In turn, many of Mama's relatives didn't like the Webbs. Helen especially hated Papa because she believed he made her abandon her Catholic roots— not so; it was her choice.

The Connors were quick to punish, but not to guide or correct, yet unmatched in affection when they *wanted* to be sweet. The Webbs as a whole were agreeable people who were slow to anger and patient to discipline, but not very affectionate at all. Both were unyielding in their approach, believing it to be the best for all children. In my wee little girl brain, I thought these were the only two ways to raise a child.

Likewise, Papa was very patient, but a cold father. He worked hard and was friendly, but rarely had time for us. He was not a warm and comforting person, even though you knew he was a good enough man who wanted the best for you. At least, you could usually count on him to be stable and consistent. I think he allowed himself only three or four strong emotional reactions per year, good or bad. Mama claimed that the only two times he had ever cried were when my brother and I were born. When I asked what she sought in him to begin with, she said that he had "a cool head about him."

Well, he did when he was sober.

The real reason she made him give up day drinking was because though he functioned and continued to provide, he often shouted when he was drunk. When he drank, everything was a big deal, and he yelled passionately as if he was delivering a powerful fire and brimstone sermon— over something as small as a chipped glass. I think it reminded Mama of her father.

My earliest memory of him drinking is maybe when I was four or five.

It was about ten o'clock, and I left my room for a sip of water. Mama always told me never to leave my room at night if I smelled alcohol. This warning rang in my ears and chilled my blood, but I tiptoed onward, led to the kitchen by a faint lamp.

He was bent over a newspaper. His eyes were very red, and I felt that if I looked into them, I would be burned.

"It's horrid," he mumbled. "It almost makes one regret bringing children into this world."

"You regret having us?" I asked, as my tiny brain could not understand nuance yet.

"No, no," he sighed, swirling his beverage around. "I say, you are the last hope for the world— you and your brother. You are too bright and too good for this life. They will not understand you, and will despise you for telling the truth, exactly as they did with Christ himself. They don't understand our intellect. Hellfire! They are destined for hellfire, all of them! All must repent: even you, if you want to be spared!"

I trembled and shrank into the doorway.

He smiled, and set down the glass, and his flaming red eyes were not quite so frightening.

"What is it that you wanted, child?"

"Nothing," I lied, though my mouth was so dry that my teeth stuck to my lips.

"Then why are you out of bed?" he leaned forward, and in that single gesture, my little body sensed danger.

"I'm thirsty. I want some water," I confessed.

"Well, that's all you had to say!" he stood very suddenly, and made a series of robotic movements throughout the kitchen, and he finally produced a glass of cool water.

"Drink," he ordered, and though I no longer wanted it, I was compelled to drink the entire glass standing right there.

"Back to sleep, then," he took the glass from me and steered me towards the hall. My unshod feet glided over the polished wood floor with that last push into the darkness.

The next thing I remember is the cold as Mama snatched the linens off of me and scolded me for wetting the bed. The verbal lashing continued to the dining table, and Papa said nothing to her nor I, possibly incapacitated by his headache, with his nose in a mug of burnt coffee.

I was told that alcohol does not change you, and it is not laced with demons, but merely brings out all of the parts of you that you repress— and I believe it. When Mama got drunk (this rarely happened— I only saw it once), she cursed her mother's name and wished she was never born. When Papa got drunk, it surfaced his fierce and unrelenting drive to correct anything he thought was wrong. As for my husband… he was probably more sober drunk than dry.

My brother James never touched alcohol.

When no longer permitted to drink to excess,
Papa began smoking. Mama smoked, too.
Sometimes, he would whistle as he blew smoke
through the big gap in his front teeth, and say he
was a train. When I was five years old, it was the
funniest thing in the world!

After my parents separated, Mama moved to the
next town, and James and I were passed between
the two of them. We spent most of our time with
her.

Am I angry about my father's adultery? I did not
comprehend it until I was maybe nine or ten. I
suppose I was disappointed in his conduct, but it
did not affect how he functioned as a parent, so I
did not hold it against him. It was between him
and my mother— and God.

I grew up with two mothers— or at least, that's
how it felt when I was very young.
Subconsciously, I split her into two people. My
mother went through many periods of great stress
when I was growing up, because a seamstress
was not in high demand out in the country; every
woman who had the money knew how to sew,
anyway. She went to a larger town to do laundry
and any sewing work she could take, and she
came home late and quite vexed. If I was in her
path when that happened, she would often find
some way to vent that fury on me. I remember
vividly when I was about nine years old: I was

trying to quietly make myself a cup of tea early in the morning, and I dropped my cup, not knowing that she was coming downstairs as I did it. She shouted at me, because I had no respect for her things, and I couldn't do anything right. I was bent over to pick up the pieces when she started shouting, but she sent me outside to clean up the mess herself, since she did everything around the house, anyway.

And when I came back in maybe an hour later, she was gay as a songbird, asking if I wanted to go pick berries with her! It was as if she had no recollection of her previous moods, and when they were mentioned to her, she always insisted they were not as bad as I made them out to be, so now, I'm really not sure anymore. All I know is that I was always vigilant.

When she was in an agreeable mood, I was an angel who held the family together. When she was at her worst, so was I; I could either do no right by her, or no wrong.

Associates never saw these two halves of her, for she was a master at composing herself for company— almost as if she was not two, but three people. I always wondered how she did it, but soon I had to mimic her. I could not afford to show weakness or shed tears, or she would interrogate me, and judge for herself whether I cried with good reason.

She often told me that I was too "soft," and that
fear and distress were a natural part of life; I'd
accepted that as the truth, but I believed that my
mother was supposed to be my one refuge from
such things— for that was what she called
herself.

For a long time, I could never be sure whether
she would breathe fire or smother me. I had to
keep my head down and read the room in order to
protect myself, but sometimes it wasn't enough. It
was difficult to reconcile these strange feelings. I
felt that to feel safe, I had to reject both of my
mothers.

By twelve years old, I had begun to withdraw
from her, little bits at a time. I began to tell her
less and less about my day, and merely tolerated
her caresses.

In later years, she had tempered, but it was too
late. She was a stranger to me, and for as long as
she would not acknowledge the past, I could not
revert back to a loving daughter. With that, came
a great feeling of guilt. It was impossible for me
to honour my mother.

After I spent a lot of time at my father's house, I
felt like a guest when I returned to my mother's,
and the inverse also applied.

My father was decent enough, but he was not equipped to understand, and unbeknownst to him, I was aware of the wedge of animosity driven between my parents from a young age. I felt that to voice my suffering would drive it deeper, and then I would have been a traitor. Worse yet, if he was intoxicated, his reply was a sermon about the child's place in the household: seen, and not heard. Meanwhile, I ventured to be neither.

It was a tough position, to be so afraid of being noticed, yet inwardly crying out to be acknowledged. I knew it wasn't fair to expect people to know what I was thinking, so I submitted myself to suffer for many years—needlessly, I would soon learn. The behaviour you take on to adapt to a tempestuous environment does not serve you so well in calmer waters.

For all that time, I had nobody to tell these things to, and kept them inside. They pricked me, like bits of broken glass sticking through a bag, because they had nowhere to go.

Since both of my parents worked much of the day, I was often left at home with James, and I was a rebellious, angry child. If I tried to go places he didn't want me to, he would snatch me by my braids, or mash me onto the floor until I stopped squirming. Again, it was difficult to tell anyone. Mama never quite believed it, because he

didn't leave any marks, but I did when I scratched
him to make him let go of me, so I was lashed for
starting fights. Yes, it was wrong to scratch him,
but I thought he should have gotten *some* form of
punishment. The most Mama did was absently
mumble, "James, be careful when you play with
your sister. She's smaller than you."

"He's not playing!" I protested.

"Well, he didn't hurt you, did he?" Mother asked.

No, it usually didn't hurt, but the terror of being
restrained was worse than any bruises he could
have given me, especially because he always told
me that he wouldn't let go of me unless I shut my
trap and stopped wailing.

One day, when I was ten, and James was
scrubbing the stove with a blacking brush, I
approached and asked him if I could go outside,
as I'd finished my chores.

"No," he huffed. "I'm not finished."

"You're doing it sloppily," I noted. "It will never
be finished before Mama gets home, and she'll
tan your hide, like she said."

(She had said that because she'd finally caught on
to the fact that I was doing most of his chores, not
him).

"I'll most definitely never be finished if you keep distracting me! Go sit somewhere quietly! Read a book, if you possess the mental capacity."

"It's almost dark out! Hurry up! How did I finish all of my chores while you're still on the stove?" I whined and stamped my feet like the little brat I was.

"I said go somewhere else!" James whipped around and threw the brush. Its blackened whiskers caught me right on my forehead, and then it clattered onto the floor.

It didn't hurt right away, yet I fumed with anger.

James stammered something, but by then, I'd already petulantly ran and locked myself up in my chamber. Now that he couldn't see me, I cried. He insisted he was sorry and that he wanted me to come out so that he could wash my face. I refused— I wanted to preserve the evidence that he was the aggressor. I waited until I could no longer hear him shaking the door, and very quietly, I opened my window and spilled out onto the grass. I waited to be pursued, but to my surprise, nobody came.

I crept out to the stream to soak my feet and think nasty things about my brother. The scrape of the

brush gradually began to sting, and it bled a lot
for a shallow wound.

When you are so young, everything is a big deal,
and you are the centre of the universe. Like the
tragic heroine in Greek theatre, I wept and
moaned about how I hated my entire family, and
myself, and wished I was dead, then I felt terrible
for even giving voice to these thoughts, because
none of it was true. I just wanted to be anywhere
other than in that house.

Until the sun set, I fancied myself carried away
by little sprites, to a field of dandelions that never
ran out of their fluff, under a warm, eternal
sunrise. Cats' whiskers tickled my nose, and
nothing hurt, or ever would again.

I was rudely shaken from my foolish dream when
I slipped on wet moss and nearly plunged into the
water, to an early grave. I would be punished
severely if I was caught being out at night,
especially sneaking away from my brother's
supervision, so I gathered up my shoes and ran
back to the house.

It took all of my strength to climb back through
that window before my mother came inside.

Judging by her pleased tone, he must have
finished his work, and done it well.

Hesitantly, I came out of my room, wondering how I would be received. Mama sprinkled kisses over my face, and asked about the scrape. I looked at James, who appeared apprehensive, and I was *almost* tempted to lie, but I could not think of a convincing cover.

"James threw a brush," I blurted out.

I thought I'd have been pleased when he was finally put in his place, but passing him in the hallway knowing that he'd been berated just did not sit well within me— especially when he stung me with that icy, accusatory stare.

I don't know what happened to him, but after that, he meekly requested my compliance whenever our mother was away. He still shouted when I didn't obey, but would not set his hands on me. I was much more pliant when he asked nicely. If I did something that displeased him, he only shouted instead of swinging at me.

If you'd asked either of them years later, they'd insist it didn't happen. It is sometimes difficult to keep up with how much of my childhood is real or not.

My father remained cool and uninvolved, as always. Somehow, these outbursts never happened at his house. I could not tell him, in case it got back to my mother. Overall, I could not decide whether I hated her temper or his indifference more.

He did pay for my eyeglasses, and they cost quite a bit back then. I was about thirteen and starting to feel conscious about my appearance, so I passively voiced that I thought I looked nicer without them.

This was a fatal error. He was in some sort of mood, and snatched them off of my face and began shouting and swearing at me about the evils of vanity— vanity was worldly and stupid, and I was not stupid, was I? He demanded to know, because if I was, he would discard them and make me pay him for the money he wasted, because I was lucky that he had not yet put me to work at my age. After all, if I wanted to speak like a grown *foolish* woman, I could toil away like one.

I answered that I was not stupid, and this cooled his wrath. He must have spent his allowance for passion in that moment, because he peacefully handed them back and was docile for the rest of the season.

Now that I am retelling all of it, there was no peace to be found with either of my parents.

Still, either house was better than when we stayed with Aunt Erinn. I liked her. She was sweet, but too permissive, and didn't like to disappoint anybody. She was not the problem. I liked some of her eight children, but a handful of them were completely without guidance. Indeed, she'd had more of them than she knew what to do with. She had Sarah with an unknown man, three with her first (deceased) husband, and four with the second. Those first four were well-behaved, for the most part.

Emerson was the second child, the first boy, and he was six years older than me. He never picked up a job or any particular skill, and rarely spoke. Aunt Erinn called him "a little silly," and "a bit slower than other boys his age." He was my mother's favourite, because he was quiet and helpful when she was around.

Starting when I was about ten or eleven, he took a particular interest in me. That was a confusing age for me, as many rapid changes were happening inside and out, and I did not fully understand them. Well, Emerson must have noticed them. Usually, I'd be out fetching water, collecting the washing, or handling the linens—something by myself. The very first time it happened, I suspected nothing, and gladly went to help him make his bed, as he asked.

This particular incident, he stood back and watched me stoop down over the corners of the bed, and told me I was very pretty. I thought nothing of it, but then as I was finishing, he came up behind me and grabbed my empty hand. His hand was damp and I hated the feeling, and I excused myself to go do other chores and slipped out before he could answer. I felt very sick, and I did not know why.

"Alma!" my mother called to me when she saw me later. "Emerson says you didn't want to play with him! You love playing with your cousins! What's the matter?"

"I'm tired from being out in the hot sun," I said.

After that, I shook off the feeling, believing it was just my imagination, and if it really did happen, it wouldn't happen again. I went to bed early, to Sarah's bed, but she wasn't home that evening. I never imagined I would have to lock the door.

When I heard the door creak very softly and heard footsteps, I assumed Sarah had come. A hand rested on my chest. It was just Sarah groping around in the dark, I was sure, but I didn't smell her orange blossom oil.

It was the distinct scent of a man, and the hand was rough.

I squirmed, and the hand withdrew. I held very still and stopped my breath. The hand came back, and the fingers reached under my gown.

I felt as though I had turned to stone. If I did not manage to move, it would soon be too late. It took all of my strength to crack the shell. Saying nothing, I sprang up and ran towards the faint light in the hall, miraculously not crashing into whatever apparition was upon me.

Mama was still awake, reading in Aunt Erinn's room (she wasn't home, either).

"Sarah's linens are so scratchy," I lied, unwilling to admit that the room was scary, as if I was a little child.

It must have been a demon, as I'd heard in church that demons sometimes tried to watch you sleep, or even perched upon your chest. To me, a demon was not as scary as the alternative, but my comforting delusion did not last long.

The next time that I was accosted, I turned around and saw a pale silhouette in the dark that could have only been him, as he was a large young man. The simpleton only dove down onto the floor, as if that would have been enough to conceal him.

Any time I lingered in bed just a little too long, it was possible that he would soon follow, and that made me wonder how far he got when I wasn't awake. I tried not to dwell on such things.

Whenever Emerson had behaved badly in some way, such as pulling Sarah's hair or looking under her friend's skirts, Mama and Aunt Erinn said, "He just doesn't know any better," which is precisely the sort of answer I'd have expected from the latter, but never the former.

I assumed they would say the exact same thing if I told them. After all, Mama would not even protect me from her own son, who was hers to correct.

Since I saw no point in saying anything, I simply tried to avoid him. Usually, it worked. Sometimes, though, I was left alone with him and the babies when the adults went out. Aunt Erinn loved how well I took care of the babies. I did this because Emerson was less likely to bother me. I couldn't always avoid him. Sometimes if nobody else was there, he'd get me from behind and paw at my clothes. Occasionally, he offered to help me take a bath. He was much stronger than I, but he usually didn't grab me too hard, so I could pull myself free and run off.

In one instance, he grabbed my apron, and I merely shed the garment. He was such a good and helpful young man for returning it to me, as I'd lost it.

I didn't always get away so easily. I had a very close call when I was thirteen.

Dearest reader, it is not for the faint of heart! Even now, it is hard to put into words, but I will spare the more unsavoury details.

This time, he was bold enough to act while little cousin Emma Louise slept at the far end of the room. He mumbled something under his breath that I could not understand, and I leaned in close.

When I did so, he snatched me by my collar, knocking me onto my back, and already had his other hand under my skirt. His fingers were so cold. My mind and body went completely stiff and numb. I only remember seeing wind blowing through the trees out the window.

But the voice in my head, which often scolded me harshly, shouted a deafening roar, *"GET UP, FOOL, GET UP!"* and that was precisely what I needed.

I had half a second to react, and I knew that I could not possibly match him in strength. The slightest misstep would seal whatever fate awaited me.

Too frightened to make a sound, my first instinct was to go limp. I became a ragdoll and fell out of his hands, and then I shot up before he realised he'd lost me, and ran for the door. I was surely raised up by the wings of an angel that day, for I had never been so light on my feet.

It was shameful to leave Emma Louise alone with him, and I still feel a prickly sensation when I remember that I did it. I acted without thinking, without feeling, and once safely outside, in the view of an elderly neighbour watering his pigs, I reasoned that surely Emerson would leave his sister be. I could have run to that old man and asked to be protected. I thought about doing it.

Still, I could tell nobody. My tongue froze when the words tried to form in my mouth. After all, I had been told that girls only got into the kind of trouble that they went out looking for.

But why me? What wrong had I been doing at thirteen? Worst of all, I feared being accused of tempting him with my maturing body.

I even had myself convinced that Emerson didn't know better, because the alternative was unthinkable. But if he didn't know better, he wouldn't have been doing it in secret. There were a lot of confusing feelings for me in those days, and another addition to the list of things I couldn't tell anyone; that is, not yet. I don't know what would have changed if I chose to speak up, but I wish I could reach into the past and tell myself that one day, I would trust somebody enough to talk (though knowing me, that would have just made me impatient). When you become a mother, you want to protect all children, even your younger self.

From then on, whenever I visited Aunt Erinn, I was always either outside or with the grown ladies, who now thought I was old enough to partake in their congress.

Even before then, I was outside a lot. At a very young age, I saw the outdoors as a shelter from inside the uneasy houses and their suffocating walls. After school, I would delay going in for as long as I could. Outside was full of endless treasures; the creek produced smooth, shining stones, and birds left brilliant feathers for me to collect. Chains of wildflowers were my jewels, and I was the queen of my domain. My imagination ran free, and so did I. I took off my bonnet and took down my hair— it was right that I enjoyed that freedom while it lasted, because by the time womanhood was upon me, I had retreated back into my hats and veils, both dreading and hoping to be seen. I must admit, that even now, it is nice to let my hair stream in the wind once in a while. By that age, I had to set an example for Ida.

I was maybe seven years old when Ida was born. Almost immediately, she was my pet. After all, somebody had to pay attention to her. My Aunt

Elisabeth gave her the minimum that she needed to survive, and then left her to her own devices. Elisabeth was tolerable as long as she was sedated. When her husband died shortly after her birth, she was given laudanum in order to function, and she barely functioned at that. Mama was already stressed enough, so I could not bring myself to tell her about this problem, and tried to take it up on my own.

I think all of the adults knew, and stayed quiet so that it did not become their business, as they often do.

I loved Ida as if she were my own child, but I had my limits. There were some things that I did not know how to teach her, and whenever she was present, I did not have a moment to myself. The adults commented on how well I got along with my little cousin, but I felt I had no choice; being conditioned by that time to be as far out of the way as possible, I could not complain.

The burden fell upon me to teach her about certain lady things, which I was not thrilled to do. Mama made sure that I was aware from a young age, because she wasn't, and learned the hard way when she ruined her good church dress.

I thought ten was a good enough age to learn, but telling her the basic, most important things opened up many other questions I could not brave answering myself, so I sent her to my mother and told her to ask away: which caused her to seek Aunt Eliana, then Aunt Erinn, then my father, and then she came back to me.

She also inherited all of the clothes that I grew out of, including gloves, petticoats, and corsets.

Back then, not too terribly long ago, ladies did not wear brassieres, as our corsets went up over our breasts— indeed, they looked much different than they do now. I did not have a real woman's corset until I was seventeen, because we couldn't afford it. I was excited to have it, even though it was my mother's from before she started having babies. It was not the fashionable shape at the time, but I appreciated it nonetheless, as my first step into womanhood. By the time I was eighteen, I bought one for myself. The old one was too small by then. In those days, we wanted to amplify our shape. I am glad that my daughter grew up before the obsession with being as straight as a set of drapes, for she has a naturally strong and sturdy physique that she is proud of.

Ida didn't like the corset I gave her, because it wasn't pretty and didn't give her a *"smart and hygienic, yet enviable form."*

I don't know where she learned that. She must have read it in an advertisement. I told her not to be concerned with such things, as comfort was most important.

Ever since she could walk, she began to follow me to Papa's house. He took to her quite fast, and allowed her to come and go as she pleased from then on.

In doing just that, she introduced me to Michael Ashley Bennett, of Ashwood Hall— brought him straight to me.

MICHAEL BENNETT, MOTHS, AND MY
GREAT FORTUNE WITH MEN

There is no greater testament to divine destiny,
than to gaze upon a person you've never seen
before in the flesh, and to whisper inwardly,
'Here you are! I have been looking for you.'

That must have been how Michael felt when he
met me.

Our fathers knew each other during their time in
the military, but I'd never seen him. For all of my
life, they corresponded only in writing. All I
knew of him was that he lived up north and had a
son, and finding him in my kitchen one morning
reminded me of how small the world truly was.

Right away, I saw he was a very big man, both in
stature and especially in breadth. This was Lord
Bennett? I didn't imagine a nobleman would be so
large. One typically expected them to have a
graceful form. He was awkward and dishevelled,
but clearly making an attempt to be stately.

Allow me to paint a picture in your mind's eye:
the ideal man of the day. He has a fair and even
complexion, and smooth hair on his head. His
facial hair is neat. His eyes are large and relaxed,
with full lashes and a perfectly pencilled brow,
and his mouth is rosy and well-formed, below a
straight nose. When he smiles, he reveals a good,

straight and shining set of teeth. His form is slender and athletic, with elegantly sloping shoulders, and his posture is impeccable.

This was not Michael Bennett.

Nothing about him was conventionally beautiful, per se, nor was he ugly. He had a wild mess of brown-red hair that swept around his face, and his eyes, though a bit lost at the moment, were intense, and were a warm cinnamon brown, framed by heavy lids and a low, thick brow— very thick, almost like a pair of caterpillars trying to kiss. His features were gloomy, though I knew his father had just passed away only a month ago. Soon, I realised that this had no bearing on his mood, anyway. He simply didn't have an agreeable face. His lips were drooping and colourless, but at least his jaw was rounded and soft.

His mien lifted when he offered a smile and introduced himself. He had large, crooked teeth, bad posture, and even his nose was bent out of shape. He had only one dimple; as somebody who fancied myself an artist, I appreciated the asymmetry.

Ida gave him a hard time. She did that to most new people in town, perhaps as a way to test their endurance, but he took it in stride. It was amusing to see them naturally snarl at each other, and it was hard for me to keep a stern face.

Papa met him, and they talked. Though my attention was divided between Ida and their conversation, I picked up as much as I could. He was polite enough, but his knowledge of the world was sorely lacking. Then again, so was mine. He was a fool: a polite fool.

The details as to how he lost the Bennett estates were greatly reduced in Grant's book, because frankly, it did not make for a riveting narrative. It was not as straightforward as law men showing up at the door unannounced, as since he was only nineteen, he'd had an older family acquaintance guide him for a small fee. So, a great many men had failed him in that interval.

He shared many stories with Papa, and eagerly told him all about a little moth he'd guarded during the train ride into town, because he didn't want it to get trampled.

And that told me everything I needed to know about him.

I spoke the bare minimum required of a good hostess, and kept my head low. Looking at him gave me a strange feeling in my chest and my fingertips.

He sounded and carried himself as an educated
man might have. I learned that he went to a
paying school from ten to fifteen, until he was
pulled out for getting into too many fights, and
then Samuel Bennett hired private teachers. He
did not do well in school because he was not
disposed to sitting still, but he seemed naturally
curious and eager to learn, despite his general
ignorance.

My school was by my mother's house, and had
only one room until I was twelve, when it was
expanded to two. Somebody I'd never met spent
a lot of money to have a second teacher offer
lessons in history and algebra. Once I was
fourteen, I aided in teaching the little ones for two
years. I often spent a week in each month with
my father, so I finished slowly.

I started to wonder if Mr. Bennett would see me
as unlearned.

As he now worked for my father, it was inevitable
that I would continue to cross paths with him. He
didn't speak much, but greeted me as I imagined a
nobleman was supposed to, and always gave a
smile. When his features brightened, they were
gentle. I wished he would talk more, because I
couldn't. I found myself seeking excuses to
interact with him. Sometimes if I saw him
heading inside from the fields, I walked just a
little bit slower so that we would meet at the door,

and he would bow his head and hold it for me,
but that was it. How annoying!

To see my suffering rendered as stoic aloofness is
quite comical and ironic, and frankly so typical of
how men think.

He never spoke to me at dinner, but what did I
expect, when I never initiated conversation? I
cursed my silence and craved to interact with this
new face. To test the water, I asked him to help
me in the kitchen. I remember I had him stir a
silky egg mixture for me. This time, it was not
merely an excuse to see him. I was tired and hot
from stirring for nearly half an hour.

When I asked, I instinctively waited to see if he
would huff and grumble, but approach anyway as
he felt obligated to assist. He never did any such
thing— on the contrary, he did so gladly. My
relief was immeasurable. He loved being useful. I
could have easily exploited this if I wanted to.

In doing so, he rolled his sleeves all the way up to
his elbows, which I did not expect! Worst of all,
he spoke to me for many minutes as he worked,
and I was not even listening.

When he called my name, I realised I'd been
staring at his bare arms. I quickly turned my head
before he could notice.

Similarly, I hated when he would come up to the house for dinner after working in the fields, with his damp shirt clinging to him just a little bit. I saw him first run and throw on a waistcoat, take off his hat and smooth down his hair with his fingers, then come into the kitchen. He ate quickly, and he ate a *lot*, and then he would graciously bow his head in thanks, and return to the fields, all while I sat to one side and tried not to look at him.

Of course, I could not help but examine him. Was this truly an aristocrat? His legs were like tree trunks, and his waist was thick and solid. He was almost too big for his height, yet it just suited him so well.

While he was working, I went to the outbuilding (as that was where he was currently being housed) to collect his clothes for washing. I always felt timid and hurried, wandering into a man's quarters, but I reasoned that any maid or nurse would do this. Besides, this used to be the toolshed. I anticipated a formerly pampered nobleman's dwelling to be slovenly without supervision, but I think he kept house as well as he could with no drawers and no light.

On this day, three shirts had been discarded off to one side, with tears and split seams.

It was stupid of me to do in every way, but I took them and set them aside to fix them, knowing I was terrible at sewing, and that he could probably go to a professional seamstress if he wanted to. I don't know why I did that, but I worked on them before bed, trying to make them as neat as possible.

That next Sunday, I sought him in the parlour, meaning to hand the fixed shirts to him, and behold his pleased face when he saw.

But as soon as I opened the door, I imagined he might have been vexed at me for possibly ruining his clothes, and then I could not speak, because I was so nervous, and thought I was making a mistake. Well, either way, I had to give his shirts back, so I dropped them, and left at once, never seeing how he reacted.

And what an idiot I was! I hardly said anything of value to him, even though I had the chance. I heard the door open after me, but I scurried to the side of the house and snuck back in through the kitchen door, silently into my room where I hid from him for the rest of the day.

After that, I went to my mother's house for a little while, and thought about what I'd done, what I hadn't done, and what I'd been thinking.

Why was *Lord* Michael Bennett any concern of mine? Impoverished, but still a lord, born from a much higher status than me! Sometimes, I heard a handful of ladies speak of him in town: his beautiful hair, his cool and brooding mien, his fine clothes, and the idea that he was secretly wealthy, sitting on a vast fortune— all these they found enticing, *despite* his rough features.

How dare they? I found his features perfectly suited to him, and he did not brood!

And how dare I? He was most certainly betrothed already, no doubt an advantageous match to a woman of status and beauty— or maybe even had a whole series of girls ready to tend to him.

Surely not— if he did, he'd have run to one of them instead of coming here.

I was always closely examining his behaviour around women in town, whenever possible. I envied how they could speak to him so freely; to do so, I reasoned, they must not have been so spellbound by him, as I was. I saw that he blushed, tittered, and clasped his hands together. He was that way with most women, and some men, so surely it was not coquetry, just his nature.

Unless he was the philandering type. Even lacking grace and conventional beauty, he could undoubtedly charm many women.

I wondered, then, why he didn't speak to me in quite the same way. Did I make him feel as timid as he made me?

More likely, he was simply afraid to step on the toes of his employer's daughter. I imagined he didn't even want anything to do with me. And why should he?

Perhaps I could draw him in with some charms of my own— if I had any. Certainly not my looks!

I was not ugly, but completely forgettable. I thought my nose was too long and sharp for my face, and my eyes were so fierce, even at rest! My hair has no form; it is straight as can be.

As for my figure— it was simply nothing special. I was not a big and buxom strapper, nor was I too thin. I'd always been just a bit on the shorter side of average, not miniscule. I had a bit of strength, yet very thin arms, and bony wrists and shoulders that I wanted to conceal, though my hands were nice enough. Most of my weight and strength was in my lower half. Walking up and down hills your whole life makes one's legs very thick and hearty. My waist was quite small, without any effort on my part. All the women in my family were trim around the midsection until they started having babies— at least that was enviable!

I think I was at my most attractive soon after I had my second child. Up to a point, many people really do get better with age.

As it stood back then, though, I did not believe there was anything there that could impress. My wit? I had none about me, especially when he was near. I would just have to hope he'd damage some more clothing.

I did not reveal any of this to my mother, for fear that she would scold me, or give me advice I didn't ask for. If one insists adamantly that they do not judge you, they are most certainly already condemning you inwardly.

I would take it to my grave.

Mother did not need to scold me, because I scolded myself plenty.

Don't sigh and get weepy, as if you're lovelorn, I ordered myself. *Don't act as if you love him. You don't even know him. This is insane and irrational.*

It was my own inward thoughts speaking to me, so why did my inner voice always sound like my mother?

I stayed with her for a few weeks, and to my utter shock, she sat me down and told me that as I was freshly eighteen, it was time to begin my search for a husband.

"Mama! You said I'm too young to marry and have plenty of time!" I protested at once.

"And you do! I'm not saying you don't," she sat across from me at the kitchen table and presented a small bundle of papers. "But it could take you five, even ten years to find the ideal fellow, and you should start early so you can snatch up a good one before they're all taken. You know, most ladies used to begin their marriage search much younger than you, so consider yourself lucky."

I didn't feel lucky. I thought matrimonial advertisements were for widow(er)s, middle aged bachelor(ette)s, and people who weren't attractive enough to meet people on their own. Perhaps I was truly in the latter category, so I agreed to look through this stash she'd put together.

"I've scoured advertisements from all over England, Scotland, and Wales," she commented, and I noticed she left out Ireland. "These are my picks. I highly recommend you choose from this collection."

"Suppose I don't want to marry at all?"

"Well, you may change your mind, but remember
I can turn away any suitor that I disapprove of
until you are twenty—"

"You said I'm too young to marry now, anyway."

She drew in a long breath and pinched her eyes
shut, as she often did when I tested her patience.

"Keep it in mind," she concluded. "I've already
done most of the work for you, so try to at least
whittle the batch down to two or three men before
you leave, so that I can write the letters for you."

"Why can't I write them myself?"

"Just *trust* your mother, please. I made sure they
were fairly close in age— the youngest is sixteen,
and I think the oldest is maybe twenty-nine."

"Twenty-nine isn't very close."

"Dear, most of the men advertising are upwards
of thirty-five. This is the best you are liable to
get. If you wait too long, all that will be left for
you are strange old bachelors and widowers with
eight children."

How old is Michael Bennett? I wondered before I
could stop myself. As far as I remembered, his
parents married in 1866, so he most likely wasn't

much older than twenty— he surely *couldn't* have been younger than me, big as he was.

"Why can't I go out and meet men in person?" I asked.

That set her off. I didn't expect it to, but as she leaned in slowly and narrowed her eyes, I anticipated the blow I was about to receive.

"Are you being deliberately naive? Men are shifty creatures— this way, you have the benefit of them making their desires and intentions plain and simple from the start, and you would not have that luxury if you went prowling around like a doe in heat! Do you want to end up like your grandmother? Like *me?* If you don't want my help, that's all well, but don't act as if you know better than me— you don't! You are a *child."*

"Why are you writing matrimonial advertisements for a child?"

She swiped the papers from my hands.

"If you don't want my help, just you say that," she said, even though I'd never asked for it in the first place.

"I'll still look through them!" I conceded, hoping to please her, but she was already storming off as she threw them back.

It was one of her cruel tricks to thrust adulthood on me and then snatch it away when I didn't do what she wished. It was this sort of game that led me to enter my first relationship with a man, back when I was sixteen. It was so short-lived and insignificant that I don't know why I even remember it.

The memory sprang upon me without warning as I sorted through those Johns, Richards, and Alberts.

His name was Arthur Campbell, and he went to the church my father used to minister to. He was twenty-eight, and not impressive to look at either which way, but exceedingly outgoing and charming to all, and very active in local charity efforts. Of course, this intrigued me— a tireless worker was attractive to any Christian woman.

He approached me one day as I was sweeping up after a Sunday service. Nobody else was present.

He introduces himself, tells me that Alma is such a pretty name (I notice right away that he calls me by my given name instead of any formal address, but I forgive it without a second thought, because he is an elder, after all), and he notes that I sure work hard, being as little as I am.

"I'm not little!" I argue immediately, and he laughs. And I certainly was not weak. I told him all of the chores I do at home, in addition to helping at church, at school, and around town. He acts impressed, and says I sure take on a heavy workload, and so cheerfully— I was definitely his kind of woman.

A woman— he called me a woman, not a little girl. This tickled me, and made me feel so special, because for once, my womanhood was recognised.

Our first encounter was brief, but I was excited that I had made a new friend, though I didn't share the details with my family.

The next time we cross paths, he does not acknowledge me, and I have to seek him out myself. I think it pleased him that I did so, because he at once became his loquacious self again.

He started speaking to me every day after church, and sometimes intercepted me in town. Why was he so fascinated by me? I couldn't help but feel special as he heaped praise upon me— I mistook those giddy feelings for being in love.

Within a month, he professed his intense and uncontrollable passion for me, and possibly being infatuated with the very idea of someone being so spellbound by me, and a grown man at that, I accepted his feelings. Right away, he pulled me into a crushing embrace that squeezed the wind out of me. We agreed not to tell anyone and meet discreetly in the evening. I went to bed feeling light as air, and a bit naughty, because I was keeping a secret.

Yet, I felt I was playing a dangerous game. On my way to meet him in the evening, at our little rendezvous out by the abandoned houses, I had an awful, sick feeling deep in my stomach. I disregarded this foreboding, because I was naturally anxious, and I was rebelling. It was soon overshadowed by a light and fluttering butterfly sensation, so I reasoned that the good outweighed the bad.

I fretted over my plain hair and clothes, but he told me he preferred a plain woman. He was quick to touch me, such as stroking my head and drawing me closer a little at a time. I told him about myself, and described my daily life, and he was quite taken, or at least pretended to be. It was unbelievable, especially since I had understated myself so much in my descriptions. Completely stepping over my ambitions and interests, he presented me with more praise and flattery, saying he almost felt guilty about having me, knowing he was taking me, such a pretty thing, away from a much more aesthetically equal fellow.

I told him that looks did not matter, and that was a lie. We can pretend all we wish, but we do like to find people attractive. That said, it was hard for me to consider anybody genuinely ugly— even if one was not conventionally handsome, I only found myself repulsed by unhygienic habits, such as drunkenness, gambling and foul words. I tended to place more value on specific features, such as brilliant eyes, a kind, friendly mouth, or beautiful hair. Though I didn't consider him a strapper when I first met him, he became more appealing the more he spoke. I guess you could say he was an acquired taste that I'm now glad I scrubbed from my tongue.

At one time, he reported a suspicious noise just outside the house, and he drew me protectively close and boldly set out to investigate. Every young girl wanted to feel safe, so this brought me nearer to him. Though I was sharp enough at that age, I wanted to believe he had the most honest intentions, and by virtue of age and experience, he must have been wiser than I. I had played straight into his hands. It is likely that he did not have the keen ear I thought he did, and there was no noise at all.

After only three of our meetings, he told me he wanted to marry me, and said I was the perfect woman— built to serve the Lord and endure many hardships, like him. The world was not

ready for people such as us. He told me about
these massive, almost fantastical plans for social
reform, and I was drawn in, though I warned him
that he was moving a little too fast, and could not
hope to do so much so soon. He became moody
and downcast for a while, and because I was
sensitive to a shifting countenance, I felt my eyes
well up with tears. He saw this and tried to
quickly mollify me, placing his hands on my head
and neck as if subduing a wild animal, and then
he kissed me.

My heart nearly leapt from my body! I can not
say whether I liked or disliked the caress, but I
loved the concept, and went home thinking I was
happier than I'd ever been before, because I'd had
my first kiss. His lips were dry and thin, and I
didn't kiss him back, but at sixteen, having never
been touched well before, it was mesmerising.

The next time, I presented myself to him with
neatly braided hair and my good brooch that I
loved. He was disappointed, condemning the
evils of vanity, and told me he wanted a practical
woman with a servant's heart; he assured me that
he found plainness of dress very attractive,
especially since a pretty wee thing like me needed
no adornment, and beauty is only temporary. At
the time, this made sense to me, so I took down
my hair and removed the jewellery. My high
collar was impractical and restricting, too. I was
ordered to unfasten three buttons and expose my

throat. My skirt was almost touching the ground. It needed to be pinned up.

Up until that point, he was endlessly shy and meek when the subject of physical closeness was mentioned. Very quickly, though, he began commenting obsessively about my body, and things he wanted to do to me. I was foolish, and thought this was charming, though I burned and hid my face. I both loved it and hated it, as my curiosity, my dignity, and what remained of my innocence were all at war with each other. I told him that I did not want to indulge in such things before I was married, and he agreed.

The comments continued, anyway. Sometimes, I expressed shock and disgust at some of what he suggested, and he called me a "prig" who needed to open her mind. I thought this was unfair to say to me, as I was so much younger than him, but he said that maybe I just was not as mature as he thought I was.

This pricked me, and I frantically tried to call him back and admit that the concepts were intriguing. He was pleased again, and asked if we at least could kiss.

I agreed to it: only for him to tell me I was no good at it, whereas he'd had practice with other women— all of whom had previously broken his heart.

"Suppose I go and *practise* with the innkeeper's son!" I retorted reflexively, because comparing me to others hurt me, though it was a bluff strike, as I did not know whether or not Mr. Briggs had a son.

My blow didn't land. He only laughed.

"Nice attempt, little girl, every *adult* knows that John Briggs's boy was murdered ten years ago. Go and dig him up, if you want."

I was too embarrassed to assert myself.

I tried to improve— I even asked a girl from school how to kiss properly.

Her suggestions were alien and even abhorrent to me, so I decided I would find out for myself. Soon, he told me I'd gotten much better at it, and that excited me! I was eager to impress him.

Not even a week after I began kissing him, he had me meet him inside one of those old houses and said he changed his mind and could not contain himself— he needed all of me— but not at his house or mine, or at the inn where people may recognise us.

Shame and insult quelled within me. Of course I told him no— in a decrepit and abandoned house,

of all places! He pressed, saying he loved me
more than anyone else ever would on this
undeserving planet, and that he *thought* I was a
grown woman. He kept getting closer to me until
I was very small and flat against the far wall. It
was dark by then. I did not want to walk home by
myself, so I felt I had no choice but to stay with
him. We grappled verbally, debating scripture and
convention, and I told him he could not pick and
choose which of God's commands he could
wilfully discard just because he was tempted. He
told me that soon it wouldn't matter, and nobody
would know because I would marry him, and he
knew I wanted to give in.

But I would know.

And then what? He would go one way, and I
would go another, and then we would happily
sing from a hymnbook, as though we had done no
wrong? How many times would he summon me
to ruined houses before he deemed me worthy of
the status of a wife?

He could not, or would not answer my
interrogations, only kept approaching and
demanding that I not beat around the bush.

Now he had his hands on my shoulders, and I
could not scream, because I did not want anybody
to find me here with him. The severity of the trap
I'd let myself be lured into was realised just then.

It is one of my greatest flaws, that in moments of great stress, I freeze and become helpless. All I could do was weep quietly.

He backed away and sat across from me, watching me with a soft expression. I mistook that for compassion and empathy. He was only studying me.

I was not just morally opposed, I was petrified by fear. Marriage was not my only reason for hesitation. Admittedly, I was so very curious, and still had some sort of feelings for him, which made me quite tempted. Still, the idea of being so vulnerable— to *him*— frightened me terribly, along with the prospect of being a parent so young. Moreover, the way he looked at me in that moment reminded me of… Emerson.

I told him all of this, because I felt an obligation to explain myself. That was stupid. He listened, and then all he said was, "Oh. I see."

After that, he was silent for many many minutes, and I shrunk myself down in the corner and wept even more.

He then told me that he was not interested in *only* my body, and that my comfort was important as well. He vowed he would protect me from anyone who meant to harm me, and then he

embraced me, and I passively allowed it. Then I
was free to go.

As soon as the house was out of sight, I ran,
feeling as if my life had been spared. I ran, and I
did not stop until I saw the lights of my father's
house.

He was surprised to see me come to the door, as
he thought I had gone to my mother that evening,
but he let me inside without questioning me.

My mother would have definitely killed me or
locked me in the cellar if I told her what sort of
nonsense I'd been up to that last two months (yes,
that whole ordeal was only two months)! But I
needed to tell somebody, and I could usually trust
that my father would not make a scene, unless he
was inebriated— then, he thought he was a pastor
again, and took to shouting scripture at the
slightest provocation.

I waited until he was seated, and when my breath
returned and I drank a great big draught of the
water I was offered, I described to him the trouble
I'd gotten into, but did not disclose the name of
the man I'd encountered. He seemed to age
twenty years. I wondered if he would upbraid me,
or tell my mother even though I'd asked him not
to.

He didn't condemn me, lecture me, or devise any punishment for me. He only set his pipe down and said, "well, you are safe now."

Arthur Campbell did not interact with me any more after that. He actively avoided me, but I always heard him speaking loudly to other churchgoers about the evils of temptation and precocious young women, while my face burned. Soon afterwards, he was shipped off to somewhere in Africa, and I never saw him again. To this day, I am not sure of his fate.

I prefer to believe his discarding me was an act of mercy, when he realised he was unfairly taking advantage of a girl much younger than him. Still, it stung for many months. Did my morals make me unworthy of finding a husband?

No. My father praised me for standing my ground, and told me to think of him as a "rehearsal," not a failure.

And to point him out if he ever spoke to me again.

Of course, later on I reasoned that of course it was all fake! I was not pretty, only passable at best, so I should have seen right through his excessive flattery. Who preferred a "plain" woman? Hopeful thinking is so dangerous.

I'd mostly been able to push him out of my mind until just then, when I was looking at those advertisements. I don't know why I thought of him. None of the advertisers really resembled him in any way that mattered. What I did not know at the time was that my subconscious mind was always comparing other men to him: his looks, his demeanour, his goals. I acknowledged that there was some good there, but at that age, it was a challenge to differentiate it from the bad.

He resurfaced again when I saw Michael Bennett. I pushed him back down, lest I confuse the two men.

I encountered him the evening I went back to my father's house.

Michael Bennett was odd and twitchy, and he invited me out on a walk. He probably did not notice, but I was always eyeing him, stealing glances as I pretended to absently twirl and turn my head every which way. He stopped and fixated on a beetle. I don't know why this surprised me, as I'd seen him enjoy animals before, but most folks don't take a liking to little creeping bugs. At best, they step over them and ignore them, but he admired them, even the "plain" ones.

I was relieved when he struck up a conversation, because I could not think of where to begin. He

listened intently, but quickly made himself out to
be even more of a fool! It was because he tried to
be cool and detached, but he could not trick me—
he blushed (the first time his face had any colour)
when I expressed contempt for his odd way of
thinking, and that was how I knew it was a bluff.
The attempt both repelled and intrigued me. What
was it for?

I told him my aspirations, and he listened, said
something stupid, and did not share any of his.
Maybe he had none— if that was so, why did he
mill about with such a determined and energetic
expression? He was all energy, yet it seemed to
be directed nowhere, and he appeared to suffer
because of it. I believed that in him, there were a
dozen different kinds of passion clamouring to be
heard.

After being so discreet and hesitant my whole
life, I'd had one full conversation with him, and
then I was ready to throw caution to the wind.
This was wholly irrational, and I was afraid of
feeling that way, so I continued to shy away from
him.

But of course it was irrational; no matter how old
we are, the part of us that loves is so young, and
so tender that it is easily hurt.

I began to make calculated efforts to be seen by
him. If he went to one side of the house, I would

make myself visible through that window, and I
would sit and read or comb my hair, pretending I
did not notice, and watching out the corner of my
eye to see if his demeanour changed. It was truly
astounding, how obvious I could be without
arousing suspicion.

He started to seek me out to listen to me read
aloud, which I gladly did, just to have him sit
close to me, even if he was just bored. He amused
me, even when he was doing something stupid,
and I knew he was genuinely sweet. You had to
be, to put up with Ida's antics, and still give her a
penny when she begged. He claimed it was the
easiest way to make her go away. Similarly, he
claimed he hated cats, but I never once saw him
do anything cruel when they got in his way, and
he even slipped them some scraps when he
thought nobody was looking. The only animal he
just never seemed to take a liking to was
chickens.

It pleased me to know that Papa liked him at least
a little, though he considered him a child.
Everyone under twenty was a child to him, after
all. When he departed to visit an old acquaintance
in Liverpool, I made an effort to appear
unbothered, but probably just looked ill. He
lightly kissed my hand, and then I really was
ailing— but it was just a gesture of reverence
from an old-fashioned gentleman.

In the interval of his absence, Mama tasked me with learning to properly sew, so that I could make my own wedding dress: a task I both eagerly approached and dragged my feet towards. She bought me such a fine and crisp, pearly linen, and gave me many patterns to choose from. I told her my ambitions, and idea to combine many attributes from different drafts, and this displeased her.

"Don't be so hasty," she warned me. "You might not like it once it's finished, and it likely won't hold up with the current fashions by that time."

This baffled me, because I thought I'd picked such a simple idea.

"I will like it! This is what I want," I declared.

"All, right. Don't listen to me. Do what you want, but you'd better not ask me for any help," was the last thing she said before she sent me back to Papa's house with her old sewing machine.

I wanted Mama to like my dress, so I changed the bodice to something a little more timeless, and minimised the draping so that it would be less of a challenge.

How eagerly I set out to work— except Mama didn't tell me how to use the sewing machine. I figured it out the hard way, but by that time, I didn't have much patience or candlelight left.

I took a few cuttings to practise with, but the first seam just didn't look quite right. On my next attempt, my hands trembled, so I put everything away, and went to bed angry with myself for getting nothing accomplished.

"I'd say learning to run that damned machine is a bigger accomplishment than I've ever made," Papa admitted. "Why, I never could learn how to sew, except to stitch up warm bodies, and that doesn't need to be pretty. Well, can't teach an old dog new tricks."

I went back to her in a week, because I could not resist showing her my meagre progress. She eagerly offered her help, in stark contrast to her previous attitude. Now I was reluctant, but didn't want to hurt her feelings. I didn't really like asking, because she did not think she should have to explain things more than once, and was easily agitated.

I could not get this one specific shape to sit correctly. I'd redone the seam numerous times, even used different cuts of the material, and it just would not cooperate with me. At the moment, I simply felt I was unfit to be a seamstress to any degree.

"Useless!" I scolded myself as I cut. "You are useless."

"What was that?" my mother barged in. I didn't think she was passing by, or would have heard me if she was.

"What? Nothing," I tried to resume my work.

"How dare you speak in that way?" she demanded. "I raised you to have more respect for yourself, and I hear such nonsense from your mouth again, I'll thrash you! I don't care if you're grown. I mean what I said!"

After that, she left. My ego was not any more elevated, having heard that. I struggled slowly onward until I could mustre up the willpower to ask for help. Since I absorbed her instructions quickly, it was not a bad experience. Very soon, I at least had the skeleton of a beautiful dress. Then I wondered how Michael would react if he discovered I was making a wedding dress…

By December, both to my delight and terror, I could not ignore the way he acted around me. Something in him had changed or been revealed when he returned from his trip. He sat near to me almost— almost— as a friend might have, yet he now turned red so easily: possibly even more so than me.

Secretly, there was a wicked satisfaction within me when he had blistered his hands from the cold, because then I had an excuse to tend to him. Of course, he acted as if they didn't hurt. It was hard to play the cool and amiable nurse while my heart fluttered to be able to clasp his fingers. I drew out of him some sort of sideways confession; he had indeed been closely observing me. He retreated to his chamber shortly after this admission, visibly flustered, meanwhile, I tidied up the kitchen, feeling as if I'd float away. It was bliss just to know that I had any effect on him— that my presence mattered to somebody.

The very next day, he came into the spare room while I was sewing and asked me some strange questions. He didn't seem terribly agitated by my wedding dress. I finished up my work and went to the parlour to read, as you know I often did, and he brought me some luxurious brand of chocolates in a wooden box. I froze, as I was not accustomed to receiving such nice things, certainly not from somebody who wasn't family. I had gotten little bags of homemade sweets and occasionally citrus fruits around Christmas, but nothing like this. It intimidated me, but I didn't want to offend him.

Once I'd accepted that this was really happening, I took them. I assumed he was about to ask me for some favour— perhaps his trousers needed mending, or he wanted me to cook something late

at night. Maybe they were a gift for his patronage
to some decadent confectionery, and since he
didn't prefer chocolate, he needed to get rid of
them.

But it seemed he'd only bought them for the
pleasure of giving them away, because he eagerly
watched me try them.

Right then, I was overcome, and really did
abandon all my inhibitions. I kissed him— not on
his lips; I wouldn't dare. My mouth only just
grazed his face. I did it faster than he could react,
and then I retreated to the other end of the couch.

He returned the kiss, and he lingered just a
moment longer than I did, and I squealed. I
couldn't contain it!

And then he left so cordially, and I went to bed
steeping in my own giddiness. I'd gotten him to
kiss me! In a hedonistic sort of way, I fancied
myself content to be caressed by any means
necessary, and I succeeded. Yes, I did feel a little
bit evil as I drifted off to sleep, but after all, he
kissed me back.

I missed him that morning, which was odd,
because it was not like him to linger in his room.
At dinner, he had a reserved and pensive look
about him, and did not contribute to the
conversation at the table. Did I leave an

impression upon him last night? I hoped so, but timid as I was, I waited to be pursued.

But what if he was the one waiting on me? What if he was sharing my exact thoughts?

I resolved to stop thinking in circles. I would go about my evening as usual, and see what happened.

Later that night, he sought me alone, and I almost dropped the pail of feed in my fright— his voice had a strange metallic warble to it in the wind, and I did not hear him approach.

He invited me on a walk, and I drew very near to him, because it was cold, and I was afraid. I'd always been easily startled. The close contact made me even more jittery.

Our walk was ruined by freezing rain, but once inside, he drew close for warmth.

He had very lovely hair, especially in the firelight, though it was soaked and dripping. It was always quite long; it hung like clumps of twisting ivy around his ears, covered his neck, and nearly touched his brow. If I pulled a coil taut, it almost reached his shoulder blades. He never sheared it short or combed it down. When I'd once asked him why he kept it so long and untamed, he said that if women could delight in their curls, so could he.

I was dreadfully fearful. I could not quite understand why he would seek me specifically, and was sure that any other woman would take him, but as much as I wanted to resist, he'd put a spell on me. I know I tend to repeat myself, but I thought these things very often.

I got him to give me a real kiss, and right away I could tell he'd never done it before. He didn't comment on it as Arthur Campbell had done; instead, he withdrew quickly to study my face, and then he tried again— grinding his teeth into mine in awkward haste. It made me laugh until I saw that we were being watched.

My father stood at the parlour door, barely visible except for the shine of his glasses, and my face turned so very hot!

I went to bed battling a dreadful feeling, but why? I surely hadn't done anything wrong. I wondered how Michael felt. He told me he wanted to pursue something more than friendship. It must have been true. He didn't give me any reason to doubt him, though my mother told me that those people are the most dangerous. So, who could I trust?

The next morning, about half of my fears were confirmed. Right after breakfast, Papa summoned me upstairs. I sat in front of his desk and anticipated an affront to my intelligence.

"I noticed you have gotten quite close with Mr. Bennett," he opened, lighting a pipe too soon after breakfast. "As a matter of fact, I've noticed for quite some time, but I've waited to say anything."

"Yes, sir, and what of it?"

"Well, you know, you are quite young, both of you— and you— you are not familiar with how men can be."

"I'm not stupid!" I protested.

"Of course you aren't!" he took a long draught of smoke, which always served as a warning that he was going to say a lot. "I'm saying that you must be very cautious. I know you must be dealing with many new and exciting feelings, but not all that glitters is gold. Men's motives are often not clear, and he may ask more of you than you're willing to offer."

"I have free will, and Michael is not Mr. Campbell."

"You do, indeed— and no, he is not. But he is a man, and—" he stopped and rubbed his brow. "I say— I don't remember— are you familiar with the natural process of producing children?"

"Don't even speak of it! Of course I am!" I cried, not wishing to hear of such things spoken of by my father, of all people.

"Oh, yes, yes, of course. You really are grown, aren't you? Hmm…" he mumbled and scratched his hair, even looking a bit relieved. "But I still ought to warn you. I understand you're having fun with yourself—"

"Papa!" I shrieked and stopped my ears.

He narrowed his eyes.

"Ahem! But if you do not foresee the possibility of marriage, I'd advise you sever those ties right now, as it'd be difficult to do so later."

It would have been difficult, then.

"And on the topic of marriage," he resumed. "Don't feel pressured. I think people should abstain—"

"Until they are at least twenty," I finished.

He said that many times in the past, and he spoke from experience. The truth is, he had been married once before, long before meeting my

mother, before he even joined the ministry—
soon after beginning his medical studies. He was
seventeen, she was nineteen, and they met at a
funeral, of all places. His parents disapproved of
him marrying in such haste, so the pair fled to
Scotland and eloped. Within four months, they
were desperately petitioning for a divorce, and I
never met this woman, nor learned her name.

"But you must be absolutely certain of his
motives, and yours," he added.

"Do you think me that defective, that I could not
be worthy of a man of noble birth?" I asked, now
growing insecure.

"No. Quite the opposite. Just take my words into
consideration, as I have a good thirty or so years
on you, after all," he concluded. "Am I *really*
that old?" he added to the side, as if this
genuinely puzzled him.

I repeatedly nodded and obediently affirmed his
advice until I was set free, and though things
could have gone far worse, I was quite morose for
the rest of the morning.

When Michael returned from his little chores, I
saw that Papa had gotten to him, as well. His
wrists trembled, and he had a funny limp (he had
been forced to sit on the wrong side of the desk,
and his legs had gone numb).

Not even a day after he'd declared his intentions, he was laying flowery prose and fantastical language upon me. Though I was flattered and tickled, I did not appreciate it. It wasn't practical. I accepted that he was just expressing his affection in his own way, but I hoped he would acclimate to my wants just a little; I didn't want poetry, I wanted touch and constancy.

As I spoke to him and drew so close, I knew all the more that I loved him very much, but I still had to wonder if I really could marry him. As it was at the time, it seemed we had very different sets of goals. Actually, I couldn't even tell if he had any. He clearly had passions, and had all the makings of an exceptional and upright man— I always knew that. The pieces just weren't all together.

But neither were mine, so who was I to say anything? Who on Earth really is all put together? I hated thinking of such things, because it only reminded me of how young and disorganised I was. Missionary work in Africa? The thought terrified me. Now what did I want, aside from him? If I sought all I desired in one man, when man is fallible, then I would never be content. I knew I had to cling to my faith now more than ever.

Still, I allowed myself to love Michael, and believe he loved me.

It was easier to enjoy the company of a man I felt safe with, and I found myself always wanting to be alone with him. Alas, despite living in the same house, he had his place as my father's hired man, and we were always working. Even though Papa knew all about it and did not discourage it, we maintained an air of propriety in his presence, and out in public— at my request. It was almost to Michael's annoyance, as he was not fond of me calling him "sir" all the time.

But once in a while, we found time to tuck ourselves away in some softly lit corner of the house and kiss. I liked kissing him a lot more than Arthur Campbell.

Even I could tell that he was not good at it. His lips were taut and he kept crashing his teeth into mine. I had to nudge him back to make him understand.

He was also easily impressed. He withdrew from me and giggled.

"You have experience, don't you?"

I started and leaned away from him.

"What do you mean by that?"

"I don't mean anything bad by it!" Michael sheepishly played with my brooch, in some sort of trance "I mean, it's so nice... you must have kissed before!"

"I have," I admitted. "He discarded me, and I haven't seen him since."

I didn't want to talk about it, and fortunately, he didn't ask.

"Well, then it's his loss," he cooed in my ear and nestled his face into my hair. "You're all mine, now."

We hid away and kissed until we were breathless (or in danger of being caught), and then we parted ways for the night.

There is a strong implication in Grant's book that Michael was a wholly pure and childlike man who wanted nothing more than to kiss me and fall asleep beside me and share my warmth on cold winter nights.

I tell you— one day, before we were even betrothed, I sat across from him (we were the first ones at the table that morning) and asked very plainly, "Do you want to bed me?"

"Yes," he replied with no hesitation.

He truly did not beat around the bush. I laughed, because I did not know what to make of his answer.

"Why are you laughing?" he asked, with his eyes wide and his frame shrinking into itself.

"Thank you for telling me. Will you wait until we are married?"

"Yes."

"You don't mind?"

He pinched his lips together, as he did when preparing to speak with a lot of pomp.

"Your beauty is demanding of more reverence than sneaking away in the shadows of your father's house— there will be moonlit satin, and—"

"I don't want a sonnet. Tell me straightforward."

"No, I'd prefer it. It would be more practical, and if it would please you, I'd be glad to do it."

"So, I am attractive, after all?" I blurted out.

"Alarmingly so," he said flatly.

And his affection never changed after this brief
discussion, nor did he try to rush me down the
aisle.

Of course, he really did simply want to sleep
beside me, and I wouldn't allow it. Not because I
was opposed, but because I was certain that I was
far more vulnerable to temptation than he was,
and I would not take any chances. I tell you, I
was under an enormous strain to keep him at that
distance!

I always teased him, even back in autumn. Part of
it was to check his prideful nature, part of it was
for my own amusement, and another part of it
was because I knew he loved it. I didn't always
want to do it. Often, it was hard not to give in to
his requests without playing any games, but he
would have gotten bored if I submitted too
readily so early in our courtship.

I knew I had a lot of power over him, and I
fought to maintain it, because I heeded my
father's words in my own way.

But I digress—

CHRISTMAS, AND THE CALM BEFORE A WINTER STORM

For the most part, it was bliss. I didn't think I could possibly be happier, and for once, I didn't try to dream away my spare time.

Leading up to Christmas, I went to visit my mother. That was the first time in a month that I would not see him for days at a time, and I really ached, but December always puts me in a festive mood, and I hadn't seen Mama in quite a while.

I brought her a fruit cake I'd made the day before, a set of exotic tea, and the decorations that Papa wouldn't let me put up around his house. I was never good at giving gifts.

I didn't tell her of my involvement with Michael, but I believe she suspected something was amiss, seeing how I'd blush for seemingly no reason at all while sitting at the kitchen table. She certainly knew it was not about one of her selected suitors, because she'd have already interrogated me.

For my Christmas present, she made me such a wonderful dress that was like nothing I'd ever owned before! Red was not a colour I'd have picked for me, but it was lovely all the same. It had fine, standing bits of lace, and a modern and fashionable silhouette. It included a separate evening bodice with a neckline so low that looking at it made me blush, and a set of draping skirt attachments.

"Oh! You made this yourself?" I asked.

"Of course I did!" she answered. "I've made almost all of your clothes. Why do you ask?"

"Well, it's just not anything I'd have expected—"

"You don't think I'm capable?"

"No, no!" I huffed, beginning to sweat. "I meant—"

"Settle down! I'm only teasing you," Mama heaped the dress into my arms. "Now, go and put it on! I want to see how it looks!"

"Right now?"

"Yes, right now!"

I'd never worn such a complicated and ornate ensemble before. Did I try on the daytime or evening bodice? It took me some minutes to be used to the quantity of skirt in the back. Frankly, I was surprised that my mother would make something like that for me. The lace trim of the evening bodice really augmented my bust. I did wish that it would minimise my square shoulders, but I'd have been too bottom-heavy without them, anyway. It was so very flattering that I wanted to wear it every day, but I wouldn't have dared.

(Actually, this dress is still in my possession, fully intact! Of course, I don't wear it anymore. Fashion has changed so quickly these past decades, I find it hard to keep up).

Mama tapped on the door, asking if I wanted help, and I declined, ready to step out.

"Oh!" she sighed, as if she might swoon. "Isn't that lovely? James, come and see!" she beckoned to him, much to his indifference. "But it's too fine to wear to church. Where do you think you'll wear it?"

"I don't know," I admitted, knowing good and well that I would find any excuse to wear it on a regular day in the house, just for Michael— or just to feel pretty. "Christmas seems a good enough occasion, does it not?"

"It certainly does, but surely you can't wear it only once a year!"

"New Year's eve, then. And maybe Halloween. These colours are too rich for spring and summer. I'm sure I'll come up with something!"

Mama roasted just a small rabbit and a heap of potatoes, since it was only the three of us. She

79

insisted that we have the tea and cake with the meal. Once we finished dinner, she went to the piano and ordered me to sing. She insisted it was no different from singing in church, and that I had no reason to be shy around her, but she stopped asking once I burst into tears, and I sat on the stool in shame, listening to her play her hymns and sing by herself.

"And after I made you that lovely dress!" she sighed. "All I wanted for Christmas was to hear you sing!"

I'd have been more prepared and willing to participate if I was made aware of this prior to arriving. She knew I was naturally timid.

She was vexed that we were going to Papa's house for the evening, because he was mostly indifferent to Christmas, anyway. I reasoned that it still just didn't feel right to leave him entirely alone that whole day, and said in jest that I was going to be sleeping for much of the remainder of that Christmas, as it was getting late, so it didn't matter all that much.

And I wanted to know how Michael was faring. He had so little family left. Not to mention, he promised me a present, and I was curious. I only made him little marzipan sweets. As I've said, I am not good at giving gifts.

He bestowed upon me such a lovely and exotic ring. Russian gold is commonplace now, but it was not so popular in the West at that time. I'd never seen it before!

Better yet was the offer attached to it: to be his wife.

Rationally, I should have been wary of such a proposal, so soon, but it simply felt right in every way. I accepted with no hesitation.

So why did I feel such dread? I was happy, so very happy, and didn't see what could be wrong.

And I already had a wedding dress! It was my very first big sewing project, and I was making it in preparation, at the insistence of my mother.

Of course we knew that we could not marry until I was twenty, and/or Michael was out of my father's house and living by his own means. We saw no reason not to be engaged in the meantime. Suddenly, he had much more impetus than ever before, and was eagerly making plans with his money. One of those small plans was making the ring all my own.

I wore that same red dress when he took me out to get the ring fitted. I felt so very pretty, despite the features I found lacking. Any ornament is more becoming when worn in a jubilant mood.

But now that he had my promise of marriage, he was getting a little too bold for my liking. The confidence and drive he dazzled me with that same morning had begun to chafe when he started imposing his money upon me. He feverishly tried to coax me into accepting all sorts of inappropriately extravagant gifts I did not want, and in view of other people. He meant nothing by it, but he likely did not realise his insult; I was his betrothed, not his favourite concubine. He did not need to purchase my attention or publicly claim ownership of me.

I tried to be patient about explaining my feelings. Thinking about it now, I knew he was not experienced with women, and as he was indulged to excess as a child, it was possibly the best way he knew how to display his love. Well, I didn't want or need any grand gestures. I wanted his real tenderness that I knew was there.

At the time, some of his behaviour did not make sense to me. Nobody told me anything! Had I known about all of his burdens in those days, I'd have approached his moods with more tact.

He was much less patient with me at the start of that new year. I knew engagement couldn't have revealed some sinister nature within him. I simply imagined that my father was placing even more pressure upon him, so I tried to be reasonable and hold my tongue when he said something that pricked me.

But the evening of January 13, 1888 would stand out to me for the rest of my life.

Friday the thirteenth… I always hated moonless nights.

Michael brought Ida into the house, squirming and squealing, and he was covered in blood! He looked awful, and I wanted to ask what was wrong with him, but he sent me upstairs to tend to Ida, and I did not have a chance to argue. I was so rattled with fear that I thought I may be sick as Michael often was when he was nervous, but there was no time to react in such a way.

I took her into my mother's old room.

"What is all of this about?" I asked. "What has happened?"

"He hurt my friend!" she cried immediately. "He's a monster! He beat him all bloody and left him to die in the street!"

That didn't sound like Michael at all.

"Tell me *exactly* what happened, and don't you tell me a story!"

She stopped herself.

"I'm not supposed to tell."

"What are you not supposed to tell?"

"I can't tell you that, either!"

"Who told you not to tell? Your friend?"

"Yes, him!"

"Well, he's not here, and if this could get somebody in danger, then you'd be *right* to tell me."

I shut and locked the door, but stepped away from it. I wanted privacy, but didn't want her to feel trapped. The look in her eyes betrayed such a familiar feeling: that she'd done something bad, but she wasn't sure what it was.

"You will not be punished, no matter what you tell me," I promised. "Just tell me everything."

She tapped her chin. While she came up with her answer, I heard clattering downstairs, and tried to ignore it.

"My friend is Albert—"

"Gillman?"

"Maybe."

Michael had beaten the town simpleton, Albert Gillman?

"Why, he's older than James! What business would you have with him?"

"He is very good and nice!" she insisted. "He brought me presents and told me I'm pretty, and he said we could get married—"

"Ida, that is not all right!" I cried.

She blinked hard.

"It's not? Did I do something bad?"

"No, you didn't— now, tell me, please— has he touched you? In any way at all?"

"He grabbed my hands once while we played in the grass, and sometimes he touched my hair."

"Nothing else? Please tell me, it's important."

"No. That's all."

My eyes welled up with tears of relief, and then terror, as the situation bore down on me. My darling Ida was possibly mere minutes away from having her childhood ripped away from her, and she may have been pulled from the clutches of a maniac.

I also considered the possibility that he really was just a simpleton with the mind of a child, who didn't know what he was doing.

Remembering that Michael had bloodied him up, and that his uncle had a great deal of power, made me more fearful than I had been relieved.

I would go and get answers from him, as well, but not before I made sure Ida was secure.

"You need to stay away from him— in fact, you aren't going anywhere tonight. You will stay up here, in this room—"

"You said I wouldn't be punished!" she interrupted.

"You are not being punished, Ida. I do not want you going home tonight. I need to tend to Michael, as well, and would rather you be here."

"Will you tend to Albert, too?"

"No!" I snapped, and then quickly softened my voice. "No, he has people who will care for him, I am sure. Don't worry about him. Please be a good little lady and stay up here quietly, and rest. For

now, don't tell a soul any of what has happened,
and I will bring supper up to you soon."

"I will."

She sat on Mama's old bed, and I turned to unlock
the door.

"Thank you, Ida."

"May I play with this doll?" she held up the little
wax-head baby that sat on the pillows.

"Yes," I was so happy that she was still inclined
to be a child. "Be careful with it."

I was happy until I shut the door and had to face
what was outside. I had no idea what state I
would find Michael in, if what Ida said was all
true.

When he opened his door, I was almost swept to
my knees by the foul draught from his room. I
smelled blood, vomit, and a mixture of strong
chemicals: about how I imagined a hospital might
smell (little did I know…)

We had quite a little tiff over whether or not he
should have done what he did. I believe he
thought I was trying to defend Gillman's actions
or say he was plainly wrong for beating him, but I
could not quite put my concerns into words, and

he was getting aggressive. I imagine his anger
had not yet burned off, but he was clearly not
himself— and I had lost all fortitude and
submitted to his temper. Worst of all, he then
drew me back to him with gentleness and
entreated me to conceal all that had happened!
His tenderness was even harder to resist, and I
believe he had good intentions, and a plan in
mind. For surrendering, I was angry at myself—
and more than a little angry at him. After all, he
was not yet my husband, and at that time, did not
support me in any way. Why should I submit to
him?

Unsure of what to do now, and rather beside
myself, I tried my best to carry on as normal. I
cleaned and fixed his ruined coat, and made a
half-hearted attempt at supper while I pieced
together a story for what had happened that
evening.

It hurt me to lie to my father about something so
dire. I tried to convince myself that it was the
lesser of two evils, but I was not sure.

And the next few days was a deathly-silent calm
before a violent storm. I knew it well, and could
not shake the terror I felt. I could not seek
comfort from anybody: not my father, because I
was reminded that I was a liar every time I saw
his face; not Michael, because lately, I didn't
know this man; not James, because he was James;

not Ida, because she needed my help more than I needed hers. And I was too distracted to seek it from God.

I definitely knew I could not seek solace from my mother, but I went and visited her anyway, just because it seemed to be about time to do so.

As I had not told Mama anything about Michael— she only vaguely knew who he was— she continued to press me about sifting through her collection of suitors. When I asked her if I could have photos of any of them, she merely said that looks do not matter.

But of course they do, just a little. We all want to be beautiful to somebody.

And I could see only Michael Bennett.

Though she pushed me to marry, she fostered my desire to take up nursing and learn to sew, as she believed every woman needed the skills to get by, since nothing was guaranteed.

"What do you plan to ask these gentlemen at the interviews?" Mama asked.

I tried to pull some questions out of the air, because I had not given the search any thought at all, and only whittled down the numbers to appease her.

"Well, I'd like to know if he is affiliated with a church, what he'd like to accomplish in the next ten years, and maybe if he'd been married before, or if he'd held conference with many women before me—"

"Why does it matter how many women he had before you?" she asked.

"I suppose it isn't all that important, but I'd like to be his first choice, that's all," I explained.

"You will never be his first choice," my mother told me, without looking up from her sewing. "Men don't marry the women they favour. They marry the women who are closest when they are ready to marry. Your only hope is to find one that will settle for just you."

My whole body ached and burned, because it wanted to reject what I'd just heard. How could I be expected to devote myself to a man who would always be pining for another woman?

"That isn't fair!" I snapped, and since my voice had begun to tremble in my throat, I stopped there.

"Of course it isn't. Life isn't fair," she replied, with her lips stiff and taut. "Stop crying! It won't change anything," she added, as she'd finally looked at me.

I tried so very hard not to love Michael. He pursued me with great fervour, said he would marry me, and at a time when I was considering marriage myself. It was too good to be true. Everything he said, I picked apart and dissected into little pieces. I was so sceptical and cautious, afraid to take anything he said for what it was, and I felt wicked for it. My mother's words echoed in my ears even as he presented me with that lovely ring. They were a deafening roar when he left me.

Grant was not sure if he should have put those details in the book. I told him he had to; Michael would not want what he perceived to be his greatest series of blunders to be omitted from his life story.

It started when the barn burned down.

While everyone was in their beds, a fire kindled inside, with all the animals trapped. The terrible heat I felt even so far away still prickles my skin when I remember it, and I can recall how hard it was to draw in a full breath. I wanted to go and just try to open the doors, as something sealed them shut, but Michael plucked me off of the ground and restrained me at a distance. I fought to pull myself free, but could not match his strength— and he wasn't even squeezing me that hard. I can tell you that it is very difficult to contain an angry child without injuring it, and it must have been about the same. At the moment, I thought it was the cruellest thing he'd ever done. Now, I don't know what I was thinking!

He lashed out at me further that afternoon. I thought I was trying to console him, as everyone had been so distressed. He used to seek me in those times, but on that day, he drove me off and berated me. I sat there and accepted it, as I'd done my whole life. Impulse wanted me to spit fire right back at him, but I held it in, because I wasn't also going to say something I'd regret. And then he stormed off, as if he was the one who'd been insulted! Isn't that always the way of it?

But the pressure was too much, and I couldn't stop myself from weeping— out in the parlour, how embarrassing! James came in and pestered me, which did nothing to help my mood. Since I did not want to talk to him, he summoned our father; that was worse. He would extract the truth from you, one way or another.

The next morning, I felt terribly ill, and was hoping for an apology of sorts. I think he was trying to come up with one, but I grew impatient and threw myself into routine to soothe my own nerves.

In the evening, I went to take a letter to post before the office closed. I must have chosen the worst possible hour to go out.

I'd walked home from town numerous times before, and never did I think I would have to fear for my life on such a quiet stroll, especially with company.

They grabbed James first, faster than I could react. I didn't realise what had happened until a strange, strangled cry caught my attention, and he was already behind me, making a fruitless attempt to free himself from one of the two assailants.

He made himself small and shed Michael's big coat that he was wearing, but right away, they grabbed him again.

And I stood there like a moron, too stunned to even scream, my body buzzing as if I was vapour.

"Run!" he yelled. "Go and get help!"

His words released me from the spell I was under. I took off my own coat to make myself lighter and turned, but not fast enough, because I was next. When I started to run, my feet didn't even get a chance to hit the pavement.

We were dragged into a nearby alleyway, out of the street lights.

I screeched louder than I ever had before, clawing, biting, and spitting like a feral cat. In the scuffle, I lost my glasses. I was tugged by my bodice, and it ripped. I pulled out a clump of hair before the man could master my hands. He must have grown frustrated, because I was flung into a wall and struck my face on cold bricks.

Suddenly, everything was as muted, murky, and slippery as if I was swimming in molasses. While spots and stars danced in my eyes, I heard James snarling, swearing he would kill them, and a string of language that is too strong for this book.

Another voice joined the chaos, and then a shotgun fired very close, disorienting me even more. After that, the men scattered, and I was dropped on the ground. The warm blood felt so wonderful on my face.

I was lifted up, and forced to use my feet.

"Oh, Miss Webb, Miss Webb!" came the voice of old John Briggs, the innkeeper. I cringed away from it. He was so loud. "You must stay awake, m'dear! We need to get you inside!"

He spoke to James about what they needed to do next. Briggs proposed he take us into his tavern to

be warm and stay put while he went and fetched
our father. James declined, insisting it would be
just as fast to take us straight home— it was far
less convenient for Mr. Briggs, but he consented
to the arrangement.

I was too disoriented to navigate myself, so I was
guided by the two men. Whenever Mr. Briggs
noticed I was beginning to slow down, he gave
me a good slap to keep me alert. Once, he caught
my broken nose, and I shrieked, now very awake,
but wishing he'd just dump me on the street to die
of exposure.

All I remember about arriving home was the
stitches. Papa couldn't give me any medicine
because of my head injury, so he only dulled the
pain with ice. He asked me several questions,
both to keep me awake and determine the severity
of the blow. I continuously had salts waved under
my nose.

Together, James and I gave our account of the
situation, and I gave my father the hair I'd been
holding on to. I was considered low-risk, but still
needing to be observed all through the night, and
then I was sent to bed while Papa set James's
broken hand.

I was tired, but too terrified to sleep. Despite
what he told me, I was absolutely convinced that
if I closed my eyes, I would never open them

again. I'd never been injured in such a way before, and almost couldn't handle it. It was silly for me to be lying there preparing myself for death when none of my wounds were so dire.

And Michael was upon me in such a pitiful state that I forgave him the moment I realised he was there. He made me feel secure, and kept a close watch over me, giving me anything I asked for, except for uninterrupted sleep, which he said was the one thing I couldn't have.

In the morning, he told me to stay right where I was, because all of my work would be taken care of. That was well, because I could hardly focus my eyes on anything, and it didn't help that my glasses were gone. Without them, I can't see more than an arm's reach away. At first, it was delightful to have an excuse to not do anything, but it grew boring within hours.

To my surprise, Michael presented to me his first attempt at breakfast: very strong tea, and toast that was uneven in every way. It tasted fine, because he scraped off most of the burned parts, probably wasting half of the bread in the process. He'd done a well enough job for his first time using the stove. Fortunately, his cooking skills would improve.

Ida came, as well. I heard her before I saw her, but she quickly understood to keep quiet. She

climbed into my bed and cried, and I tried to
share my breakfast with her. She didn't want it.

"Why would somebody hurt you? Who was it,
Alma?" she asked, and I didn't have an answer.

"Well, there are just some people whose motives
we can't understand, nor do we want to."

"When will you be better?"

"I don't know. Probably in a week or two."

"What will you do then?"

"I'll go to London for my nursing training, and I'll
come back here for a little while, but soon I may
be going away."

"Going away to where?"

"I am going to marry Mr. Bennett," I answered,
and I felt right in saying it.

She started, as if this was dreadful news.

"Why are you marrying him?" she demanded,
tugging at my bed clothes. "What did he say to
you?"

I laughed. It hurt my nose.

"He loves me," I told her. That was the plain and simple truth.

"You don't have to marry him just for that reason!"

Presently, I didn't think I needed any other reason. I thought love on its own could overcome all things, but the world doesn't work that way.

It didn't stop him from leaving.

I would have done anything at all to keep him there even a moment longer. I sat up in my room and waited, believing he was perhaps delirious or confused, and would come right back. Because of the cold and my injuries, I could not keep myself awake for very long, and I dropped off to sleep as soon as I sat down. I awoke, and he still wasn't there.

Regardless of his intentions when he departed, I only knew that he was gone, and I couldn't make him stay.

What I did in that time is not signified in Grant's book. It's about Michael, after all.

James hated him, and pretended he wasn't surprised. My father was confused and hurt, but not cut as deeply as I was— in every sense. He sent us to our mother so that I could be away from that miserable house while I recovered— or so he said. Mama bought me a bundle of sweets and cooked me anything I wanted (whether I wanted it or not) while she diligently tended to my wounds, but was indifferent to my mental anguish, and thought it was insignificant compared to how I was hurt.

Most of all, she was angry at me for fraternising with my father's hired boy, and at my father for allowing it to happen, and went on to say that had she known about it, she'd have kept me with her the whole time.

"See what happens to you when you don't heed my warnings? Well, you've had your fun, and for your sake, I won't reveal such sports to any potential suitors," she decided. "Once you heal up and take your training, you ought to get serious about your search, so just you forget about him."

She thought I should have been indifferent to the whole thing, so I resolved to appear so, and wept secretly, as I put myself to bed.

Outwardly, I handled it with grace and dignity, but inwardly, I thrust myself into work and studying so that I didn't have to handle it at all. When I showed distress about all that transpired, Mama blamed my head injury. Soon, it would heal, and I would no longer have it as an excuse.

All the while, I desperately tried to piece together what had even happened that made Michael leave, but my brains were batter, and some nights, it felt as if they were leaking out of my nose.

Reader, I did not go to London with my mother. I had originally planned to, but that is not the reality of the situation. In fewer than two weeks, that image was ruined.

In late February, I had gotten new glasses, and I began work on a fashionable walking suit for that trip that we planned to take in spring, with crisp and airy grey cotton that my mother eagerly purchased for me. Since I was going to be a professional woman, I simply had to have a brand new dress.

It made me remember my wedding dress that I would never wear, and the memory broke me down. I had at least one of those moments per day for a long time.

My mother caught me crying on the floor while I was meant to be sewing.

"What's wrong with you? Why are you crying?" she asked, standing in the threshold.

"I'm not," I turned my head and tried to discreetly wipe my face. "I'm tired."

"You are! I saw you. So, why are you crying?"

"It doesn't matter," I insisted, stooping over the sewing machine, hoping she would just let me work.

"Oh, it doesn't?" she stood over me now.

"It never mattered how I felt, as long as you were at ease," I spat without thinking.

"What are you saying? Look at me!" she grabbed my face and thrust it to meet hers. "When have I ever said that?"

I withdrew from her grip and tried to conceal how my lips trembled. "Any time that I—"

"Don't toss your head away from me, like you're better than me!" she moved to face me again. "When have I said that? Well?"

"You never did. But—"

"Then how *dare* you speak to me that way, after all I've done for you?" she snarled, and her eyes were very red. "How I suffered to keep you comfortable? Did that mean nothing to you?"

"Of course it didn't! I'm only saying that I've never felt safe being honest."

"That's on you, and you only! Only you are responsible for how you feel and reac—"

"But the same can be said for you—"

"Don't interrupt me!" she leaned close, and I nearly stumbled over my own skirt trying to step back. "You may be a grown woman now, but I am your mother— we are not equal. You would have nothing if not for me. That cotton you're cutting up was a gift from *me,* that I worked for, so that you could look so nice for your new profession. For *you!* I've done everything for you, and this is how you repay me!"

I will spare you most of the redundant details. It was a lot of *"you said—"* and *"no I didn't—"* tossed back and forth, and I just wanted this little discussion to stop.

And stop, it did.

"Well, if I can't measure up to *your* standards, then— then—" she threw up her hands and frantically looked every which way except at me, and I had my eyes fixed low on the wallpaper.

She was gone from the room by the time I looked up. I heard her say something to James, and then a few doors slammed.

Unable to repress all that I'd endured any longer, I fell in a heap with all of my dress material and howled— scratching the fine fabric into shreds, clawing at my face, my arms, my neck. I had never shrieked like that in my entire life. I thought I would die right then and there. I hoped I would. I didn't want to be seen alive after that exchange.

James tapped at the door. I didn't want him there. I wanted to be left alone.

"Oy there," he called in a tone I'd never heard from him before. "What's all of that? Let's get you cleaned up."

I braced myself to look in the mirror and see all of the ugly bruising on my skin, and my red, blotchy face.

"Good God!" I cried reflexively. "I look horrid."

"You don't," he thrust a cool rag onto my neck, and kept it there until I took it. "Listen, I'm going to take you to the Doctor."

"Why?"

"I think you should just stay with 'im for a while."

I didn't protest. I walked without any of my belongings, saying nothing. I didn't want to speak at all, and thankfully, he respected it.

He paid for a ride back to our father's house, where I felt forced to tell him all that she'd said, possibly ruining his game of cards and evening pipe.

"God," he mumbled, and set down his still-smoking pipe. "I hope you realise, she doesn't mean anything by it. Still, I think you should stay out of her way for a little while."

"I'm going to London," I insisted. "I'm going tomorrow."

He raised an eyebrow.

"Are you certain? You haven't fully recovered yet. If you wouldn't feel well staying here, you could perhaps stay with Minister Coleman and his wife, or maybe your grandmother, or Elisabeth, even."

"No. I want to go to London."

"And you have a plan for this?"

"Yes," I lied.

"Well," he sighed. "I can't stop you, but I can give you a little money if you need it."

Probably money from Michael. I wouldn't take it.

"No. I have plenty, and I will make my own way."

"For how long do you plan to be gone, then?"

"I don't know. Until I graduate from training."

"Please," he produced his pocketbook, pulling out a ten pound note. "Just enough to get you established somewhere halfway decent."

Reluctantly, I accepted.

"She didn't mean anything by it," he repeated.

I was tired of people justifying those who'd wronged me. I was even tired of myself doing it. I excused myself and went upstairs.

"Put some salve on your neck!" he called.

But I still needed to grab some things from her house. Though I was bitter and I could not think clearly, I knew I still needed to be smart about my exodus.

I hid in Papa's study, and murmured, *"Be not far from me,"* over and over until I had no more strength, and I slept in his chair for an hour. At five o'clock, I saw him downstairs, making toast on the stove.

"You will go, after all?" he asked, offering me toast that I didn't take.

"Yes. I said I would."

He nodded.

"When you settle, give me your address at once, and the names of the people you are with. Write me if you need anything at all, and I will come no matter what."

"I know."

"And your mother would, too. She is still your mother, that has not changed. I know she'd rather be pulled limb from limb than talk to me, but I will see if I can reason with her."

Maybe she had not changed, but I had.

I went back at eight o'clock the next morning, when she was usually out doing washing for folks in town, and I tapped on my brother's chamber window.

He opened it.

"What are you doing?" he hissed.

"Is she there?"

"No. Why do you ask?"

"I need some things out of there, and then I'm going off to London."

He let me in the house. I scurried into my old bedroom as quickly and quietly as a mouse, and recklessly stuffed what I needed into a bag, evading windows as if I was a burglar. I sure felt like one. There was some jewellery on my table. I took only what I'd bought with my own money. That meant sacrificing my beloved brooch, but after all, it wasn't mine.

Nothing in the world was truly mine, except my wedding dress: a horribly cruel trick fate had played on me.

I purchased a ticket, and since I was meant to depart in the evening, I had time to spare, so I went to be more meticulous with my packing.

I heard the front door open and shut. It must have been her.

"Where have you *been?*" I heard James demand.

"You're not my father!" was the reply.

It seemed she had never returned last night. Muffled discussion ensued. I dove over my bed and stooped down, mashing myself flat to the wall. She spoke to James for a long while.

"Where is she?" I heard footsteps draw near, and held my breath.

"I didn't see her come or go," he lied.

"She's probably hiding! She's such a child."

Then she opened my door.

"I brought those little sweets that you like. Come out and eat," was all she said to me.

I didn't. I would take from her no more. Instead, I waited until she was in her room, and then I stepped out with everything of mine that I could carry. All I had to do was slip out unnoticed, silently over the steps, and then I was free! I was sure she didn't see me, and if she did, she wouldn't stop me.

"Oh! So you're leaving!" she squeaked in a sickly sweet chirp just as my foot touched the last bottom step. I turned to face her.

She looked awful. Her eyes were red and drooping, her hair was dishevelled, and her shoes did not match her dress.

"Yes."

"Where do you think you're going?"

"London, to train and do as I please."

"To do as you please? When have I ever held you back?"

"I didn't mean tha—"

"You did. Don't talk to me as if *I'm* insane! I'm not my mother!"

Motherhood, at that time, appeared to be a generational succession of "at least I'm not my mother."

"So you'll go to London, and then what? You don't have any clue how horrendous it is there— because we saved every bit that we could to leave before you were born. Not that you care! Nothing I do is enough for you, it seems."

"I didn't mean that, either!" this time, I was determined to speak calmly, and never say more than I needed to.

"If you didn't, we wouldn't be standing here, having this conversation, *dearest child.*"

It was hardly a conversation.

"You'll live in deplorable conditions," she continued. "Likely with strangers, barely scraping by. You think you can live on your own, on a nurse's salary? A seamstress's salary? I've tried it! But go right ahead. If you'd really rather live with strangers than here with me, where you don't have to worry about food, because you hate me that much, then go ahead."

"I never said I hated you."

At that moment, I probably should have just left, but I couldn't. I could not move my feet.

"You didn't need to. I know we struggled, and I know sometimes I was distressed and took things out on you— and I'm *sorry* for that, but that's life! Maybe you're too young to realise it, but *nobody* is going to be mindful of your feelings. I'm *so sorry* I actually sent you to school, and didn't let you do whatever you wanted, like your good-for-nothing father."

"This isn't about him."

"Oh, it isn't? Your talk of London didn't even start until you finished school and started spending more time over there. Well, go on. Go be with people who won't *bully* poor, poor little Alma, and don't be surprised when you realise you can't make it on your own, or you die trying!"

I didn't reply, and so she spoke some more.

"So you can't be honest with me, *my dear?* Well, now is your time. What do you have to say?"

I had many things to say, but I kept them to myself, because none of it was nice. By keeping my composure while she spoke to me in that way, I felt I had triumphed over her. At the moment, I *did* feel better than her.

Even I knew that passionate confrontation was not always worth it. I did everything within my (limited) power to keep the peace, and may God bear witness to that. Even if she didn't respect me, I respected myself, all the more so, the fewer attachments I had.

"Well?"

"I don't have anything else to say."

"Of course you don't!"

She turned around and headed for the door, and I got ready to leave, but she stopped and pointed a finger at me.

"You are a bitch," she murmured with cool conviction. "I left, and you never once asked about me."

"I thought you wouldn't want to talk to m—"

"You don't care about anyone except yourself. You couldn't even face me as a grown woman. You were going to leave silently, as if you'd stolen everything that wasn't nailed down. I'll bet you did, too! *Spineless! Useless! Get off my steps!"*

The door slammed shut. That was that.

I walked slowly onward until the house was no longer in view, and then I ran, stumbling and tripping along under the weight of my bags. It was dark, I was very cold, and I hadn't eaten since yesterday morning.

Sometimes, while writing these events, I feel bad, knowing that she will most likely read them. Then, I remember how I felt having to experience them myself, and I don't feel that bad. I spared the worst details, anyway. Besides, our feelings are solely our responsibility, so if reading her own actions makes her feel some type of way, that isn't my fault.

LETTERS, LAURA, AND LONDON'S LAMENT AND LANGUISH

Before boarding the train, I pulled my standing lace collar up high to conceal the unsightly scratches on my throat.

I tried my best to feel nothing, and I succeeded until I took my seat. As soon as the train began to huff onward, and the gravity of what I'd done settled upon me, I convulsed with silent sobs. I buried my face in a book that my eyes were too cloudy for me to read. I wanted Michael. I wanted him to hold me, and though I knew I could never have that again, I could not perish the idea. I thought of his warmth as I rubbed my chilled fingers, and how he let me put them in his coat when I went out without any gloves.

Silently, I begged and pleaded with God, for nothing in particular. I only inwardly wailed *'God, help me!'* over and over, with my head bent over my clasped hands. Any little thing would do. Even just a glimmer of hope would have sustained me: anything to lift my spirits, which had never been lower in my life.

To me, that meant death. To my late grandfather Ronald, hitting bedrock meant there was nowhere to go but up. He told me "all will make sense in the end; if things don't make sense right now, then it just isn't the end yet."

I don't know if I believed it back then, and I still don't know if I believe it now, but he hasn't been proven wrong, yet.

London was… vertical. That was the most I could make of it so late at night. Dogs barked in the distance, and I could hear somebody weeping.

Immediately, I was fearful. My mother's stories of how horrendously dangerous this place was resurfaced within me, and I wondered if I'd made a mistake. I was a horrible child for leaving her, and leaving Ida. I could have just stayed quiet and made everyone happy. I tried so hard to make everyone happy.

But I refused to go home in shame, so soon after I'd left. I knew she would gloat that I couldn't make it without her after all, and then I would be further indebted to her. I walked, because that was all I could do. Since I went at an easy pace and did not look too meek or too eager, I did not catch anyone's attention.

I went to the first inn I found. It looked fairly clean, and didn't have too many drunken men or loose-looking women slithering around, so I deemed it safe enough. I paid a middle-aged dark-skinned lady for a cheap room. She knew by my accent that I was not local. She did not mention or look at all surprised by my injuries. That's how I knew what sort of place this was.

"Looks to me as if you're on 'ard times, baby," she noted as she counted the coins I offered.

"Oh, things could be a lot worse!" I answered, and that was true. I was then sent to a room upstairs.

"You lock your door, little Miss, y'ear?" she mumbled, without looking up from her newspaper.

Once I'd settled in my cramped little chamber and shut myself off from the world around me, things didn't seem so bad. I even felt confident and sure of myself, and I slept well even in that damp and frigid stall. I didn't think I'd be tired, but sleep overcame me as soon as I lay my head down.

'What will be, will be,' I thought in that moment.

I awoke much calmer than I was yesterday, but I still wondered what I was going to do next. I put Papa's ten pounds in a stocking full of face powder that I bought a year ago and rarely used, and then I combed my hair neatly, put it in nice plaits coiled on my head, and smoothed my collar, pinning a plain tin brooch under my chin. If I was going to be a disaster, I was going to be a pretty disaster.

I came downstairs for a flavourless runny porridge and burnt coffee that I was too ravenous to turn my nose up at, and I asked the inn mistress for her newspaper.

For half a penny, I could take it up to my room, as she was finished with it, but somebody else wanted it next, so I needed to be quick.

My eyes went straight to the crime reports. It was mostly petty theft and skirt flippers. I then skimmed over the cartoons to make me smile a little.

In the advertisements, I saw that three ladies were soliciting a fourth woman to share their apartment. The Madam in question needed to be punctual in paying a quarter, thus have proof of employment, to keep to herself, and be skilled enough to keep up with her fair share of the house work.

Well, I'd planned to be a nurse, but I was not employed just yet. I needed an occupation until then.

I asked the mistress, Mrs. Green, if she needed any assistance in the kitchen, and she admitted she could use an additional set of hands.

"But your hands is so soft, wee gal," she commented, pointing a chipped nail at my hands folded neatly over my cup. "How much use could ye be?"

"Oh, I'm sturdier than I look!" I promised, placing my hands in my lap. "I can peel potatoes, make a good broth, or do just about anything you need, or I could sweep and help wash the linens!"

She agreed to make use of me. The pay was barely enough to keep up with the expenses of my stay, and I was harshly scrutinised at first.

"Dat porridge is too tick! We're not tryin' to fatten guests up to roast 'em for Christmas dinner, we're honly feedin' 'em enough so dat dey won't complain," she warned as I prepared breakfast.

"You're takin' too long to clean de tables!" she barked at me as I meticulously scrubbed the grooves in the wood. "Dey don't need to shine!"

"You're goin' to wear dat dish down to powder. It's clean enough."

"Are you kneadin' dat bread, or givin' it a massage? May'aps you should be servicin' the drivers that come through 'ere."

Since my pay did not change with the effort I applied, I didn't think she'd have any reason to complain about cleaner tables and softer bread, especially on slow days. That first week was very stressful! I'd been so used to doing one thing at a time, doing it *thoroughly,* and then moving on to a new task. I admit, I sometimes wept silently as I worked, and contemplated giving up more than once. Maybe I could go back, slip past my mother somehow, and hide in my father's toolshed, working at the pharmacy.

It was truly not all bad. I had some pleasant conversations with Mrs. Green, as best as I could understand her. Her accent was very thick, probably Londoner with traces of many others, and I couldn't be sure of her ancestry, except that she was darker than a Sultan and grew up in an orphanage as a foundling. There just wasn't a great demand for little dark babies, so no family ever claimed her, but she'd managed to work for her freedom and become an independent woman.

Hearing of her trials, my grievances suddenly seemed insignificant.

A lot of travellers came through, young and old, and they watched me. They hadn't seen such a fresh face in these parts, they said. Why did my eyes seem so lost, they asked.

A few of them asked me to have a drink with them, sit in their laps, or sing to them. I'd never gotten this kind of attention before, and did not know how to react.

"Oh, I'm engaged!" I almost said a few times.

Sometimes, they did not ask, they just pawed at my skirt. I pretended I did not notice, and tried to discreetly pull myself free as I was serving ale.

"Oy, ye leave dat baby alone!" Mrs. Green barked at one of the men, holding her butcher's mallet in a menacing sort of way. "She is only fourteen! You touch 'er, and I'll smash yer knuckles!"

I opened my mouth to reflexively correct her, but decided I'd better not. My assailant did it for me, anyway.

"No way is she fourteen!" he grinned, bearing a set of broken teeth, still holding my clothes. "She's a little one, but she's all woman!"

"Would you bet yer life on dat, fool?" she came out from behind the counter and waved the mallet under his nose. "I ruin your 'ands, an' ye starve! You's too ugly to beg."

"Bah! She ain't worth fightin' over, anyhow," he released me.

Anyway, most of the men left me be.

"You ain't in te country, wee Miss!" she told me off to the side. "You gotta be meaner 'an that."

This would have never happened at Mr. Briggs's establishment, but that's just a matter of probability. If fewer people pass through, you simply won't come across as many slimy types of men. Additionally, he was not shy about the fact that he was armed and ready to shoot.

I found time to answer the advertisement, and write a few letters. First, I wrote to my father, just to announce my whereabouts, my intentions, and my well-being— it'd been several days. Hopefully, he hadn't chewed up his pipe yet.

I wrote a letter to Ida next, and made sure she knew that my decision didn't involve her, though I was sorry to leave without telling her. She could talk to me any time she wanted. I didn't expect her to write back— she could not sit still enough to even write her own name, but maybe she'd put a word in while Papa wrote to me.

Papa's heart nearly gave out when I told him I was working at a hotel, but he still sent me the money for my nursing training, along with a letter:

'It pleases me to hear of you. I was growing worried when a week went by, and I didn't get a letter. Why are you working in a hotel? If you

urgently need more money, your mother and I have old acquaintances in that area who would help you with no questions asked.

James told me what he heard of your last conversation with her. She is earnestly penitent, and would like to see you again, but I will only reveal your whereabouts to her if you consent.'

Then she should have written to me herself. She likely meant to ensnare me so that she could spit more venom. Whatever her intentions, I was not ready to see her face. As for her acquaintances, she had likely already told them what a terrible child I was.

"Have some patience and compassion for your mother who raised you!" was the best they would say to me.

I'd been patient enough with her. If her devotion to me had really been the cause of all her burdens, then it was fine if she hated me.

I perished the thought, because it sounded all too familiar, and that frightened me.

On one hand, I still tasted that awful bitterness. On the other hand, that weak little child within that needed to be held would have sickened herself trying to swallow down that poison, and accepted her without question.

I hid the money and wept until I felt my ribs would crack, as those two halves of me tried to pull apart and gain autonomy. Even within my own body, the adult and child fought for control.

Years ago, my mother was intricately woven into the centre of my life, because she was all that I knew. Maybe it was nobody's fault, but I had slowly begun untwining myself from her little by little, and by then, there was only one lingering thread left that had recently snapped.

I sorted all of my things in preparation for relocating and meeting those ladies, and then I undressed to thoroughly wash myself.

Michael's ring was on a cord around my neck. I must have put it on without thinking before I left. I didn't take it off when I saw it, either.

Now, did I want to look as neat and well-dressed as possible, or would that make me look presumptuous? I decided I would wear my best daytime dress, but plain hair and no jewellery (except the ring, tucked away under it all).

Today was not a busy day, so our interview would not be disturbed. One of the ladies arrived at the inn herself, as a representative. She introduced herself as Carol Fletcher, a seamstress.

"How do you do, madam?" I greeted her,
presenting her with fresh coffee and roast
potatoes I prepared from the kitchen at my
expense. For the coffee, canned milk would have
to do— as I was used to the fresh stuff, I could
not stomach it, so I made it black for myself.

"Oh! You are a gracious hostess, I see! I thank
you, I desperately needed something hot!" she
took her coffee at once, and I prickled with joy to
be praised for my hospitality again, and see
somebody devour my real cooking.

I gave a very brief description of my background,
and the best recounting of my employment
history that I could, sparse as it was, trying to
focus more on my plans for the future: to be a
nurse, of course.

"Ah, you don't say? A young lady with us named
Laura is a nurse herself, and a practising midwife.
She works at a hospital not far away."

"My! Then I won't be alone in that regard! Will
there be company often?"

"No, no. We keep to ourselves."

"Good! Smoke or liquor?"

"Marie has one pipe a day. Laura occasionally has
a pint."

"Ah, those are just fine. Do any of you regularly attend church?"

"I do. Laura does not. Marie is a Jew."

"No men and no children, I'm guessing."

"No, none of us. Marie and I are spinsters. Laura is a widow."

"Oh, dear—"

"It is fine. I don't think she liked him all that much, anyway."

They agreed to have me, and I agreed to be had. After many frantic letters asking my father what I was supposed to do next, I registered for my training, at Laura's very hospital, and brought my things to their dwelling. I moved to Western London. It was a bit more… decrepit.

I accompanied Laura to the hospital and watched her, and my training came in ten hour shifts. I was first charged with sponge-bathing patients, bringing their food, and changing out soiled bedding.

I now knew why my father made house calls. Hospitals were dreary environments. It was as if they were engineered to punish you for being sick. Clearly, nobody with any authority to influence the law had ever been inside of one. The stench of death was impossible to avoid. Despite what people may tell you, it is a stench you do not actually get used to. I had to wear a rag soaked with perfume on my face. There was always at least one moan of despair echoing through the halls. Sometimes, ignoring their anguish was the only option. I saw nurses faint from repeatedly administering chloroform.

Worst of all were the children. I saw them wasting in every way imaginable, or having been burned, beaten, and/or chewed up in factory machinery. Nobody was too young. If possible, I made sure to learn their names and address them properly.

The strain was so great that I wept right before and right after every shift for the first week, and after that, they set me on more complex and meticulous tasks. I was able to keep up, but just barely.

Once in a while, there was a birth in the hospital. I'd bore witness to every range of emotions a human was capable of when women laboured. Sometimes, it was the greatest joy of their lives, and sometimes, they grieved yet another mouth to feed.

I'd seen bodies shredded by all manner of man-made horrors, and I'd seen syphilis eat away someone's scalp, but the process of birth, indeed a woman's most natural profession, was a sobering experience unlike any other, and I imagined that birthing in a hospital only made it that much worse.

It made me grateful that I was scarcely touched by a man, and I was already taking mental notes of the arrangements I desired when/if my time came to give birth.

Even alongside Laura, walking from work was stressful. No matter how safe our surroundings seemed at the moment, my head was spinning, trying to look at everything at once— after all, I'd already been attacked on my way home once before. To this day, I feel a shiver up my back if I hear footsteps behind me.

Once or twice, I tried to take a walk by the Thames, to be soothed by the sound of a rushing current. It was too dull to make a habit of it. I didn't think it was possible for a body of water to be dead or dying, until I beheld that open-air sewer. Michael would have wept. Both my parents claimed it used to be far, far worse, which I cannot comprehend, even now. I saw many young men and a few girls wading up to their chests in the putrid lifeline of London, scavenging for anything that could be sold— with their bare hands and feet! It could not be faulted; they did what they needed to do to survive, but I knew that I would see some of them in the hospital soon enough.

I never thought I would enjoy inside more than outside, but I established a bit of a home away from home with these three women. We lived in two rooms, and each had a stove and a pair of cots. Bathing took place by order of seniority; of course, I was the last. Laura had the least shame out of us all. She would walk around in any state of undress, and sit so close while talking that you could see the veins in her eyes. I hated it, because she was tall, well-built, and beautiful, and I was none of those.

Together, we tried to make our little corner of squalor tolerable. In order to have a vague understanding of me, they asked me a standard list of questions: Where was I from? Did I have brothers and sisters? Were my parents both living? Was I married? Did I have any children? I'm only eighteen? Well, that's old enough to have children.

"Oh, Marie!" Laura stopped my interrogator. "There's no way she has any children."

I froze, and felt blood rise in my face.

"Pardon?"

"It's obvious you're a virgin!" she insisted. "The hair and eyeglasses are practically a chastity belt."

My face grew hotter still, but this time from indignation.

"What's the matter with them?" I demanded.

"My, you won't keep any man except some middle aged Quaker who wouldn't be any fun at all. You're in desperate need of fixing up."

The mere mention of keeping a man brought bittersweet reminiscence to the surface, and I retreated to my corner of the room.

"Why, Laura, you hurt her feelings!" Marie cried. "You come on too strong, you really do!"

"My, my, my!" Laura tried to smooth over the blows she'd landed by stroking my back as I sat and pretended to practise my sewing. The touch angered me. "I only meant that you're so lovely, and you mustn't hide it!"

"There's no need to lie to me," I chuckled through my tears. "That isn't even my problem."

"And what is, hmm? Come, tell me, tell your Aunt Laura," this strange lady brought my head to her perfect bosom and patted my hair away from my face.

Since I couldn't lose a reputation I didn't have, I explained my silly plight to them.

They cursed his name, and all men of his status. I protested that they did not know him as I did.

Their advice, surprisingly, was a bit helpful, once we got past "burn everything you can't sell," and "go and bed every gainly young man you find until you don't miss him anymore."

"Write him a letter," Carol told me. "You don't even need to send it to him. Write down everything that you feel, and hold nothing back, but don't keep it! Drop it in the Thames, burn it, or tie it to a pigeon, as long as you let go of it."

That sounded so romantic, and yet so practical! I set to work on my letter once everyone else had gone to sleep. I wrote down exactly what I felt and thought, no matter how irrational I knew it was in that moment, only for me to find myself unable to discard it.

I took it back home with me, and I went into his room. Everything was untouched, and scattered about as if he'd been there yesterday. I tidied the place up, because it would have driven me mad if

I didn't, and I put the letter in one of the drawers, as if he would come back and find it.

What caught my attention was a heap of opened letters from an Abraham E. Reed. I remembered that this was Michael's butler, and an acquaintance of my father's. Just when I'd finished up my letter of severance, curiosity and a fierce longing overtook me. If anybody knew of his whereabouts and well-being, it'd have been him! I wrote a letter to him next, introducing myself, explaining the situation as I saw it, and asking if he knew anything at all. If I could only confirm that he was alive, I could leave that letter behind, and I could live again.

Abraham Reed was such a tender and gentle soul. His letter began with an outpour of sympathy and remorse, as if he was the one who'd wronged me, and only a footnote dedicated to his own fear. He knew nothing of Michael's whereabouts, and didn't even know he'd left.

He didn't tell his beloved Abraham?

I borrowed a little money from Papa to visit Mr. Reed in Liverpool. He knew at once who I was when I knocked at his door.

"Dear little girl!" Abraham cried and took my hands. "You have to be Miss Alma Webb, to be upon my house at this hour! I knew it was you!

You are every bit as lovely as Master Bennett described you!"

"Oh, no, sir! I am nothing special," I protested, brushing over his mention of Michael speaking of me, because it was too sweet, and too horrid, and because in those days, I did not feel lovely.

"Nonsense!" he rasped sharply, and took my bag from me. "You *are* pretty, just lovely, fresh as morning dew! You are far too pretty and too precious to be slaving away in the gutter of London, panting that foul air, no doubt beating men off of you with a stick."

"Hardly so," I tried to snatch my bag back, but he was already taking it into a guest chamber, chattering to himself about tea needing to be finished.

He brought me into his neat and spotless parlour, and offered me the aforementioned tea, which I was not in the mood for, but I accepted in order to be a gracious guest. It was a cinnamon and walnut breakfast tea brewed very bitter, and nearly half milk, the way Michael liked it (yet he hated coffee).

"My dear, my dear!" he sighed some more as he laid out bread and butter that neither of us touched. "I cannot tell you how it pains me to meet you under these circumstances, but I welcome you. You are a little darling to pay a visit to a lonely old man."

"It is nice to meet you, as well," I replied, and that was the truth. Michael spoke of him often, and it was only good things. "I'm sorry to be so much trouble, coming late at night—"

"No, no, you sweet thing, you are welcome here at any time," he insisted. "You are free to stay here for the night if you would not feel well boarding a train so late, or staying in one of those inns all alone. And if you would not want to stay here, I can give you a ride to anywhere you'd like— free of charge!"

He was so unflinchingly kind to me, a stranger, because he loved Michael that much.

I agreed to stay the night, but I had to answer many questions for him in the morning. Before I'd had a chance to get out of bed, he was at the door with eggs and toast, demanding to hear anything I knew that might have involved his master's disappearance.

As I'd hit my head at around that time, it was hard to remember the fine details, but suddenly, it occurred to me— I recalled our secret, about his run-in with the magistrate's nephew. Terror seized me. He did say that he was sure people were looking for him, and I sensed he shared my

foreboding of the inevitable consequences if they
knew it was him. Did he leave because he feared
for his life? For mine?

It was so dreadful that I didn't want to even speak
it, but I felt I had to tell Abraham all about it. I
asked him to sit at my bedside so I could explain.

The more I spoke, the older he got. He aged to a
hundred before my eyes, and before I'd touched
my breakfast.

"My, my, my!" he cried and tugged at his fingers.
"I never imagined things would get so out of
hand! Who knows what state of mind he's in
now?"

Or if he'd even lived to see twenty, we both
thought, but could not bring ourselves to say.

Though my mind tended to wander to the worst
possible places, I knew he was alive even then. I
felt it in my feet touching the earth.

And off to the side, I thought: *Did my mother feel
the same things that we were feeling since I left?*

No, it was not the same. I'd gone well over a
month without seeing her before. Most likely, she
didn't even miss me. And why would she? Last
we "spoke," she couldn't even stand the sight of
me!

"He loves you," Abraham said after a long while, noticing my thoughtful silence. "He still does, I know it. Whatever his reasons were, you could not have prevented it, and are not at fault."

I knew it was true already, but it was good to hear.

We spoke of other things, as well, because wringing our hands did no good. He asked if he could see the ring, and it was always on my person.

I cannot say enough how much I adore this perfect ring. In those days, pearls as a gift were considered bad luck, but recently, they have been designated as the gem of June, my birth month, which pleases me! To me, pearls are the jewel of true love. Unlike cold and ancient stones from the earth, they are the direct creation of something living, and they require so much care, as they must be touched so that they shine. The wearer becomes a part of them. They are the most fragile of gemstones, but when treated well, they shine for centuries. Russian gold is unique and never tarnishes, and opals glitter as though you captured the surface of a lake in your hands.

Oh, but I'm getting ahead of myself.

Abraham was wonderful company, and I felt I'd
known him for years after only one visit. If he
were a man of the outdoors, he'd have been the
mirror image of Grandfather Webb. I told him
where I was staying in London so that he could
write to me there, as well.

That afternoon, I returned for another stretch of
long shifts. If my mail wasn't dated, I'd have
been completely unaware of the days going by,
because sometimes the sun was up when I was
finally able to get some sleep, and I could not rely
on counting my meals, because I simply ate
whenever I could, *whatever* I could.

My diet in the country was lavish compared to
what was available in the city. The primitive
wood stoves that we had were not suitable to
bake bread, so it was rare that we had it fresh.
Stewed vegetables on dry toast sustained us for
most of the week. Meat and butter were luxuries,
and of course, we did not cook with lard. I
definitely ate more fish in London than anywhere
else. I adapted to it with grace, though, because
we were often found wanting when I was
growing up and we struggled. In fact, I found
myself going back to old recipes I'd learned when
I was very young, and I shared them with the
other ladies.

Always, I prayed over my meals, as I was
thankful for what I would get. This is a good

practice no matter your circumstances. Even Michael prayed over his food, because no matter what you eat, it is a part of something that was alive, thus you should show gratitude for its sacrifice.

That is not to say that I didn't really miss food from home. I took advantage of that oven every time I visited.

And Abraham, the thorough fellow that he is, sent letters to both locations. I am not sure where he found the money or the energy, but I had one waiting for me at the Webb residence, which I saved for later so that I could bake a loaf of bread to eat hot with my bare hands. After my dissolute repast, I read by dim candlelight with eyes half-shut:

'Dearest Miss Webb,

Michael is alive! I have gotten word from him, and have his letter on my desk as I write to you. He says he is not destitute, nor is he rotting in some ditch in the countryside, though there were some days that he wished that were the case. He is well, and with friends, making more permanent arrangements for his future.

I was so elated, I could not stop myself. Forgive me for being so crass— I hope you are well, and that you are successful in your pursuits. Please

*give all my best to your household, and visit me
some time.*

Abraham.'

Such precious words! I felt as if I could breathe
again. I relayed this information to Papa, and
asked him if he'd gotten any letters from Michael.
He had not.

At once, my rapture crumbled. Had he forgotten
us? Were his more permanent arrangements
rebuilding a new life without us, while so many
of his things remained— while I still had his
ring? Did he ever plan to tell us?

It's true that my mind often assumed the worst,
but these ideas were not even that; they were
perfectly practical and realistic, and not
particularly ghastly in nature. Despite being too
bitter for me to dwell upon, I could not stop
thinking about it.

The best case scenario in my mind was that I was
the proverbial unattainable woman canonised in
his heart, that could not return to, forcing him to
seek another for a wife. And yet, that was so
much more painful than being forgotten.

But whatever happened, I was determined to live
my own life, and trust in God's will for me. It was

all I could do now. I was able to save little bits of money, and I was getting better at my work.

First, I threw myself back into mind-numbing routine, so that I didn't have to think. I reasoned that I was exactly where I was meant to be, so it was alright to settle in that space for a little while, even if it wasn't ideal. It was much better than where I was before, and I was glad to take the independence of London over the infinite comforts of home, where I was viewed as a baby. I suppose that's easy when both are readily available to you. I'd probably have loathed living in London if I didn't have the choice to leave it, as many people unfortunately did not.

The biggest test was going to other places. Once in a while, I travelled a modest distance by myself, just to behold the new surroundings. I had my father's wanderlust, but it was at odds with my timid nature. If I didn't challenge myself and go anywhere other than those two destinations, I'd never thrive.

Additionally, I finally allowed my father to disclose my London address to my mother. I hoped she wouldn't arrive unannounced, but if I did see her again, I'd have preferred it be in a home I paid for, where I had authority.

All she did was mail me a box of assorted tea biscuits, with a note expressing concern that I was not eating enough. I accepted this as her own way of attempting to make amends, because I was no longer trying to tell myself cruel things to protect my feelings.

I visited Abraham sometimes, as promised. He told me that he would eventually live with Michael, and try to "straighten him out," whatever that meant. It set me at ease to hear about him.

I loved Michael. That had not changed. However, I could not pour all of my time and energy into grieving what we had. I was finally able to think of him without plunging into some distraction to keep myself intact, and content as long as I knew that he was alive and well.

It is, of course, foolish to pine for things you cannot have, but I allowed myself a little foolishness. Oh, yes, I pined for him, but life was going to march onward, with or without him. I could live without him. I didn't *want* to, but I could manage it, and the more I did it, the easier it got.

Still, I kept that door open, so that just a sliver of light escaped. I prayed in earnest over it, and I did not receive any warning or great revelation against it, so it must have been safe to do. Yet I could not even begin to think of how to contact him, or if he'd want me to. I did not have the courage to ask Abraham such a thing. To do so would make my presence known, anyway. I would *not* make him aware of my state of mind. I had too much pride.

I didn't talk about him with my fellow London inmates, because they hated him. They were ready to believe that there was no genuine good in him, and that to think of him was self-abuse. Oftentimes, we arrived too exhausted to make conversation, so it hardly mattered, anyway.

And Abraham sent me a shocking letter:

'Sweet child,

I have taken up residence with Michael, as you know. He lives in a large, old ancestral house by himself, except for me. His profession is a strange one: he tends to snakes and lizards for a Mr. Kelley, an eccentric Bohemian in Bristol. I don't see the appeal, but it pays well, and he seems to enjoy it.'

Of course he would. Michael loved all creeping things, because, "Somebody has to."

'He lives well, but his friends reside far away, and he spends days at a time away from home. You are under no obligation to take my word for it, but he feels terrible for having left you. He does not speak of it often, because he believes he has

done an unforgivable thing that he can not take back, and is worried he would trouble you if he reached out himself. I told him that he should find out for himself! He is either too fearful or too proud. He does not know that we are speaking. I don't know if I should tell him. It is in your hands, whatever you would like to do.

Abraham.'

I did not know what I'd like to do! But I didn't need to make any major decisions right that second, so I told him I would think long and hard.

And then I thought about it as little as possible.

I tried working with my father, as his assistant on house visits. It was awful! He would not let me work, intending to shield me from blood, vomit, tears, pus, bruises, and bare skin. Whereas I was there to do my profession well, he was merely taking his little girl to work with him. And that was where he wanted me! I told him that I could not sit and be a display while people really needed my help, and returned to the hospitals, even if it was harder.

In London, we saw less frostbite and less pneumonia as the world warmed up. But just as soon as it was warmer, we had a handful of people collapsing from working long hours and being unable to cool themselves. Even the nurses were susceptible. Some of my patients were my colleagues.

You surely know of Jack The Ripper, the legendary and infamous icon of London's criminal underbelly. Well, to us, he was a real terror. Though he only seemed to strike in Whitechapel, the working women of the city reasoned that he would not necessarily stay there. Despite these crimes happening so near to us, I never came across such a scene myself; there was no shortage of people dying of exposure on the street or wasting away in the hospital, but a fresh murder, not so much. Still, nobody in our flock went out alone at night unless it was absolutely necessary, and at least one of us always had some sort of weapon.

In fact, anything in your hands can be a weapon. A slimy sort of man skulking around the hospital waiting to get a handful of skirt instead got a mouthful of hospital waste water. I was not in the mood to be pawed at. Such is the hazard of merely being a young woman in the city.

But it was right that I was there, as I finally found a real calling to serve.

I was an idiot for fancying running off to Africa to do the work of God, when my countryman needed me right at my doorstep— a great and dire need, at that! I did what had to be done in the hospital, and when I had time to spare, I took my efforts out into the greater city.

I even began to spend my money differently. Each time I ventured to put a little extra on a good cut of meat or a box of sweets, I thought really hard about it. When was the last time I afforded myself such luxuries? Two weeks? I could go longer than that, so I set that money aside for another day.

Together with Laura, I collected funds to go into the local churches and distribute much-needed supplies to families who could barely afford flour. Laura and I personally ministered to the young girls, and we taught them about sanitation, babies, and various preventive measures against disease and other conditions. Maintaining cleanliness was a challenge when many of them lived stacked on top of each other. Laura taught girls how to sew, as she was better at it than me. She told them that it was the best skill for them to feed themselves, because people always need new clothes.

Of course, many seamstresses in the cities were being replaced by factory workers who produced hundreds of near-identical garments in a day. I knew it well, because sometimes we had to assist in the amputation of fingers and whole hands chewed up by dangerous machines. Some of the ladies coming to see us in that church worked in those places, themselves. It astounded me, what people could be subjected to just to have barely enough to survive. *'In the sweat of thy face shalt thou eat bread,'* indeed, but this was hardly short of slavery— yes, it had been abolished only on paper. They did the work, and they were not too proud, so they had a greater degree of humility than I'd ever possess, and they were entitled to more than what they received from their employers.

It was awful to see little children's filthy, cut up feet. I entreated many family members to mail me any children's shoes that nobody was wearing, even if they were worn out. Myself and all the ladies I was with knitted hundreds of stockings.

Naturally, I drew closer to Laura, since I spent so much time with her. Our relationship was a peculiar one. She always had a nice thing to say, even if it wasn't always sincere, and she questioned you more than your own parents. She was obnoxious and best taken in small doses, and she did like to gossip, but she was a fantastic nurse who would do anything for someone in need, even if only she saw the necessity.

She tried to get me to let her pierce my ears, even though it frightened me.

"You like earrings, so just do it!" was her reasoning.

I did always like earrings. When I was very little,
I used to press tassels, feathers, beads, and
buttons to my ears until they stuck, and admire
myself in the mirror before they could drop off.
As a child, Mama wouldn't let me wear them,
citing some incident that happened when she was
fourteen, when Eliana offered to do her ears for
her. When I got older, I just didn't have the
courage to maim myself. Laura promised that it
didn't hurt, I just needed ice and a searing hot
needle.

Instead, I applied a little ingenuity and insanity in
a way that would have made Michael proud: I
took a pair of lightweight earrings that were
gifted by Aunt Sophia and worked the hooks with
facial grooming tools after heating them on the
stove, then coated them in wax. They hung from
my ears like clothes pegs. Earrings that you
attached with screws and levers were not
common in those days.

"It would have been easier to just let me pierce
your ears," Laura complained, seeing me revel in
my crude and primitive experiment. It was
perfectly fine as long as nobody looked too hard
at it.

"And when are you going to go and catch
yourself a man, making yourself so pretty like
that?" she asked as I put the jewellery away. "All
that energy, going to waste!"

"Oh, well—" I couldn't think of a good way to put my feelings into words, so I kept it short and simple. "I don't think I'll ever marry."

"I didn't say marry! I said get yourself a man! Nineteen, and never touched! It's about time you had a taste, don't you think?"

"A ta— oh…" I don't think I'd ever blushed so hot in my life.

"What do you have to lose, except what you should have lost already? You're not getting married, you said," she continued to plead her case.

Well, first and foremost, I was hoping to go through life with as few chronic diseases as possible. Secondly, my values were not here to appease anyone on earth, but to honour my Lord. Thirdly, and most importantly to me, I just didn't want to. Laura understood after only needing it explained four times.

I was always giving and receiving letters in those days. I passed a birthday and a Christmas in London, much to my family's dismay, but to my secret delight.

I started to write my mother a letter in January, as I knew her birthday was near. It had been nearly a year since I'd spoken to her, and I thought that I had healed enough to write without too many strong feelings.

'Hello, Mother

I am well.'

That was as far as I got before things became complicated. I couldn't shun her forever. It's not even that I was doing it on purpose. I hadn't opened the tin box of biscuits she'd sent, but I hadn't thrown them away, either. They were in a locked chest under my cot. I considered sending them back, but that'd have been in bad taste. I could give them to the children at church…

This was the one issue that I did not bring to anybody else, ever. It was difficult to make people understand what I felt, so I didn't even try.

I stared at the paper for many minutes, and those minutes became an hour. It just shouldn't have been so difficult.

I finally went to church to seek answers from a man of the cloth. I don't think I ever had before. I fully anticipated being called a sinful woman for failing to honour my mother. Whenever strife between parents and children was revealed, barring fathers that were useless drunks, the burden to reconcile was placed on the offspring, as we must seek to reconcile with our Lord, who is perfect… but our fleshly parents were not.

I had not come to a regular Sunday service in a while, and on that day, I slipped inside an hour after, just as the last lingering attendant had left. I knocked and waited for old Reverend Ryan Mulligan.

The door opened, and a young man I'd never seen showed himself.

"Oh! You are not Reverend Mulligan!" I blurted out, stupidly. At least the heat of my shameful flush warmed me up a little.

"No, Madam, I am John Bailey," he stepped aside, inviting me in, out of the cold. "I have studied under the Reverend for ten years, and I am here every other week. I don't recognise you. What are you called?"

"I am Alma Webb," I offered my ungloved hand.

John Bailey shook my hand. His snowy white fingers felt cold and waxen. He had flared nostrils, an assertive nose, and very rectangular features, all made even sharper in the light of the lamp we stood by. Even his eyebrows were boxy. His eyes might have been green; in the fire, they were golden. His features were beautiful, but unnerving. I imagine that is how angels looked when they walked among men.

The door shut behind me. On the piano, I saw music open to the hymn, *Come Thou Fount.*

"That is my favourite piece to play. It speaks to me," he declared, following my wandering eye.

"Does it? May I have a look?" I was then unfamiliar with it, and I had only asked to buy more time, but as I read on, it would soon be my favourite, as well.

"It is always a pleasure to see a new face," he began very slowly. "What brings you to the house of God today?"

"Oh, well," I cleared my throat, realising he was *still* holding my hand. I gave it a light tug, and he let go. "I wanted advice on familial matters, or at least somebody to talk to."

"Somebody to talk to? Well, talk away."

"It isn't exactly inherently spiritual," I tried to explain. "It is more personal troubles."

"You may find that the root of the issue is spiritual, after all. It would perhaps help to speak them aloud, and give them a voice."

"Perhaps you're right! I hope that you don't mind—"

"No, no. It would delight me to listen," he said, without a hint of pleasure in his tone.

"Ah, it's sort of about my mother," I started, and he took my hand again, leading me to a set of chairs by a window and a little stove, where a kettle sat. He silently offered me tea while I tried to piece my sentence together, and though I was thirsty, I shook my head, because I wanted no distractions.

"I have many conflicting feelings about my mother," I admitted.

I waited for him to condemn me or recoil in shock, or comment on womanly rivalry. He did none of those.

"Whatever for?"

"Well, it's— she—" suddenly, it seemed my tongue was stuck to my teeth. Maybe I should have accepted the drink. "I don't want to speak ill of her…"

Mr. Bailey signed, put down his tea, and folded his hands.

"She isn't here."

At first, that seemed so obvious. Of course she wasn't! However, I sat and pondered that statement for a minute. Almost every move I made, I wondered what she would think. She had been the voice in my head for my entire life. *"She isn't here,"* was a powerful incantation that freed my lips and lifted the *geas* over me.

Out of me poured a torrent like no other, describing, in great detail for the first time in my life, all that I'd carried, and the two mothers and half a father who raised me, my brother— even Emerson came up, which not even Michael had known about. All the while, Mr. Bailey helped himself to a second, third, and fourth cup of tea, leaning close and listening. Why was this stranger so much easier to talk to than anyone I'd met?

"That brings us to today," I choked out the last words of my testimony.

Mr. Bailey took the other cup. "You are quite hoarse. I don't suppose you've changed your mind about the tea? There is a little left."

"Well, just a drop, thank you."

He filled the cup halfway, and I just pressed the warm rim to my lips at first, letting the steam caress my face.

"Your plight is a unique one," he said at last. "But by no means is it singular. A great many people, especially young girls, have complicated mothers."

"Am I wrong for feeling this way?"

"No. We cannot control our feelings— only our actions. And you, my dear, have conducted yourself better than many. God has been calling you to act on these feelings for many years, and today, you heard Him— just as He has heard all of what you just said to me, long before you ever spoke."

"With respect, sir," I cautioned. "I have already found salvation, and am not here to be converted. You need not state the obvious to me."

"Ah, but what is obvious to you may not be obvious to somebody else. You asked me just now if your feelings are wrong, seeking validation for a truth that would be immediately apparent to another person."

I didn't know whether or not that made sense, but I did know I was suddenly embarrassed.

"Yes, I suppose," I murmured and sipped the tea. It was now lukewarm.

"Well, what do you want out of it all?"

"I just wanted this burden alleviated a little. I already have that, thank you, though I'm sorry for talking so mu—"

"No. As I said, I am here to listen."

"Oh, yes, that's true," I finished the tea and set the cup down. "Moreover, I'm thankful that somebody understands. I wish I could make her understand without pushing her further away."

"But I'm sure you know by now that this is not up to you."

"I… yes."

"It is right to grieve for your childhood. Make the answers for yourself. Pray for her in earnest, but take her or leave her. What happened to you—you cannot change it. You cannot change her: only yourself."

"Figures that I'm the one who must fix it all," I mumbled, knowing what I had to do, but allowing myself a moment of self-pity and petulance.

He smiled, with a pleasant crinkle around his eyes. So, he was human after all!

"It seems unfair that you are the one who must make adjustments to right these wrongs, but it is for you, and nobody else. Likewise, if you forgive her, it is for your benefit, and yours alone."

"I can do my best."

"That will just have to do. She is probably doing her best, as well."

I believed it. He prayed over my circumstances, and I stood and shook his hand, but the contact broke me. As soon as my fingers folded into his, I felt my face grow hot and reflexively contort, and I wept shrieking sobs like a famished infant as he lightly entwined me into his arms. His whole body was cold. My cries echoed in that empty church.

Several minutes passed before I could say anything.

"This is so humiliating," I retched, nearly choking on my own tears and saliva.

"Why?"

"I don't even know you! I came here uninvited and unloaded all of my problems on you, and now I'm crying all over you!"

"Nonsense, your invitation was set apart long ago," he produced a pocket handkerchief to wipe my face. He pressed it into my hand. "There are still some hours of daylight left. Go and take a walk. It is lovely outside."

"Oh, yes, it is," I chuckled. "I think I will."

I removed myself from his grasp and headed to the door, then turned around to see him still standing at the window.

"Goodbye, Mr. Bailey! Thank you once again!" I called.

"It was nothing, really."

"God bless you, sir!" I called once more, with one foot on the threshold.

"You as well."

"Take care of yourself!" both my feet were out the door.

"Of course."

"Stay warm tonight!"

"Yes."

"Goodbye!"

"Goodbye."

I slammed the door and hoped I'd never see him
again, after a departure like that.

I still have that handkerchief. I found it in my old
wardrobe at my father's house only a week ago. It
is still crisp and bright blue. Finding it summoned
many memories within me, so I took it home and
put it in my jewellery box. Sometimes, I even
entertain the idea of returning it one day, not that
I had any idea how.

I heeded his advice, and took a walk. Away from
the sprawl of the city, it truly was lovely that
day— it was lovely just about any day. There was
still a light dusting of sugary frost on the ground.
I loved all types of weather, and was reminded of
that just then. I missed the outdoors. I walked
outside all the time, but it had been a long while
since I really took in my surroundings.

It was in nature that I found myself again. That
sounds too romantic, but it was the truth. I took
long walks into the fields, as I did when I was
very little, just to feel that amazement again. I
rediscovered childlike wonder, and took little
pieces of it along with me like I used to. It was
like collecting pieces of myself that I'd lost along
the way— a little blanched and weathered, but
still right where I left them. Birds singing in the
trees sounded the same as they always did. I still
took a simple delight in splashing in the shallow
creek, cold as it was, and chains of flowers

looked just as pretty ten years ago as they did now.

I thought of the quilts my grandmother made of old dresses that had been worn down to rags. She said, "If you can't make them the same as they were before, make something better."

Out by the creek bed, I began rebuilding myself new and better.

At home, I cut my hair. It wasn't anything drastic. I cut a nice, pretty fringe above my brow, and I liked my features a lot more when I did that. The ladies in London approved of it too, which was splendid, but not necessarily required.

With the money I did not spend on treats, I got new eyeglasses that didn't take up so much of my face.

And with practice, I learned a few modern hairstyles that could be done quickly, and added my personal touch.

Inwardly, I spoke gently to myself. It was hard to get into that habit.

It is alright. Put it down and try again later, I told myself when my sewing did not turn out quite how I wanted it.

By spring, I was brand new— but not finished. You see, we are always repairing ourselves, little bits at a time.

However, once you change what is happening on the inside, some of the things that surround you naturally follow.

In March of 1889, Abraham Reed presented me with an oddly-worded request:

'I hope this message finds you well! I am in need of some assistance, I'm afraid.

If you would be willing to help an old man, there are many things I left behind at my residence in Liverpool. Some personal effects need to be packed up and taken out very soon. If you could name a time and date that would be convenient for you to go there for me, it would be greatly appreciated, though I cannot pay very much.

Young Bennett will be there to pick those things up. I will not tell him you are coming— he is so sensitive. Of course, only speak to him as much as you would feel comfortable doing so.'

It pleased me that we were on good enough standing that he could ask me to take up such a task, but it annoyed me that his intentions were crystal-clear, and he could be so reticent about it.

I told him that I could arrive on April 19, and stay for the afternoon, but I would take no payment. I needed that entire month to mentally prepare myself. I absolutely wanted to speak to him, but what did I say?

I considered digging up the letter I wrote him a year ago. I did not, but I continuously wrote and rewrote all of the things I was certain I would say to him with a firm countenance and a solemn tone— I said none of it. When I saw him, my words failed me, and I forgot them in an instant. It seemed like a lifetime since I'd seen him.

And he had changed, indeed; he was a bit thinner, his eyes were more tired, and his hair was quite long, touching his shoulders while wet, but it was still him. I thought he was lovely. Immediately, I became conscious of how I had transformed. How did he view me?

Did he have another woman already? I couldn't help but wonder. No, if he was groomed so poorly, he couldn't possibly.

I wondered if he mistook my demeanour for coldness. I bore no ill will towards him, and couldn't possibly have been angry, but to stand near him and not touch him, nor bear my heart was agony. Now was not the time. I could hardly trust myself to speak.

He always did put too much power in my hands.
Whether or not he would see me again was left
entirely up to me.

ROCKS, TOADS, AND OTHER THINGS
FOUND OUTSIDE

Mainly, I was fearful of making myself
vulnerable again, but I took the risk, and invited
him back to my father's house, with his consent.
Again, I had an entire script for the encounter that
I'd all but published, and did not adhere to it.
Talking to him was just natural, even after all this
time. He was so remorseful, that I had to forgive
him on the spot, and I was able to believe his
promise of better things.

I wore his ring on my hand again, though not out
and about in London, as I was not interested in
being robbed.

With the understanding that our engagement was
ongoing, I needed to prepare accordingly in my
spare time, even agreeing to go to his house. I felt
bad about bringing Ida, especially on such short
notice, but I hadn't yet gotten her used to the idea
of me being married, and quite honestly— her
presence would surely be a deterrent from
temptation.

I was warned before I arrived that the house was
full of spiders.

Many people do not understand spiders. My
father was fascinated by them, and often read me
books about them. As for my awareness of the

little creatures, it began when I was fifteen. I knew I shouldn't have been, but I was a little afraid of them throughout my childhood. It was completely irrational. One day, I was cleaning a window and saw a leggy spider making its way up the wall beside me. Without thinking, almost in a panic, I thrust a shoe onto the little thing and killed it with a horrid crunching sound.

After that, I stared for a long time at the remnants on the plaster, and pondered its place in the world, along with mine. It had done nothing to me, and was much weaker than I. Obviously, I was not going to eat it. It was probably doing our house a great service by catching real pests. What gave me the right to snuff it out? Doing so did not benefit me in any way, and yet I had ended its life in a single second, with no forethought.

All at once, I was so full of remorse, I sat on the floor and cried, inwardly begging God to forgive me for treating one of His treasures with such disregard.

I scrubbed out that awful spot, but I still see it, even though it is not there anymore.

From that day onward, spiders were friends. I still took flight when they came near, but I regarded them with respect, and admired their intricate movements, and beautiful webs.

Michael liked to pick them up and let them crawl on his face. I think one of my favourite things about him was his admiration of that which many people would overlook, or even scorn. He did not need to play up their mysticism or dress them up in prose to make them appealing. He was able to appreciate exactly what they were. For that reason, his tendency towards poetic language puzzled me. I suppose that's just the way he was taught to express himself. It was vexing, and yet I grew to like it, which is well, since I intended to marry him.

Marie and Carol caught wind of it, and disapproved, no doubt anticipating losing a paying inmate, but did not pester me. Laura was in favour, under the impression that I was after his property and planned to financially ruin him.

I had a lot of letters to write… including one to my mother… I could not put it off any longer.

'Mother

I am well'

That was still written on a piece of paper on my desk. It was about time that I finished it.

'I hope you are well, too. I will be married soon, and could not have picked a better fellow to

*cleave to. He is called Michael Bennett. You
surely know of him.'*

Did that sound spiteful? I didn't mean for it to. I'd
always tried to soften my words as much as
possible.

*'I would not object to a meeting in London. There
is a decent inn near where I live. If you have the
means and can make the time, I will be there all
morning and afternoon, on July 8.*

Alma Webb'

On that morning, I went to Mrs. Green's inn. It
wasn't terribly crowded that day.

"Ohhhh, the little Miss Webb, is it?" Mrs. Green
chirped between puffs of a cigar. "It's been a
good, long while, yes indeed!"

I greeted her with a kiss and asked for a little
coffee, if it was fresh.

She happily brought it to me, and it most
certainly was not. I needed canned milk to make
it palatable.

I read the paper of that day and yesterday three
times over, and spoke with Mrs. Green whenever
she asked me questions as she worked. When not
occupied in some way, I stared straight out the

window and let my coffee get cold. The more I waited, the more I began to dread the exchange.

"Are ye wantin' to stay for the night?" Mrs. Green finally asked, refreshing my cup.

"No, I don't think I will! I'm supposed to be here for a meeting!"

The smell of the coffee now made me ill. I pushed it to one side. My nerves were too taut for me to eat anything. It was getting to be the time when men started bothering me if I stayed in one place for too long.

Ellen Webb arrived at five o'clock, when I was on my ninth cup. I was just about to leave. I sat for nearly ten hours. Somehow, I'd have been both disappointed and relieved if she never showed up.

She was dressed quite sensibly in grey and green, with an ornate feathered hat dropping a veil over her shoulders.

I stood and pulled out a chair for her, and I succeeded in remaining solemn and composed for the whole greeting. She kissed and embraced me, and I allowed it.

"There is coffee if you want it," I said as I sat back down.

"Is it any good?" she asked, sitting across from me, taking my hands without my permission.

"No, but it's coffee," I answered, straining to keep my face firm.

She tasted it, and immediately put it back down.

"And you worked here?"

"Yes, for a little while. I needed immediate employment to be allowed to stay with these three ladies, and I did save a little money."

"You slept here, as well? You didn't have a home?"

"Not at the beginning, no. But plenty of people don't."

"You could have asked to stay with any one of my friends."

"Well, I didn't. I'm tired of being a leech."

"You aren't a leech. You never were."

I looked away and sipped the terrible coffee. I thought this would be easy. Even now, there was an unbearable urge to tear into her, gnaw into her throat, and leave, like a cornered dog, but that would have only made me feel better for a moment. And it would only solidify in her mind that I was a spiteful child. Since I couldn't do it, my voice just stopped.

"I know I often say regrettable things out of anger," she continued.

"Those *'regrettable things'* did not come out of nowhere," I said, because after all, this was Mrs. I Mean What I Say.

"Do you like it here?"

Now I was actually angry, mainly because I could not determine the exact reason she changed the subject.

"This inn? It is fine."

Something that might have been a smile rippled across her features for only a second.

"I mean, are you happy with what you are doing?"

"I'm happier than I've been in a long time."

She nodded.

"I'm glad."

"Though," I looked over my shoulder to make sure nobody was listening. "It was frightening and stressful when I first began working here."

"How so?"

"My room was cold, and there were always men eyeing me while I cleared the tables, sometimes grabbing at me. It is a bit unsanitary compared to what I'm accustomed to, but, as you say, *life isn't fair.* Generally, I was just afraid, because coming here was unlike anything I'd done before, and I did it half in a panic."

She lowered her eyes, as if the description of my livelihood filled her with guilt. That wasn't my intention (at least, I hoped it wasn't), but in a moment of wicked spite, it didn't bother me even a little.

"Additionally, the porridge here is practically broth."

"Is it?" she smiled again.

"Yes. And I think the paste they use to seal cracks is the same mixture that yields the bread."

That made her laugh, and then I began a detailed recounting of my peculiar experiences. It seemed we got along best when we weren't talking about things that mattered. I'd take it, all the same.

"I am not around much, but I suppose James will be working in the fields again, soon," I guessed.

"I wouldn't know. He does not talk to me as of late."

James always had a preference for her over our father, and spoke to no-one else. Was there anyone left on earth whose company he enjoyed?

"He doesn't really talk to any of us, though, does he?"

"He does not come home anymore, not since last February."

"Pity. I wonder why!" it probably sounded sardonic in that tone, I didn't mean for it to.

At seven o'clock, I needed to leave, because I had work in nine hours, and I'd not slept. That wasn't her fault. I just couldn't bring myself to send her away, but I finally excused myself.

"You aren't coming home?" she rose hastily, as if she absolutely expected me to go with her.

"I am! I have to work early in the morning. I'll come visit some time," I replied, feigning ignorance. "Do you need some money to stay the night here or go back?"

"No, no! I got here on my own, so of course I intended to go back on my own," she chirped in a dangerously cheerful tone. "It was nice to see you again!" she grabbed my hand and squeezed it, hard.

Then she was gone.

In that moment, I felt as if all I'd done to better myself was for nothing. I was already weeping when I got through the door and took off my shoes. I knew some things were never meant to go back to the way they were, but sometimes, I wanted to feel like I was ten, and could freely love again. I felt as though I was never truly feeling at all, only acting the way that I thought I should, back when I did feel. Why was it easier to be nicer to strangers than my own mother? Was I the unfeeling beast that she'd called me as our prior parting words?

It was a hollow feeling, as if I was being eaten alive, from the inside out.

I was mourning. Why did I mourn? Nobody was dead.

This sort of process is agony in the very beginning, and yes, a year is only the beginning. I promise, once you start to understand, you will get better at handling your feelings, and it will get easier. Tomorrow, I will wake up and realise that this order of things is normal.

Still, I began writing my mother letters. She agreed to attend my wedding, and didn't even make any comments about how my dress wouldn't age well, or how she did not approve of Michael Bennett.

Raising children is more than wearing your fingers down to the bones so that they can be comfortable. That is the bare minimum, because they have no choice but to depend on you.

Consider this a desperate warning from both a mother and a daughter. The burden of turning the other cheek is on you. That is the cross you took up when you had children, whether you believe it is fair or not. They are not miniature figures in the likeness of adults, and they are not you. Your anger is too much for their little bodies to handle, and the words you scald them with will be the fire they seek for warmth for the rest of their lives.

I emerged into adulthood full of anger and doubt that I did not understand until I stepped out of my parents' houses.

I'd seen numerous caretakers who never learned how to hold their feelings. For many years, I carried a deep and personal spite towards those people— a very raw, primal rage burning my insides. I wanted to crush them and force them to endure the terror they inflicted. Now that I am older, I just pity them. They don't know what they're doing.

Oh, yes, I used to be Mama's little pet, her best girl. I sought her for solace and security, and never shied from her. She was my world, and I was hers.

It only took one second for that to change.

That was the first time she struck me across the face. That was upsetting, but even after she'd hit me, I reached for her, and she sent me away, because she did not want to see me.

The safety of her presence evaporated in an instant, and has not since been restored. The embraces that I so badly ached for suffocated me. Kisses were no different from being branded with a hot iron. Even though I did not feel safe near her, I kept going back... I needed to.

Distance tempered my bitter feelings, yet it also made me need her less. It helped to tell myself that I did not miss her; I missed what I thought she was.

Maybe not. I don't really know.

But it was not all bad, and that is what made it so confusing.

You know, metamorphic rocks are my favourites. Michael is partial to sedimentary and igneous rocks: the former, because the layers tell a unique story, like the rings of a tree; the latter, because he just thinks volcanoes are fascinating. I cannot tell you how many times I have scooped rocks out of the bottom of the wash tub before I learned to check his pockets. I have a lot of his rocks in a box in the study, and lining the back garden.

But let me go back to what I was saying— metamorphic rocks were once igneous, and/or sedimentary, and were transformed into something completely different through prolonged heat and pressure. How interesting! It helps to think of our trials in such a sense. We still mend and become something new, even if we crack— and we will crack many, many times. It does seem insignificant to be endlessly sealing cracks, doesn't it?

In early autumn, I visited Michael once more, to lift my spirits, and to make sure my engagement was still real, and not a dream I'd had for months.

Or years.

"You did not sever the betrothal when you left," I told him, and he cringed when he was reminded of it. "Has it been ongoing since 1887?"

"That is for you to decide. At the time, I thought I would die in a month," he replied, preparing water for tea, as he had company due to arrive that evening.

"I kept the ring, so I suppose it is so, but you also proposed twice."

"Then we shall marry twice."

Michael introduced me to one of his friends, known in Grant's retelling as Ruth White. Her name, and the names of many characters close to her had been changed, to protect them from certain scandalous associations possibly being tied to them.

Regardless, I saw immediately that she was very lovely. Every feature was warm and inviting, and she was tall and graceful. Lack of finery did nothing to diminish her beauty.

I was well until she kissed Michael, and he kissed her back. It was an innocent gesture (she kissed me, too) but I could not fight the envy that stirred within at once.

As we sat and talked over tea, I contemplated
these thoughts, and tried to pick apart what
precisely pricked me. I did not feel as though she
could take my betrothed from me (after all, she
had a husband, and Michael was wrapped around
my finger). She was so effortlessly sweet on top
of it all, I should have just liked her— and I did,
very much so, but there was a faint feeling of
resentment tickling the back of my head. I
suppose it is foreboding, when somebody forces
you to see all that you are not, without even
meaning to, but it is true that you can't control
your feelings. I didn't try.

There was one solution: in order to learn to
appreciate how she'd been blessed, I would make
her my muse. Yes, I would draw her, and she
allowed it! I did greatly enjoy drawing her
portrait, and I knew I would, because I had such a
fine and willing model. Better yet, I was able to
draw her curly hair loose around her shoulders,
and I decorated it with roses. She kept the picture,
but it has since been destroyed by moisture.

Soon, Michael took Ida and me to Mr. Kelley's
estate. As you know, it is a very old gentry
settlement made into a massive zoological
garden— mostly Asian and European reptiles,
and it is now called the *Kelley-Bennett Zoological
Garden*. Michael praised it as his favourite place
to spend summers as a child, and he teased me,

saying that here, I would overcome my fear of toads.

No, I was not afraid of toads, nor have I ever been. I simply was not inclined to pick up and caress them, and you would flinch, too, if something leapt at your face so suddenly!

As expected, Ida took to the place immediately.

Meeting Mr. Kelley was certainly… an experience. Michael warned me that he was "a bit of an eccentric fellow," but I was not quite prepared. He intimidated me, but did not frighten me. Michael hailed him as an example for mankind, at least at that time.

He'd admired many men in his life. Of course, my father was one of them, as were Abraham Reed, and Samuel Bennett. Grant's book makes him out to be mostly resentful towards his father, but in truth, he spoke very highly of him even in spite of his shortcomings, and described many fond memories of him— even wishing that we all could have met him. He was deeply sorrowful because his parents were not alive to attend our wedding.

If you readily retain what you read, you are possibly wondering how my past associations (especially with a cousin who shall not be named) would paint my anticipation of marriage.

I finally told Michael about that ordeal very
shortly before, during a visit to Brownwall,
because I felt he was entitled to know about it. I
made sure he was calm and content first, though I
hoped I wasn't ruining a pleasant mood.

At nine o'clock that night, I found him seated in
his chamber with a late cup of tea. I sat beside
him, and then I explained it very plainly and in no
soft words, but I was able to remain steady,
though retelling those details made my heart race.
I made sure to speak without any long pauses so
that I could finish what I had to say without
interruption. As I spoke, his expression shifted
endlessly, and he wriggled in his seat.

When I finished, he had this strange and dark
look in his eyes, and he said, "Well, don't invite
him, if you want him alive."

That startled me, of course, hearing such harsh
words from him.

"Pardon?"

"I don't ever want to see him. I'd kill him, most
definitely," he said it as if he'd have no choice.

He touched my hand, and an involuntary shudder
rattled my frame.

"Why do you recoil?" he asked.

"Well... I did not think you would react in that way."

"You thought I would be delighted? Thought I would not care at all?" he cried out, and that dangerous expression was still etched into his rock-like face, but he stared through me, at some imaginary threat.

"I don't know."

Michael lunged and snatched at my arms, as if to steady himself, then started and released me, chewing his lip and averting his eyes. I drew him back to me and placed his head in my lap. He pressed his face into my skirts.

"I wish I could offer you an untainted body," I mumbled.

He raised his head up and pulled me closer, almost to the point of crushing me. "Don't say that! That's rotten! You could never be tainted."

Now I almost wished I did not tell him, because it pained me to see him this way.

He was calmer, now, and lifted his face up close to mine.

"Tell me it is so," he demanded. "Tell me that you are not sullied."

"You already said it yourself."

"I want to hear it from your mouth. That is more important. You need to be able to say it."

"I am not…"

"You are not—?"

"I am not tainted."

A painful smile spread over his face.

"One day, you will believe it."

"Perhaps," I frantically darted my eyes around the room, looking for something else to talk about. "Do you have other curtains for this bed?"

He knew my intentions. He humoured them.

"There is heavy damask for winter. Have you decided you don't like them after all?"

"No, they are cool and pretty. But I think they are not suited for cold weather— on the subject of bedroom arrangements, I'll be getting ready for bed now."

I stood and went to the door.

"Will you be coming back for the night?" he asked and gave my sleeve a tug.

"No."

He pulled harder.

"Alma… do I frighten you?"

After a moment of clarity (foolish man), he loosened his grip.

"No," I answered, and that was the truth. "I like my bed to myself."

Nobody shut the door. I saw him sitting in deep thought as I passed— neither furious nor sorrowful, simply contemplative, and swirling a stronger beverage in his hand.

Strangely, I don't think I was affected very much in that way— not when it came to him. If anything, it made me delight in him even more, for he was most assuredly one of the few safe men in the world.

And if you anticipated a romantic quest for vengeance fuelled by manly pathos, then I'm afraid you picked up the wrong book. I have no desire to seek violent retribution against my attackers, and would not have approved of it on my behalf. I am content to simply be rid of them, with the knowledge that they will not escape judgement.

As the date drew near, I had many preparations to make, even more than Michael. You surely know of my catastrophic blunder while wearing my original wedding dress.

It's true that I sometimes put it on to strut around like a little peacock, because I loved it so much. Unfortunately, I had put new paint on my desk, and had forgotten that it was still wet when I leaned over it to grab a stack of books. The entire front of the bodice was ruined, and when I realised this mistake, it was already beginning to set.

Terror made my hands fumble with the many hooks on the bodice, and I nearly tore myself free in desperation. I then had to throw on my work dress and hurriedly run out to pump water. I soaked the bodice in every solution that I could think to concoct, panting and moaning feebly as I did so, and I had only managed to spread the stain.

Papa laughed at my plight, and told me that this was my rightful punishment for my vanity, and since I had only two weeks left, I ought to simply

wear my old green church dress. A wedding was
only one day of a life sentence, after all.

This seemed terribly unfair, as my wedding dress
was the first fashionable dress I had ever made
with my own hands.

Well, very little of what I petitioned for turned
out exactly how or when I wanted it, so why
would this dress be an exception? The same could
be said for the occasion tied to it.

I decided to cut up the skirt, take the collar and
cuffs, and use those scraps to decorate the old
church dress. When I'd gotten over how sore I
was about ruining my creation, I realised I liked
this one better. The pearly shades of the bridal
fabric complemented the celadon so beautifully,
and since I had material to spare, I sewed myself
a lovely chemise and a pair of garters that I
decided would have to be part of my ensemble.

The week before the ceremony, I returned to my
mother's house— she begged me. Before I left
London, I announced my marriage to Mrs. Green.

"Oh, 'ow sweet!" she chirped as she was stirring
a big pot of porridge. "And what is your Mister
like? He a baby, too?"

"Um— he is about my age," I replied.

"Aye, sweet baby," she mumbled, tasting from the tip of her wooden spoon.

"Will you come to my wedding?"

"No, no, little Miss Alma. I live on dis street my 'ole life, an' I don't tink I shall leave it, but I wish yous all de best, you and yer dear boy."

I gave her a sovereign and a kiss before I departed, but I admit, we were not on close enough terms that I was pressed to reunite with her any time soon. I am grateful for her time in my life.

I brought Laura with me; the other inmates did not wish to attend. James was furious, and silently fumed that whole time. Ida was ecstatic, possibly only because she was enthralled with the idea of weddings. I promised her my good blue dress that did not fit me anymore. It suited her better, anyway. I purchased a brand new corset, so that my dress would form the most modern silhouette. That week was spent breaking it in.

On December 17, two aunts and two uncles came to the house, with four children that we were not warned about. I complained to my mother, but she said,"What will you have me do, send them right back? They're already here."

Despite how busy that night was, I was sent to bed at seven o'clock in order to be awake and alert by three the next morning, but I could not force my eyes to stay shut until ten. Mama also climbed into my bed for a little bit, while I pretended to sleep.

I woke up at two, and did not bother trying to go back to sleep, because in those days, I was perfectly able to function well on fewer than five hours of rest. I doubted anybody else would be up, so I lit a lamp and contemplated my future, staring at my new dress, laid out on my wardrobe.

Oh, my dear reader, the anticipation was like nothing I'd ever felt before. Dread is not the right word, but the day, the lifetime hanging over me was so daunting. I felt light as a feather, and sickened with many clamouring emotions.

Around three o'clock, I smelled toasting bread, and realised that above all else, I was just hungry.

And Laura forced her way into my chamber on the stroke of the hour.

"MA!" she cried, thrusting a candle under my nose. "Oh, you are awake! Up! Get up!" she was already taking my hand and dragging me to the threshold, scarcely giving me a moment to throw on a dressing gown.

"Five minutes! You have five minutes to eat a
light breakfast!" she continued, sending me down
the hall with a hearty push.

My mother, and all the aunts and uncles were
seated at the table, tightly packed like canned
fish. Coffee and toasted tea cakes were laid out. I
ate standing up, and still had one more mouthful
between my teeth when Laura apprehended me,
and she and my mother brought me to a
lukewarm bath and scrubbed me until my skin
was red.

I reached into my modest trousseau for fresh
underclothes, and Laura volunteered to lace me
up, without actually waiting for me to answer— I
could not, as she had forced the air out of me.

"Stop! No more!" I choked out with the very last
of my breath.

"Was that too tight?" she clawed at the strings,
and then I could breathe again.

"Yes, fool," I huffed. "I'll do it myself."

I dressed myself with nobody's help and arranged
my hair into a simple but elegant updo, with only
a little heat applied to my fringe, but Mother
desperately wanted to pin my veil, so I allowed it.

185

We ladies all had a quiet understanding that making up the face was not "proper," but we did it, anyway, in subtle ways. In those days, lipstick was brand new and not readily available for most. We either used a liquid rouge on our lips, or made a red concoction in our kitchens. I used almond cream and a beetroot extract. It made just a faint tint that was probably not noticeable to anyone except for me.

James was coaxed out at the very last minute, but he at least shaved and put on a nice suit. I didn't know he had one of those.

As for me, I'd never felt prettier— that is, until Aunt Eliana ordered me to remove my eyeglasses. She told me that I looked better without them. I obeyed, fighting back tears of frustration as I struggled to see past the length of my outstretched arms.

We all took an early morning train, and then a little caravan to Michael's old family chapel. Papa was so grim, he might have been marching me to my grave. I'd never had so many eyes on me in my life. The chapel was deadly silent, except for me. My clothes, my footsteps, and my breath were deafening. I then wished I'd eaten more and drank less coffee, because I was in danger of swooning. Hardly being able to see what was in front of me put me all the more on edge.

A priest who looked older than the building itself joined our right hands. Michael did not wear gloves, of course. His fingers were cold, damp, and trembling.

I would later learn that the little Presbyterian chapel was fairly new in the Bennett family, as they were mostly Catholic until the late 1700s. However, as the old inhabitants of the surrounding village were disappearing, congregations seemed to be miniscule, yet the priest remained at his post.

Papa was a fiend for photographs. He made us stand in that ghostly chapel for a dozen portraits, which must have cost a pretty penny. I knew that my family would fight over them later.

Brownwall was nearly six miles away, and we had to make the journey on foot. I asked Michael why he did not simply commission the priest to perform the ceremony in his home. He turned very red, saying that he just really wanted it done at the chapel for the sake of tradition, and he did not expect small children to be there. That was not his fault, of course. Little Emma Louise was the eldest of Aunt Erinn's second brood, then about eight years old, and she carried her infant brother Jacob, while her parents had the other two boys. Michael pitied her, and plucked Jacob out of her hands, then scooped her up in his other arm, as easily as if she were a kitten. She did not mind, and even took to him quite fast.

Likewise, Ida and Laura quickly formed an odd friendship. They both had strong personalities, after all. My father was delighted to see old Abraham, and was passively cordial to my mother's relatives.

At Brownwall, an elderly lady had a thick vegetable stew ready, and Abraham told her in a hushed voice to add a little water. He did not need to be so concerned about the portions, because it turned out that there was more than enough for everybody to eat. It was a bit too mild-tasting, since it was watered down, but I was ravenously hungry. Despite this, I managed to neatly eat a modest portion so that I did not make myself sick with my uneasy stomach, or become sluggish from overeating. Michael kept trying to feed me from his plate, with his own spoon— I accepted one bite to appease him, when nobody was looking, and returned the favour.

Coffee and tea were made fresh. I served tea to Michael the way he liked it, which prompted him to pour my coffee, and do nothing to it, as I preferred.

The two boys screamed and ran through the halls. Aunt Erinn shouted from her seat as she nursed Jacob, but delivered no discipline, nor did her husband. Emma Louise climbed into Michael's lap and begged him to teach her some French and German. He was happy to, but Aunt Erinn ordered her to stop bothering him.

Michael told me to put my glasses on, seemingly bewildered that anyone thought it significantly changed how I looked.

Early in the afternoon, he shooed out the guests, and then, completely alone except for Abraham, who wanted to stay out of our way, we were unsure of what to do with ourselves, and at once grew very shy. At Michael's insistence, we took a walk until the cold no longer permitted it (for him), and then fled back inside.

I was so nervous to be alone with him, even though I had been several times before.

I had my first taste of expensive red wine. It was fine, not great, but not terrible. I'd had a sip of light ale before, as my mother had insisted, but I did not like it. This was much better. He waxed poetic, and I allowed it, since he enjoyed it so much, and then we turned in at about seven o'clock— very early yet again, because we had to rise promptly, have a quick breakfast, and catch a ship out of Liverpool in the morning.

That is what was written, anyway, but it is not quite all that transpired.

Michael was completely unserious about punctuality, for the trip that he had planned himself! At breakfast, he ignored his own meal and kept trying to feed me, reaching over our plates to kiss my hands, and praising me as if I was Venus herself— in front of Abraham, who pretended not to see it, and took his tea to his room.

You wouldn't find any such things in Grant's book! The truth is, Michael (of course) wrote about it in great, meticulous depth, but I removed those passages, because even though Grant would never retell such intimate details, I didn't want him reading them.

Michael was taking me to New York. I do not know what possessed him to go there. It seemed impractical, but I was enticed nonetheless, so I consented to the long voyage.

For the first three weeks, I wished I hadn't. I detested sea travel within an hour of departing. Most of the time, I was too dreadfully ill to do much of anything, and I especially could not hold still for very long. Of course, it was incredibly difficult to sleep, more difficult to eat. I could tell Michael felt terrible, and was likely bored of watching me be sick for most of our waking hours. He often paced the ship on his own if I was languishing, but he would come back with toast or water and brush my hair. Relief came to me when we finally touched dry land.

New York City was not unlike London.

New York winters, however, are entirely different from England. Michael leased some old homesteader's cabin in the north of the state, and it was fortunate that we stocked up on provisions before we arrived, because by the time we'd settled in, the snow began to reach above our knees. Neither of us was adequately prepared for the cold, and these two elements combined kept us indoors twenty-three hours in a day. The grease paper windows were not sealed well anymore, so the shutters were always latched. The only light was from inside. That made our sleep patterns completely irregular.

Michael had envisioned adventure, excitement, and gazing upon animals you'd never find back home. He imagined the American frontier as much more romantic than it actually was, and thus befitting a celebration of marriage— how wrong he was. One may have considered this trip a complete disaster, but it was not all bad, or even significantly bad.

Though the cabin was well-insulated, it was still cold, and very little furniture had been left behind. This meant that we spent a great deal of time huddled in front of an iron stove in the middle of that one room. The wind whistled and howled all hours of the day. We slept in a heap of blankets on the floor, and we washed and cooked with melted snow. We even ate sitting on the floor; a crate was our dining table. I could not understand why anybody would lease this place on purpose, except as self flagellation.

In order to make the best of it in his own mind, Michael likened it to camping, though I could tell he suffered, being unable to go outside for more than ten minutes at a time, with twenty minutes of preparation. When he did go out, it was usually to gather snow. Later on, he would say that the trip was worth it, purely because he saw coyotes out in the wild.

In that interval, I had become lax about tending to my hair, and slept with it loose numerous times, on those wool and fur blankets. I paid dearly for this later.

Really, we didn't do anything that we couldn't have done without leaving home (aside from seeing coyotes). Even so, I was sorry to leave, but happy to return to more familiar territory— and not one bit happy to board the ship again.

THREE YEARS, IN THE BLINK OF AN EYE

Abraham had returned from his own trip when we arrived at home. It was good that he was taking advantage of his remaining vigour.

Upon returning, we had only a few days of leisure. Part of that time was spent making preparations to travel more, but this time, we would part ways for a little while. It was a mutual agreement, as at that point, our professions still demanded that he go one way, and I go another. Also, Michael's job required him to stay in Bristol for stretches lasting up to several weeks, and I was not quite ready for such a thing, in addition to having found an advantageous position as a physician's aid. We wrote every single day (even if the letters did not arrive punctually), and came together at least once per month.

I would be lying if I said that it was not difficult to maintain a marriage that way. Our leisure time had to be coordinated perfectly, sometimes many weeks or months in advance, not to mention simply longing to be touched. I tried to make the most of it, as it was a season of my life like any other, and I did not want to miss such a long stretch of time by trying to dream it away, so I got as much accomplished as possible. There were still late nights and early mornings of fitful distress and impatience when I had too much time

on my hands— which made for some very
interesting, very angry letters.

In those days, you took a day's trip to phone
somebody, and it was quite costly, especially over
long distances. I think that hearing his voice once
in a while would have eased my mind a little.

No matter what, every reunion was sweet, though
I knew I did not want things to stay that way
forever, and neither did he.

In fact, some of our acquaintances told us that our
union was doomed to fail, because we were not
close at hand during the first, most important
formative year— of course this was not the case.
It survived, because we wanted it to, and we
worked for it— for we were indeed perfectly
matched as a whole, but still two separate halves.

To remedy some of our marital woes, Michael
took me to Bristol with him one summer,
promising a "second honeymoon." This was
hardly so, as he worked the entire time, and
though I was allowed plenty of leisure and gifted
new pencils and pastels, I saw very little of him
except late at night, and was not permitted to
cook for him. Going to the markets to buy food
for only myself was unfamiliar to me, and
Michael would not eat what I cooked except on
Sunday, when he didn't work. I spent much of my
time talking to Miss Gaye, the secretary. We were

not exactly fast friends, but we shared an affinity
for flowers and art.

While residing in Bristol, I saw just how
fastidious Kelley could be. He was intensely
passionate about his animals and his
establishment, and expected perfection in every
sphere— he claimed that this was a testament to
Michael's reliability, and that he wouldn't expect
it from any other man.

I suppose his practice was an objective force of
good, having turned his family's vast fortune
(ironically accumulated in part by trophy hunting)
into a sanctuary and centre of education. Started
in 1854, it is one of the first of its kind in the
world.

And maybe that was true, but I still hated him. It
seems, at least according to what Grant has
written, that the feeling was mutual.

Truthfully, the moment I laid my eyes on him, I
got an awful shiver up my spine, and the hairs on
my arms stood up, as if I gazed upon the devil
himself.

I saw in him a profound and even eccentric sense
of justice, much akin to Michael's. In reality, the
true philosophy that he adhered to was entirely
different, and Michael told it to me as we settled
into bed:

*The world does not care one way or the other,
and it owes you nothing. There is no justice or
injustice, only the individual and what he has the
power to obtain, and what will be will be.*

He believed his philosophy to be the ultimate freedom, if such a thing existed. This, I found to be far more bleak and horrid than even the idea of inherent evil, and could not fathom anybody taking comfort in such thoughts.

According to Michael, Mr. Kelley believed it was up to the individual to create a purpose for himself, and his was to revere nature, his only love that had humbled him as a young man many years ago.

Michael believed that we are all born owing a tremendous debt, and that debt can only be repaid by being better than our parents.

I asked him if he thought this was fair. He merely shrugged, and said, "What is fair? I've been given far more chances than anybody is entitled to."

After a long pause, he asked, "Do you think God is fair?"

"No. If He was fair, then His son would not bear all of mankind's sins, and He would not have allowed humanity to continue after the flood. I think we are all very fortunate that He is not fair."

After that, we went to sleep, and let it be known that a mattress of densely packed straw is not very comfortable when you are too light to sink into it. Michael always preferred a firm bed, though. It still surprises me that, exacting as he was, Mr. Kelley allowed me to sleep beside my own husband. I knew he had an intense visceral hatred for the institution of marriage… most institutions, for that matter.

I can not believe that Grant left out the alligators, though I suppose they are common knowledge to anyone that has visited the garden.

Those creatures arrived that summer in 1890, as Mr. Kelley had received news that nine juvenile alligators purchased as pets had been discarded, and they were growing quickly and encroaching upon farmland. Three had already been killed. He recruited Michael for the rescue mission, and they followed the farmers and fishermen into the marsh with nets, ropes, and long sticks.

And Michael invited me.

"You must have a hole in your head if you think I'm coming with you to play *lacrosse* with the Angel of Death!" I said, but I went anyway, because I was going to make sure that if Michael

was to die in anyone's arms that day, it would not
be Mr. Kelley's.

Michael mostly had me stand to one side and
draw pictures of anything I found interesting. I'd
never seen alligators before, except in drawings,
so of course I was fascinated, but kept my
distance. They were only the size of a small child,
but they were already fearsome! As for Michael,
he was spellbound by the mighty beasts.

I will give credit where it is due: Mr. Kelley had
an incredible gift to handle dangerous animals,
whereas I was close to swooning with shock just
watching the men work, terrified at the thought
that somebody could lose a limb or a life.

"Then it is fortunate that we have a physician's
aid with us!" Michael assured me, though I was
not sure if I would know how to act under such
conditions.

We trekked miles into the marsh and brush,
scouring the waters. Only four were found living,
and three bodies… two have never turned up…

The alligators are still there. They grew quite
large, each the size of a grown man! They eat
whole chickens— really, just about anything that
they could catch on their own. Witnessing the
process still makes me ill, and Mr. Kelley said
that he'd seen crocodiles get much bigger. I've

grown to respect them as the impressive creatures
that they are, but I am glad that we have not
acquired any more. They do not belong in this
climate, and moving them to indoor enclosures
during colder months is stressful to both the
animals and the humans undertaking the task. I
both loved and hated watching Michael handle
them.

After that first very difficult year, we both spent a
long time at home, and took up projects on our
own property, so even during that time, we were
hard at work.

It was also during this interval that I discovered
even more of his strange habits: with the
exception of sitting at the dinner table, Michael
did not like chairs. While reading or handling
paperwork, he could often be found on the floor,
or even stretched out in the grass outside.

Apparently, the reason he did not do this with
company or at Papa's house was because he was
told it was rude— but this was his home, and he
could do as he pleased.

I found it mildly annoying at first, but he would
sit beside me on a couch if I asked him to, and
sometimes I sat on the floor if I found him there. I
expected different from a former aristocrat, even
if it was Michael, but Abraham told me that he'd

been trying to break the boy of that habit ever since he could walk.

Most peculiar was when I retrieved a cup for myself in the kitchen, and he stopped me.

"This one is mine," he insisted. "You can have any other."

"Why is that one special?" I asked.

"It is the first one I drank out of when I came here," he ran his finger along the rim, revealing an almond-shaped blemish in the glazed surface. "See, I dropped it and it left this little chip. That's how I know it."

"What if we chip more of them?"

"It won't look exactly the same."

Only a madman would concern himself with such a thing, but I humoured him, because now that I saw the chip, I knew I wouldn't be able to stand it. I made sure that I chose it for him when I set out tea.

Other than that, he gave me free reign of the ordering of the house. Decor meant very little to him, as long as I didn't create clutter or plaster the walls with horribly bright colours. While I still did a lot of work outside, I did not spend all of my time indoors wanting to leave.

Finally, I lived in a home that I loved.

As you know, it was also during that time that he brought Jeannine home. We'd never had dogs anywhere I'd lived, certainly not large ones. Though we suspected she was some kind of sighthound mongrel, Jeannine was not fit to be a hunting dog, not remotely, but despite her size, she was determined to be a lap dog.

I was timid about dogs, but no man was a better fit to be their master— after all, Michael wasn't that far from being a dog, himself, so he must have understood them well.

I grew to love Jeannine, though likely not the same way Michael did. Their bond was unique, and I still remember how he wept and could barely stand on his feet when he had to bury her. Her passing really ripped him up. All of the animals' deaths did. He'd swear over and over, "No more pets. No new animals."

And within a week, he'd bring a new creature to the house, without fail.

With Jeannine, Abraham, and the two of us, we came together as a quaint little family tucked away at the edge of the woods.

As Michael returned to Bristol, work soon slowed down for me, and I spent more time at home. I kept myself busy by working in the gardens, tending to Jeannine and the chickens, and still participating in charity efforts from time to time, but I was not working as much as I was before, and I was growing terribly bored! I thought I'd feel better at home, but I missed Michael even more, having our bed all to myself— I admit, this was sometimes nice, because he was quite large and threw off heat like a furnace. Abraham was good company, but his mind wandered, and of course, he was not my husband. I was not able to mustre up the willpower to ask Michael to stay home more often, but as it turned out, I did not need to.

Autumn was a surprise— not unwelcome or unwanted, just unexpected. We saw so little of each other in those days, that we did not think we would need to plan for a child. Of course, we spoke of it, but we did not see it happening so soon. Michael was certainly in no hurry.

That stretch of time we spent mostly at home made me really think about it, even if I was too shy to seriously discuss it. We liked our life the way it was— but I was starting to think that we could have a lot more. Sometimes, when helping those ladies in the lodging houses, with their babies— I was the slightest bit tempted to take them home.

Well, it was in January that I grew suspicious. In February, I was certain.

At first, I was mortally frightened. After all, it was a place I'd never gone before, and did not expect to find myself in so soon. Moreover, I was afraid that Michael would be distraught if I asked him to stay home. It could either make things far better, or far worse for us. I tried to conceal it from him, and went to my mother to consult her about my suspicions. In her frank opinion, it was "certainly possible," and after about two more weeks of waiting, it was "most likely."

Great terror seized me, but also a dizzy sort of joy I could not put into words. My main fear was that I would have a difficult labour, and then I'd be maimed by the surgeons trying to fix me, so that the scarring made me unable to give birth again— exactly what happened to my mother.

I went home and contemplated how to tell this to Michael. I knew that he liked children, and would have stayed at the house if I asked him to, but I was too timid and giddy to tell him outright, so I decided I would drop little hints, and see how long it took for him to notice.

I began knitting, even though I absolutely despised doing it by hand, but that meant it was sure to get his attention.

He was at the piano, so it took a while.

I admit, it was greatly amusing to watch his face as he pieced everything together. His features underwent a dozen different expressions in only a moment.

I also admit that I was startled when he sprang upon me. I expected him to be merely fine with it.

He knew at once that there was a great deal of arrangements that needed to be made, and went about it with bustle and enthusiasm. I imagine he was glad to be busy, as always. Immediately, he constructed a very ugly but functioning cradle, and even tried his hand at making toys— he quickly gave up.

I switched to crocheting the blanket as soon as I was able, because that was easier for me.

Lady readers, I feel I will be doing a great service to society if I describe my pregnancies exactly as they were, instead of how we are told we're supposed to feel about them. It was a most singular and spiritual experience, and I spent half of it cursing my existence.

It started as just a peculiar little feeling in no specific part of me: a delightful flutter that lasted for many days, and was unlike anything I'd experienced before. I even felt very beautiful. I wish I'd taken advantage of that feeling while it lasted.

I remember I had bad heartburn between five and eight o'clock every morning, for three months. I could not have anything for breakfast except curds, milk, and jam, and Michael, perplexed that I would make such a sumptuous breakfast over a hot stove and eat none of it, kept shovelling meat, vegetables, and mushrooms onto my plate until I was able to make him understand that I could not digest what he offered me. Even coffee was no longer desirable. Alongside everything else, I had terrible shakes and chills while my body adjusted to tapering off my coffee intake. I was not an avid tea drinker before, but it eased the transition. Most times when I'd had it, it tasted of little more than hot water to me, but Michael made it very strong.

"Then how is it that you don't like coffee?" I asked as he offered me another cup.

"Tea is mild and earthy. Coffee is so pungent," he explained. "Besides, I simply don't like how it makes me feel."

"If you drank it more often, you'd get used to it."

"I don't want to get used to it."

He always said that coffee did not wake him up, only make him feel as though his heart would explode, and then it slowed him down.

As it became more and more difficult to sleep comfortably, Michael handled my late night fits without complaint. He slept less than I did, anyway, and if my tossing about disturbed him, he simply surrendered the bed to me and slept on a sofa somewhere, or on the floor— never in any of the guest chambers, as the beds were too small for him. My irrational brain felt rejected. My rational brain knew that nobody wanted to be kicked all night; I certainly did not!

In deep summer, I did not always need to toss and turn in my sleep, I just wanted the bed to myself, because Michael is so hot. I admitted this to him later, and he thought it was funny.

I did not mind being away from work, because it was so hard to think in those days. I would leave a book on a table somewhere and immediately forget where it was. My eyeglasses did not seem to work as well as they used to, so even reading a clock became a chore— my vision would become clearer again when Autumn was two months old. That is still a mystery.

The first time I clearly felt her stir within me, I was cutting up new spring blossoms at the kitchen table. It was akin to a swarm of butterflies, or a little fish caught in your hands— I even felt it from outside of my body. I squealed and threw down the scissors (don't do this) and ran to find Michael, not caring that Jeannine was now eating my flowers.

The little flutters continued, and he needed to discover them before they stopped. Whatever he was doing was not as important as what I had to show him.

He was only sorting papers in his study. I climbed onto him without disturbing his pile, and demanded he feel my abdomen. At first, he searched thoughtfully with his fingers, almost as if kneading bread.

Up until then, Michael did not seem to fully grasp imminent fatherhood, even though he was adamant about being as helpful and accommodating as possible. Finding the child and feeling it move made it real.

He gathered me even closer and pressed his face into my clothes, and his features illuminated with a new understanding. From then onward, he would find any excuse to have his head in my lap, and talk to "her."

Even though I insisted that the child was a boy beyond a shadow of a doubt, Michael was not having it. What did he know? The baby was in me!

On top of my intuition as a new mother, I had substantial evidence: my complexion became shiny and rosy, whereas a girl syphons her mother's beauty (he argued that I had more than enough, and quite simply, motherhood becomes me), I had a great deal of trouble sleeping, Michael had put on a few extra pounds recently (he raised an eyebrow at that one), and finally, I carried quite low— so much so that many mundane tasks had become a great undertaking. Eventually, I needed Michael to fasten my boots— or Abraham, which took much longer with his shaking hands.

Sometimes, I abandoned footwear altogether, and walked barefooted in the garden. That was easier on my ankles, anyway.

Michael would often cast a glance at me while I spoke to him and suddenly start laughing, and when I demanded to know why, he said that because I was so short, my belly concealed my lower half when he looked at me standing up.

I still enjoyed making myself pretty, but not at the expense of my comfort. Only three of my dresses fit me, so I made the best of them. By then, my hair was long enough for me to sit on, and I cut it to my waist. I wanted it to be more manageable when I had the baby. Michael did not mind me cutting it. He even helped, and he guessed that less hair coiled onto my head would be better in summer.

Of course, I shed a tear while it was cut, even though I wanted it, and knew that it would make my life easier. They say that the hair holds feelings and memories.

I had actually shorn off enough hair to make a pretty penny! It was a good fifteen inches, and the money went to the church's charity efforts, as I was not active during that time.

There were additional changes to my looks during that time. My face and the tip of my nose became rounder. I was glad that my features were not so sharp, but it did not last long after the birth. Even my hair changed. Some new strands grew in dark and coarse, and the hairs stayed for many years. I treasured some of them as a beautiful memento.

Michael still often worked for weeks at a time, and always made sure he saw me right before he departed, no matter what. In June, I spent much of my waking hours outside. Usually, he walks with me, but he'd been packing all morning. He sought me out as I was picking berries in the garden— I like them just before they are fully ripe. I heard Jeannine first, so I knew he had to be close.

"There you are!" he approached and gathered me and my basket to his breast, then picked me up and carried me up the walkway. "Your little feet are so red!" was his excuse for toting me around.

"So are my hands," I replied, revealing my stained fingers.

He explained what he was going to be doing in Bristol for the next week while I fed him berries from my basket, and he deposited me on the steps.

On that day, I decided to go with him to the train station, even if it meant putting on shoes and departing by myself.

It was just me, Abraham, and Jeannine for nearly two weeks, until one day, when I heard a great commotion in the front while I was in the back garden.

A lavishly decorated and cushioned carriage was in the gravel, and a lone horse was in the new stable that Michael hadn't gotten to use yet. Chatter could be heard inside the house. I was sure that these visitors were no relations of mine.

Hopefully, they were not there for Michael, as he was not meant to be home for another day.

Though it was improper to meet a guest this way, I entered through the side door by the garden, and fled up the stairs, into the bedroom to quickly make myself more presentable: after sponging away the sweat on my neck and brow, I put up my hair, and donned lilac kids and a pretty silver watch, as if I'd been expecting company the whole time— of course, I hastily put on my easiest shoes. Those days, I often did not wear a corset, as though it took a tremendous weight off of my back, a doctor told me that it would limit my baby's movement and growth.

I descended the steps as gracefully as I could with my awkward gait, wishing I'd stopped to have a sip of water.

Everybody had gathered in the parlour, and I already smelled tea. I heard the middle aged woman before I saw her, and I practically heard her clothing, too. Her dress was a red and blue Oriental pattern, with gold lace trim, and sleeves that nearly consumed the seat she was in. The false front of ebony curls was just as voluminous. She was flanked by two servants, and Abraham sat across from her, as gay as could be, laughing with this woman as if he'd known her for years. She shook her head a lot, and her large earrings danced. She was even stroking Jeannine, who was content to lie at her feet. A stack of papers sat on the table.

She fixated on me before I could welcome her and introduce myself.

"Ah! You have to be Lady Bennett!" she sprang up and curtseyed, and so did the young lady standing beside her, while the gentleman bowed his head.

Then this was most certainly an associate of Michael's family.

"Oh, yes, indeed!" I tittered nervously, thinking only of that tea, because I was parched. "I am Mrs. Bennett, though hardly gentry— the Bennetts have fallen from their former status."

"Hush, hush!" she raised a hand, as if she was the mistress of this house. "Nobility is not merely a rank, but a way of life— how you carry yourself as a powerful woman! I say, you have a lovely face and strong shoulders, but where is the air of fortitude? Put out your chest and speak with authority!"

Putting out my chest hurt my back.

"I welcome you to my home," I tried, speaking not with authority per se, but mild annoyance. "I see you have met Mr. Abraham Reed."

"Oh, I met him long before you, my dear!" she insisted, taking my hand as she seated herself again.

"I am not your dear," I murmured, too thirsty and too pregnant to be polite. "Actually, who are you?"

"Ah!" she clasped her hands over her very ample bosom. "How rude of me! I am Hannah Lavigne, formerly Hannah Alice Bennett, of Ashwood—the sister of Lords Gabriel and Samuel Bennett, children of Nathaniel and Berthe Bennett: that is, I am the aunt of Michael Bennett; I say, that makes us family!"

"I did not need an entire pedigree, but I suppose it does," cynical, nasty creature that I am, I anticipated her asking for money.

"She is the real thing," Abraham confirmed, beckoning me to sit beside him. "She has presented me with a series of tell-tale documents, and I'd never forget that face!"

That was all well, but no matter how you spun it, I did not know this woman, and did not know how I felt about having her in my home. How would Michael react to finding her? He mentioned an aunt he'd never met, but he'd not heard from her his whole life, and even expressed concerns that she didn't really exist. I was afraid her presence would trouble him, and was hoping she'd be long gone before tomorrow.

Abraham served more tea, while Hannah Lavigne told her entire life story to me: she'd cut all ties with her family because of her parents' disapproval of her involvement with a divorced Frenchman twice her age: Adrien Marcel Lavigne, whom she met as a brand new debutante at sixteen. Within two months, she'd renounced her dowry and fled to France, and had lived there ever since, having her every whim indulged and raising nine children, happy as a lark— a stark contrast to Elisha and Helen Connor. Monsieur Lavigne passed away in 1882, leaving his widow, seven living children, and now fifteen grandchildren with a sumptuous fortune.

"It is such a relief," she continued, even though nobody was talking to her. "To find the family name intact, even after Sammy's passing! Abraham tells me you are with child! It must be a recent undertaking."

"Actually, I discovered it in January," I replied.

"Lord have mercy!" she cried, fluttering her hands about her breast. "It can't be! You are so little! What are you eating? You need to get fattened up, or you won't have a good, hearty baby!"

I'd already put on a bit of weight, so at what point would I have been fattened up enough to please her?

"I eat plenty," I asserted. "We have chickens and a wonderful vegetable garden, and Mr. Bennett brings home game birds year-round."

"Those birds must be skin and bones— as you are! I'll have Sandra make you my favourite stew tonight."

... tonight?

I only allowed this woman to stay beyond our introduction because she was Michael's family (allegedly), and because she and Abraham obviously adored each other. That being the case, I did not dislike her, but I found her presence to be a burden on my tranquil afternoon. She was brazen and forthright in such a way that only a wealthy dowager could be, and while Michael could be both of those when he wished, his temperament was often checked by a natural meekness.

In short, he knew when to shut up.

"No, no, I will prepare supper—"

"What! You have no servants to do it for you?" Madame Lavigne's face turned very red. "You should not be on your feet!"

"Many women get on just fine without servants."

"And they and their little ones are such puny things— no wonder you are only just now with child for the first time, your poor delicate body. When I was your age, I was carrying my fifth!"

"I haven't *known* Mr. Bennett long enough to have a fifth child with him."

"And is he equally as frail? No Bennett man has ever been fragile, nor had a skinny little wife!"

And the man we spoke of arrived at the threshold as she began to ramble about how the Bennetts select their mates— it is not noteworthy enough to recount.

Completely fatigued by this encounter, I made my escape as Hannah Lavigne descended upon Michael. For what it's worth, I felt bad about it.

Seeing that she would not be leaving that evening, I began to prepare a large supper: or, I tried to. Sandra, Madame Lavigne's attendant, had inserted herself into my kitchen and took up a knife right under my nose, setting to work on a dish I hadn't planned for. She was only doing what she'd been told, so I just held my breath like an angry child and trusted that she was a competent cook.

I resigned to spreading butter on bread and making Michael's favourite tea, but I admit, she prepared a splendid roast with vegetables from the garden.

Madame Lavigne retreated to a guest chamber to spend almost an hour dressing for supper, and questioned why the Master and Mistress of the estate had not done the same. Who went to so much trouble for a private country meal?

"Don't tell me you passed the entire day in that faded wrapper!" she sighed, as if she was about to swoon after bearing witness to a heinous crime.

"Not the entire day!" I replied. "I was in only a chemise and stockings until about ten o'clock."

"Oh, my…" Abraham hid his face.

I retired to bed soon after eating, which was the one thing Hannah Lavigne approved of, given my *condition*. She was already horrified to learn that I'd not had my sacred afternoon nap.

Michael followed in about an hour, after trying to speak French with the dowager.

"There's my Alma, my little country flower!" he sang out and lifted me out of bed, as he'd not had a chance to delight in me since he'd returned home. "Light as a feather, she is!"

"Do you think I am too thin?" I asked reflexively.

"No!" he responded just as naturally, giving me a gentle shake. "You fit perfectly in my arms."

And about seven years later, soon after having Ashley, I asked, "Do you think I am too fat?"

Again, he said, "No! You fit perfectly in my arms," and lifted me up high, even with his bad knee.

Hannah Lavigne departed that week, and the house was peaceful again. By then, I was obsessively consulting the calendar, preparing for my child, who both couldn't come soon enough, and was arriving at a frightening pace.

All the while, I was terrified of myself; though I prepared diligently and anticipated this baby's arrival, I was not always a bubbling fountain of unbridled joy, as I thought I was supposed to be. I was afraid that this meant I would not love my child. Would that make me some kind of monster, to reject the most natural undertaking of a woman, after planning for it all this time?

I'm ashamed to say that I once took this frustration out on Michael, while we were trying to have a relaxing dinner after walking in the hot sun. He only mentioned work as a passing thought, and I exploded, telling him that he could not abandon me for his work, and that he needed to be present for the arrival of the baby, or I'd never forgive him.

He blinked hard and bit his lip, and after a minute of painful silence, he told me that his plan all along was to take leave in September and stay home until the first frost. At once, I was contrite, but he did not take it badly.

Mr. Kelley granted him three months of leave with surprisingly little fuss, though, of course, things did not quite go according to plan.

My mother and many aunts continuously pressed me to choose a midwife, and preferably one of them.

I chose Laura. For all her jests, I knew she would respect my wishes and intervene as little as possible, and she was just familiar enough to be a comfort, but detached enough for me to feel that I'd be in the hands of a professional. I believed that childbirth was a completely natural process I could handle on my own, as any mammal could.

Young lady readers, let no-one impose their will upon you in your birthing process, because it belongs to you, alone. Males, read on and learn how to accommodate your wives and sisters.

My first labour was stressful in many ways. Admittedly, I think I slept through much of it, but when I awoke and had to accept that it was really happening— and at such an inconvenient time— I nearly worked myself into a panic, because I expected my baby a whole month later!

I called upon my mother to confirm my suspicions, but she became more involved than I'd have liked, first ushering me into an empty room, and then forcing me to sit still. Sitting made it hurt. Before, I only felt giddy and agitated, and it was manageable as long as I could stand and move when I was inclined. Being confined to that stiff chair felt cumbersome and unnatural. How my heart raced!

"I don't want you here, touching me!" I admitted, writhing in that chair.

"And I don't want to be here," she replied, shutting the door. "But somebody needs to."

"I can handle it myself!"

"I know you think you can, but it is not so. Don't make me strap you to that chair."

Being in such an undignified and uncomfortable position, in such a state of undress was embarrassing enough, but being unable to check my panic compounded the humiliation. The gleaming surgical equipment on the table was not a soothing sight.

My mother insisted that this was all for my benefit, and then she was adamant about separating me from my husband, who was the only person advocating for my feelings. By the time I was in active travail, the whole house was stirring, and now Hannah Lavigne was a witness as well as my mother: both insisted upon what was right for me, and ignored my complaints, telling me to sit still and focus.

As for the contractions, I do not intend to describe them more than once. It is akin to the ache of your menses— lady readers know what I'm talking about, but for the gentlemen: try to imagine how it would feel if somebody folded up your colon to make paste.

This was not the most intense, but it was the hardest part, because it went on for so long.

With my intended midwife unavailable, and my hopes to give birth in tranquil privacy completely dashed, I was acutely distressed. I'm sure this was

the cause for my prolonged efforts— fifteen
hours!

Hannah Lavigne arrived nine hours in. As I'd
been awake for a long time, I asked for only a cup
of coffee.

Worse yet, the women were arguing over me
almost immediately. Madame Lavigne insisted
that immobilising me with my legs up slowed my
labour, whereas my mother said that confining me
thusly would protect me from bleeding or
swooning, lest the baby come too quickly.

By then, my patience was wrought to its limit,
and I wailed, because nobody was listening to
me. My mother completely missed my point, and
told me she understood that I was in pain, but
needed to be still— be still, be still, be still!
Michael was dismissed when he tapped at the
door. I heard him shouting in the gallery. I would
later be told that Sandra had tried to stop him
from reaching the second storey, and Papa and
Abraham needed to settle him down, as his tirade
of swearing reduced her to tears.

Mrs. Lavigne hardly allowed me room to breathe,
and gave me kisses and nonsensical loving words
that I didn't ask for. I asked for coffee and
solitude, and received neither. She told me to
embrace the thrill of my natural uptaking as a
woman, and I could not spare enough moisture to

spit in her face, so I only set my teeth and turned my head.

I was only accommodated when Michael was permitted to fetch things for the two women. I would have gladly traded their "help" and "experience" for his naivete. I caught a glance of his face as he came to the door; it looked stalwart enough, but sweat formed faster than he could sponge it dry, and I was tucked away in a corner where he could not find me. I could not make a sound, as I was in the throes of a powerful contraction that took all of my air.

I nearly fainted at the sight of my own blood, and I really would have if I was not sitting down. I just knew that I'd be torn apart, and stitched back together all wrong, like my mother. It really wasn't a lot of blood, but the smell and sight would have made me vomit if there was anything in my stomach. I thought I would die. I really wanted to.

"Help! I can't do it, I cannot!" I cried, repeatedly. And who could help? Nobody.

"Oh, my girl, you are simply growing restless!" Hannah assured me. "This means your troubles will soon be over."

At the very least, I was offered a little dignity in being allowed to wash myself; indeed, I had never been so filthy, and the rising summer sun made me sweat until I had soaked through my clothes. I didn't even want the hot coffee anymore, and my mother called me flighty for rejecting it when I'd been begging for it for so long.

Now, I was in such a state of discomfort, I could not eat or drink what was offered, and thought only of passing through this ordeal. Instead, I occupied myself with the names I'd thought of: Joseph was such a pretty name; Alexander was proud and stately. Joseph Bennett; Alexander Bennett; Joseph Alexander Bennett? Samuel Bennett? Was Michael correct? Definitely not.

I did not believe in delaying the naming of a child, because if it died before or shortly after birth (God forbid) with no name, that seemed horribly cruel.

Oh, I howled when that baby started to come out, not from pain, as my nerves were too taut to feel pain, but from the horrifying sensation of my bottom half being forced down and my upper half trying to float away. There is no feeling quite like it. At least it was easier to breathe, and I needed every bit of that extra room in my lungs.

"You're almost finished, *ma chérie,* do you want to see?" Hannah asked, brandishing a hand mirror.

"NO!" I shrieked. I did not even want to imagine how it looked. Feeling it was enough.

Maybe it was for the best that Michael was not there, because curiosity would have gotten the better of him for sure.

I knew when it was over, because I had spent the very last of my energy, and in an instant, my relief was immeasurable.

I was denied being the first to see my child. Hannah Lavigne cooed over the lovely, healthy-looking baby, but as I was now more exhausted than I'd ever been before, I could not even lift my head. My muscles were gelatin.

"Let's get her cleaned up," my mother declared, and they at once took her (her!) away to the far end of the room to wash her. I tell you, I saw nothing, but I heard the most tiny and breathy little cry there ever was.

Suddenly, I could sit up, and I was inflamed. I wanted her back! Let me clean her myself, she is mine! She was presented to me wrapped in white linen, not the blanket I'd prepared for her.

It was then that I wholly believed in love at first sight. I did not care that she wasn't a boy. I freed her from the tight swaddlings and laid her on my breast, and she stopped crying.

Hannah and my mother hung over me and pawed at us both. I'd had just about as much of them as I could take.

"Get out," I ordered them.

They shared the same bewildered expression.

"Alma, you are tired—"

"Get out!" I repeated, and the baby cringed and trilled at the sound.

They left without protesting further, and then there was a lot of noise downstairs. I prepared to be mobbed very soon, and tried to savour the little morsel of privacy I was allowed for the moment.

This was no stranger, of course. I knew these little hands and feet. They'd been beating me into pulp!

The eyes squinted and frowned, as if she was not sure she liked what she was seeing. I must have looked as though I'd been through the wringer.

"Well, hello," I puffed, as that was all I could think to say.

At once, I felt very sheepish and ashamed.

"I'm sorry. I don't have a name for you yet."

She smacked her little lips and rested a puffy red cheek on my bosom.

I chuckled, and I could feel again.

"Oh, don't I know it! Being born is hard work."

They let Michael in, and thankfully only him. I was glad to see him, or anybody who asked me how I felt. He first tended to me, and made sure I was secure and recovering, and then he turned his attention to the child. I was happy to let him take her.

I'd never seen his face transform in that way— I watched his countenance shift from relief, to utter amazement, to mortal terror, to heavenly rapture, and everything in between. It truly must be seen to be described. He brought her close enough that their noses touched, and many times he opened his mouth to speak, and could not form a proper sentence.

If you really want to know what truly transpired, he grovelled, wept, and kissed my hands and feet, and thanked me repeatedly, and I tell you, it was nowhere near as articulate as it was written.

Fortunately, he had thought of a name for her.

Autumn was not a family name. I'd never even met anybody with that name. I didn't mind, because that meant it was singular. She was special. Her full name is Autumn Rosanna Bennett. I chose Rosanna with no particular significance, except that it sounded pretty. My first choice would have been June, but since she was Autumn, it'd have been a heinous crime.

I fed her after a great deal of coaxing, but my energy was entirely depleted. I did not have the fortitude to go and use the stove, and at the moment, I did not want to ask somebody to cook for me— Michael would have made it terribly spicy, which I wasn't in the mood for, and Hannah Lavigne would have attempted to dictate how the meal was meant to be prepared— or worse, tell me what I could and couldn't eat. Michael readily brought me anything I wanted.

I asked for only berries and milk, then slept for a very long time, and chose the next morning to eat to my heart's content, because four people happily worked on a sumptuous breakfast, and I finally had a good cup of coffee. Ida begged me to let her hold Autumn while I ate. She was very careful. Michael breathed down her neck the entire time, and he policed how long each person could hold Autumn, and how much they could bother me. Even Sandra was in high spirits. I suppose she simply wanted to partake in this good mood. Michael was meek and submissive around her, even though she didn't seem hurt anymore.

I expected to be much more fatigued after the birth, but my strength had returned after a good meal, and as you can imagine, I felt a great deal lighter!

The untouched bliss lasted for only three weeks. That is not to say I was unhappy, but gravity caught up to me.

In those first few weeks, waking up every three hours to feed Autumn was a task that I carried out with enthusiasm, and believed I would never tire of it, always able to persevere without allowing myself to be fatigued.

Things began to stack up. Sometimes, she was well-fed, and cried only because she needed to be held. Michael readily volunteered on some of those occasions, but there were nights that we got two hours of sleep between us. He never complained, except that the cradle he worked so hard on was scarcely slept in; he complained, but would not put her in it as long as he had the energy to lift his arms (this vexed Hannah Lavigne, who insisted that this was how babies were spoiled).

Grant really made light of my ordeal in those days! Maybe he thought the book was getting too long. Maybe seeing me in that way would have broken my pedestal of pristine womanhood.

Much of my suffering came because I just was impatient. I did not know what to expect, because the period after birth was not discussed very much. I expected my body to take its original shape inside and out, and do so within a month. I knew Autumn would not sleep through the night right away, but I was already counting the days, and pretending I wasn't.

I thought Michael was going to stay home for the rest of the year, but he returned to work in November— the three months he'd requested had been used up, and he was not going to push his luck.

Two weeks passed, and he did not arrive home as he said he would, and his letter explaining why he was held up was also late. Again, I was asked to be patient, and I thought I could do it.

I managed it for another week. On some nights, while Autumn wailed and could not be comforted unless I paced through the house, I swallowed a great deal of bitterness, imagining that Michael had only gone back to work to get out of the house, away from all of this noise. Maybe he saw us as a burden. As hard as Mr. Kelley pushed him, I envied that he had set hours and a full night of sleep.

Maybe my body had not recovered fast enough for his liking— maybe he'd never find me appealing again. Maybe this time, he was gone and all that remained was the smell of his hair oils on the pillows.

He came back home after nearly a month, just as I was ready to snap like an old harp string. After giving him a cold word, I wiped my face and made myself presentable for him, even though I had my hair in the same coiled plaits from the previous week. He took Autumn off of me so that I could freshen myself up, but still, he did not touch me very much.

We were not short on money, and never were. In fact, we still have not spent all that he left behind. Even when he worked for Mr. Kelley, we had plenty, and yet, he was always worrying, and consulted his banker many times in a month, feeling that he could die at any time, and leave us penniless, and so his workload never lightened.

He pushed back against Kelley and managed to keep his days consistent, but I still had a great deal of trouble adjusting on my own.

Winter was worse than I imagined. I was trapped inside for most of the day except to do chores, and it was always so dark. It felt as though all I did was feed the baby and feed the fire— and rarely feed myself.

In January, Autumn was breaking in teeth, and she screamed all of her waking hours, barely nursed, and when she did, my breasts chafed. She slobbered on everything all the time, and sponging her mouth with clove oil for the pain made the torrent worse.

Dinner, clothes, and dishes remained constant through it all. While I sliced vegetables and used my brand new stove, I became engrossed in the glimmer of the knife in the lamplight. I gazed into the golden shine, cutting recklessly, and marvelling at how sharp the blade was. I wondered how easily it could pierce my hands. And how long would it take me to bleed to death? That would be quite a mess to clean up. I was just one of the messes, wasn't I?

The tea kettle was howling, and so was Autumn. I put the knife down.

Sheepishly, I came upon Abraham's chamber, with Autumn weeping on my shoulder. My arms trembled, but they were secure.

"Please, Mr. Reed," I whimpered pitifully through my tears. "Would you please hold her so that I can finish preparing dinner? Would you take her, please?"

"Oh, give her here! Give her here, let me have her!" Abraham cooed and brought her to his bosom without question. Once she'd settled a bit, and I was content, he seized my hand and turned me towards the door.

"And as for you," he began. "Dinner can wait a moment. Go and have some tea, and start again later."

"You think more of my feelings than Michael does. He does not even want to live here anymore."

"My! You don't mean that!" Abraham stepped out of his chamber. "He would stay home more if you asked him to, I know it! You never asked him, did you?"

I felt as though I shouldn't have needed to.

"He barely even touches me when he's here," I huffed.

"Oh, um… ah, hmm…" the old man shifted his feet around, since he could not pull at his fingers in that moment. "I imagine he thinks he would be

a nuisance at this time. Did you… invite him to
do so?"

"I never had to before."

"And now you do!" Abraham chuckled. "There's
a great many things you've never had to do
before, that you must get used to doing now! I'm
certain that you did not always have to wake
every two hours to tend to this little butter pat!"
he brought Autumn up close and peered at her
over his eyeglasses. She was starting to fuss
again, so we paced the gallery. It was well that he
did most of the talking, as my voice had not
steadied yet.

"She'll sleep through the night before you know
it. You must persevere. Lady Mary Bennett had a
dozen women on the duties of the house so that
she could focus solely on tending to her little
ones, and you do not have that luxury. If the
dishes are not washed right away, or dinner is half
an hour late, it won't be the undoing of the
household. That is— did you ever know Michael
to be so exacting?"

I did not, not even once. If there was no dinner
when he was hungry, he just prepared something
cold from the larder, or his brutal curries. He
never took up unfinished household chores, but
he did not complain about them, either. I
considered myself lucky that I had a husband

willing to even set foot in the kitchen on his own accord.

After we had tea standing up by the stove, I felt more willing to prepare dinner. Hunger had made me weak and irritable. Having two biscuits with my tea gave me enough energy to continue.
My fascination with the knives did not leave, but I was able to brave it as long as Autumn was in someone else's hands.

Rest assured, not for a moment did I think of harming her— strangely, it was the fear of having those thoughts that put me in a dangerous sort of mood. I'd heard awful tales of new mothers who'd gone completely mad from exhaustion, and drowned or smothered their babies. Sometimes, in a most dreary delirium, I told myself that I would die by my own hands in order to protect Autumn from me.

More specifically, I never thought of harming her intentionally. I was always afraid of doing something by accident; I could not descend the steps or even lay myself down in bed without thinking every second that I was going to drop her or roll on top of her. In fact, Michael initially did not want her in bed for that exact reason. He was deathly afraid of crushing her, and it made him such a light sleeper, that he'd have awoken if a pin dropped— but for me, it made nursing so much easier.

Michael was in Bristol two weeks at a time, and home for four days. I begged for him to stay just one extra day. He was missing so much, and surely he could find work closer to home.

His compromise was to hire a housekeeper, both for my benefit and Abraham's. I was not wholly pleased, but I accepted this resolution peacefully… for a time.

I admit, I greatly appreciated Mary Jones's help and companionship, even if it wasn't what I wanted. She entertained and kept a close watch over Abraham, who was happy to have a housemate closer to his age, and she did most of the dusting and polishing around the house while Autumn was in a disagreeable mood and I could not go far from her.

Even so, Grant's retelling of this ordeal is much more pretty and to the point. In reality, there were many weeks of huffing and puffing and nearly choking on my own tears, and Michael begging me to hold out for only a little while longer. That interval of the two of us working separately was easy in comparison. Now, there was even more to pine for. I wanted my husband, and I wanted Autumn's father. Oh, when he was present, there was no better father in the world. Grant could not truly capture it, not even I can.

Hannah Lavigne insisted that Autumn did not need the guidance of a man, and would be spoiled by seeing too much of her father. Children, especially little girls, needed to stay by their mothers, and be allowed to meet with their fathers only at tea times and meals— that was how she did it, and her children turned out marvellously. It was a testament to their good training that they did not bawl and pout when they were taken from their father.

Michael paid her no mind. Admittedly, I did restrict him from partaking in many child-rearing duties in the beginning. I was afraid he would resent them, as my father secretly did, but he was more injured by the fact that he was not viewed as an equal parent. It was hard to think of him as one when he was hardly home.

Once again, a bizarre series of circumstances put us back on equal footing.

INDIA, INHERITING GENERATIONAL CURSES, AND APPROPRIATING AN OLD MAN'S HARD WORK

Have I made it clear how I loathe Mr. Kelley?

Michael confided in me about the circumstances around Abraham's death nearly a decade later. I could not find fault in him, especially knowing how it weighed on his heart, and how easily swayed he was by men of authority. Well, nobody who was involved in the crime can be accounted for now, and its exposure to the public has since raised many ethical discussions that doctors and nurses have pondered for centuries.

It could have been justified as an act of mercy, especially to somebody who saw man as equal to or even beneath animals, but Kelley's conduct afterwards was entirely inexcusable. I vividly recall Michael's panic when his employer abandoned him during a vulnerable time and left the business to sink or swim— living things!

And poor Miss Gaye was also a victim. She really thought that Michael and Kelley were both playing a trick on her when he begged her to stay at her position after the latter's callous and cowardly dismissal.

I know for certain that it was an act of spite, because he knew that he could not control my husband anymore. His ego could not handle Michael submitting to anyone other than him.

The Kelley-Bennett Zoological Garden operates to this day, with Michael's reputation overshadowing Mr. Kelley's, even if in death, so perhaps I should thank him if I ever run into him again. He is probably still alive… men of that sort are hard to be rid of.

I agreed to move the family to Bristol. It was unexpected, but I saw a silver lining, and I really needed to get out of Brownwall. The house was so dreary and oppressive ever since Abraham's death, and I know it was so much worse for Michael.

He did his best to make these transitions easier on Autumn and me, and life became more stable straight away.

Whether or not the move brought on the change, I do not know, but I thrived. I had more energy than ever before, and I was active in the community. I was pleased to wear corsets and slender shoes again, and I felt that I was reclaiming my figure. Motherhood really did become me. I felt beautiful with Autumn on my knee— after all, I had knit together such a lovely creature.

I admit, I never had much contact with the animals myself, except when I fed some baby birds with my hand, which I really enjoyed.

Michael's work ethic is unrivalled, and it was fuelled by his mentor's influence until it grew almost into something ugly. Even before Mr. Kelley's garden belonged to him, he was waking up before the sun rose whenever he had some sort of project. I voiced my concerns about him going nearly three hours without breakfast; he told me that he didn't like to eat first thing in the morning, anyway.

This behaviour carried over after Mr. Kelley left, but Michael then had more freedom to do the things that he felt needed to be done.

Some have considered it barbaric that Mr. Kelley and Michael kept animals captive to be on display for entertainment. It is not mentioned in Grant's book, but the truth is, most of them were unfit to live on their own. Mr. Kelley quite often acquired creatures that were deformed or injured, and it just so happened that he used them as a demonstration to common folk. I suppose it is less awe-inspiring to tame debilitated snakes, but Michael and Mr. Kelley would both tell you that it was no incredible feat on their part, anyway.

That besides, even healthy creatures are hard to put back in the wild, as animals establish territories that are disrupted by new arrivals.

He'd taken animals from just about every form of mistreatment imaginable— most discarded, but allegedly, he had even stolen some of them from the upper class's exotic animal collections.

Potentially illicit means aside, it was admirable work that I consider a privilege to behold, but I still did not like the man. In my defence, he never got along with many people. He respected Abraham Reed, but did not particularly enjoy him. Abraham disliked the outdoors and was very concerned about Kelley pulling Michael into his line of work.

Another major accusation he faced was that he was heartless for helping animals, when human beings, God's children, needed aid all over the world.

Well, I was a missionary first and foremost, so he asked for my frank opinion.

"No, both undertakings are sacred," I answered. "We are called to be stewards of the earth— that is, we are not the owners, merely the caretakers, and I think we will answer for taking it for granted."

You cannot please everyone no matter how hard you try. Even while I did active charity work for people, I was asked, "What about the people in the north? Why don't you adopt some of these children? Why do you give *them* this and not *that?* Why do you help women and not men?" (I helped anybody who had the humility to seek it, and that was mostly women).

Furthermore, Michael did plenty to help people. He employed anybody willing to learn, and paid his workers generously. As you know, there were many young widowed or unwed mothers coming to work, and he sent them to me to make the necessary arrangements to provide additional assistance.

On multiple fronts, he was a force of good.

After Abraham died and Michael received Mr. Kelley's decrepit property, he decided there was nothing left for him at Brownwall— a stark contrast to the obsessive youth whose entire personhood hung on retaining his family's estate. It was shocking, but I saw it as growth; he had shed the chains of nobility and was his own man.

When asked if he believed he was betraying his forefathers by selling their estate once again, he simply said, "I don't think they'll be coming back for it any time soon."

He also rightfully decided that Kelley's compound desperately needed renovations; the infrastructure was well cared-for, but primitive and inefficient, thanks to Mr. Kelley's fear of modern technology.

Since all of the money was gone with its master, I wholeheartedly think that he forewent necessary renovations in order to hoard the cash and run, and that meant that Michael and Dolores needed to start over on their own.

With the help of many professionals, he drafted plans to remake the entire facility, and then he needed money; without Mr. Kelley's familiar presence, it was difficult to solicit donations.

The majority of what remained of the Bennett estate was gathered up and sold, and not just the jewellery. Though most of it was lost to new money in America, a great deal of treasure remained in that dower house.

So I was told, Great Great Grandmother Adelaide Allard-Bennett was a drunkard. It was reported that she spent a third of her short and sad life hiding away in a much newer Brownwall, accumulating a hidden stash of fine liquors that were well over one hundred years old by the time they were rediscovered. Even after so much time had passed, and many relatives had come and gone from the house, a fair few cases of whiskey remained untouched.

Michael gathered them up (though unable to resist keeping one for himself) and sold them for hundreds. Even though his mind was made up from the start to renovate Mr. Kelley's garden, he set aside money for Autumn's future before he did anything else.

Though he did poorly in school, he was not unteachable, not even close. I think he simply had an unconventional way of learning that was best nurtured outside of a schoolroom. What distracted most children stimulated him. When he was able to pick books that were to his liking, he was an even more voracious reader than I, and he could read in a tree or sprawled in the grass for hours, but he told me himself that would have rather been burned alive than be confined to a desk.

As such, he taught himself as much about repairs as he possibly could, and did much of the construction with his own hands, which saved money, but took much, much longer.

He spent long hours soldering, and sometimes he had little pinpoint burns because of his refusal to wear gloves. When he received these burns, he merely licked them for a moment and continued what he was doing, if he noticed them at all.

Many times, I saw him take a few minutes' rest from the task, and eat a cold sandwich stooping down right where he was, without washing his hands. It was also not uncommon to find him napping in a ditch.

The secretary, Miss Gaye, stayed on. I grew to like her. It was nice to have a woman my age close at hand. He kept her, but never made her do any hard labour, and hired many young people from the city, as long as they knew what they were getting into, and were willing to work at any time of day. Pay was fair, and shifts did not exceed twelve hours— ten, if they were still in school. At first, he used them as an extra set of hands during those big renovations, which he was determined to finish before summer, and it was already early March.

Of course, that meant long, long work days, with brand new workers who were barely competent enough, and he was the one to pay for their blunders.

The worst of the burns were on his face and left hand. They had weeping blisters and white leathery spots that soon fell away. Patches on his right hand, neck, and arms were singed pink and hairless.

He refused any drugs for the pain, even though he was warned that it would reach its peak in a few

hours. His only request was that Autumn didn't
see him like that.

Mary Jones spent a lot of time with her so that I
could tend to him myself. For a whole day, I
continuously sponged at his face and arms with
cool rags, until he could finally fall asleep.

It was awful, seeing him writhe and pant. I knew
it was bad because he would not leave that room
unless he had no choice— he often paced from
wall to wall, trying to distract himself. I wiped
the ever-present sweat on his brow, and when it
was more than he could withstand, I dried his
tears. This was a man who'd finished a shift with
two broken ribs.

On day three, it was bearable enough that he
could talk and think clearly without my nursing.
Since he could finally sit still, I cut off most of
his hair. This would make his wounds easier to
tend to, and it was uneven from being burned,
anyway, so I made it neat. I'd never seen his hair
so short before. It coiled into perfect red ringlets,
like a bunch of roses.

"You do have such pretty hair!" I told him,
hoping to raise his spirits a little, but to no avail.
He only grumbled about how he didn't like the
feeling of hat bands against his head, and I had
shorn off his protection from sun and wind chill.

Papa came soon, as that was the only doctor that Michael wanted. Immediately, he did not like the look of his left hand, and recommended it be amputated.

He refused, the reason being simply, "It's my hand."

Papa warned him that it would never heal correctly, and would be a burden to him for the rest of his life.

"It's my hand," he said once more.

"It's only your left hand," Papa replied.

"It's my hand!"

So the hand remained. I truly did not know what was best, so I did not try to sway him one way or another. After all, it was indeed his hand, not mine. He never regained all of the fine motor skills in that one hand.

For a month, I washed his burns daily, then applied menthol jelly, and I made sure that nothing I prepared for him to eat required widely opening his mouth or using two hands. By then, he still had a long way to go, but there were no more open, weeping sores, and he was ready to be out in daylight. Being indoors all that time made him morose. He started work at dusk and stayed out until midnight, despite the cold. Knowing that he would begin climbing the walls if he could not be out in the sunshine, I saw that his insecurity was deadly serious.

His face healed with minimal scarring, regardless of how horrid he thought he looked. The initial swelling made it seem far worse. It only drooped a little, and was quite pink, with a faint sort of cobweb pattern. The left corner of his mouth drooped, as though it was paralysed. He wore a patch over his left eye on especially bright days, and could not see very well at night. People did stare, but his workers stared because they knew what happened, and they felt terrible, and strangers stared because they were rude— as if they'd never seen a burned man before! If I caught them looking and whispering, it was all well, because while in London, I had perfected my cold, accusatory glare.

The worst part for me to see was not those first few nights of agony, but seeing his frustration as he learned to use his hand again. One of his greatest fears was being an invalid— he'd have rather been dead. I watched him dissolve into tears as he struggled to button a shirt on his own.

He scarcely allowed me to touch him, and was just about willing to die to avoid me looking under his bandages. Even Autumn's entreaties for

him to play with her were rebuffed, and he did it
as if he had no choice.

Finally, I had to be harsh.

"Michael, get out of this house!" I ordered him.
"You have a perfectly good set of limbs, and
you're letting them waste away— that's right, you
still have working arms and legs! People who've
been hurt far worse than you are still able to make
a living. It's all well that you feel bad, but you
mustn't stew in it! You would even scorn Autumn
because of your brooding! I know that inwardly,
you are grateful that your injuries were not more
serious, so act the part! Go and take a walk. It is
lovely outside."

And as soon as I closed my mouth, I felt like a
cruel witch, and wanted to drop balm where I'd
cut him, but restrained myself, because he needed
to hear it. I still don't know if it was the right
thing to say, but he did go outside and take a walk
with Autumn, and came back telling me about all
the baby toads they found by the creek, as well as
the flowers: especially the yellow ones.

I knew for sure that my lecture did not magically
draw him out of his despair, but very slowly, it
became easier for him to manage it, even if some
days were harder than others.

He was afraid of Autumn being frightened by what she saw, but she was too young to even understand it, and once she was old enough, she was used to it.

To the children, Michael's burn scars were not a deformity, just another feature, as familiar as his sweet brown eyes. When Ashley was three, he got a bad stinging nettle rash on his face and arms, and didn't want me to put cream on it because he thought it made him look like Daddy.

It took him a long time to even let me touch where he'd been burned, though that was partly because he had lost sensation in his hand and face, and did not want to be reminded of it. The beard he'd wanted since he was seventeen would never be realised, because hair did not grow on that side, anymore.

Honestly, it hurt to know that he feared I would find him unappealing, though I knew he couldn't help feeling that way, and I tried not to take it personally, but I did explain it to him, in one of those conversations you have at one o'clock in the morning that feels as though you'd cut open your abdomen and exposed its contents.

"Really!" he cried out, though there was no hint of anger or distress in his voice. "But were you not afraid of the same, and not even having been maimed, but merely carrying a child— my child?"

At the time, it did not matter to me that he insisted he still liked the way I looked; I wanted to be exactly as I was when he first saw me, until I was able to accept how dramatically I had changed. It must have been the same for him.

"So… we understand each other," I concluded.

He chuckled.

"You've aged. So have I— but it's not quite the same. I've aged in addition to being scarred beyond repair."

"Suppose it happened to me."

He tapped his chin.

"I would only feel that I'd failed to protect you… looking at you would trouble me for that reason, but that would be my burden… I could learn to live with it."

We had both changed quite a bit, and though he was never a terribly vain fellow, he was definitely affected by how people perceived him. Since he was fairly large and with a thick waist and legs, and he often wore loose clothing, many people thought he was fat. He insisted, of course, that it was all strength. He would later be vindicated by his post-mortem examination, which revealed to the physician that he was indeed a wall of solid muscle (I already knew this). However, it was also reported that the condition of his knees and one shoulder was that of a man twenty years his senior.

I must admit… due to a degree of self-abandonment, he was in poor health at the end of his life, and aged rapidly.

At thirty-five, many a passerby had mistakenly believed he was the grandfather of his own children. He worked himself into quite a mood for the rest of the day, and kept asking me if he truly looked so old.

It's true that the sun aged him fast. Additionally, the fatigue he brought home caused him to grind his teeth in his sleep. They chipped, and that made them appear even more crooked, though he took better care of them than most people I knew. His fear of dentists made him completely unwilling to seek treatment even when one of his molars had split down to the root.

He ignored the offending tooth for as long as possible, insisting still that he could drown it in clove oil and whiskey. This went on for a month. He went to bed with bad headaches, and chewed with only one side of his mouth. Sometimes, the pain was so horrid that he could not let air in, and once scolded Autumn by grunting and wildly gesticulating.

I came in from doing the washing one day, and saw him sprawled out on the sofa in the parlour, fast asleep, with all of his working clothes on. This was not abnormal, especially on days when he worked over fourteen hours. What stuck out to me was that his face and neck were soaked in sweat.

"Michael, you're boiling alive!" I shook his foot. "Take off your coat and tie."

He did not stir.

He must have been exhausted, so I elected to loosen the scarf around his neck myself. In doing so, I moved his head to one side, and felt a hot and swollen knot in his jaw that was not there before. I gently massaged it.

This roused him. He jumped and gave a cry of alarm.

"You need to go to a dentist before that tooth kills you!" I admonished him, while he was still coming to his senses. "You're probably already in the early stages of blood poisoning."

"Alright, alright," he mumbled.

As you know, the tooth did not kill him.

Instead, he assigned *me* the ghastly task of helping him pull it out.

This task had to wait until the children were asleep.

He got quite intoxicated, and my role was planting my knee on his chest and steadying him while he yanked it out little by little. Even as strong as he was, it took several minutes. It had to be extracted in two pieces, and the process nearly broke his jaw. There was a lot of blood when it finally came out, and I had a few drinks myself afterwards. We shared a drunken laugh by the fire while he recovered and I packed the open wound with cotton and salt.

For two days, he was so delirious from the pain and remaining fever that he could not go to work, and was very upset that I would not kiss him at all in that interval, but if you watched somebody spit a blood clot and half-chewed bread into a napkin, you wouldn't be in that sort of mood, either.

I remain so disturbed by that ordeal, I would never consider performing dental work on myself. I have four gold crowns that suit me just fine, and the process was mostly painless.

Michael's incredible collection of scars and injuries was what caught the attention of Grant Abernathy, and most peculiarly, it was the beginning of a life-long friendship. It was at about the same time that Michael had finished the major renovations on the garden, and opened it up to the public again.

Grant, though much different from Michael, is a charming fellow. They complement each other well. He is a conventionally handsome man of average stature with a hot temper, in contrast to large and gentle Michael. Still, they had much in common.

He had found work in journalism while building towards his career as an author, and he drew people to Michael's tricks: how he would let snakes, lizards, and spiders crawl all over him without being harmed— how he handled alligators seemingly without fear. They paid to see it. To the English working class, it was unseen outside of a sideshow attraction, so you can understand how it would attract the public.

In truth, Michael could not embrace this image, no matter how hard he tried. He did not see it as any great feat, and was hoping to draw people in with a desire to learn, not parlour games. He would not muck about with the animals on demand purely for entertaining the masses. He

used the snakes and spiders as a demonstration,
and only agitated the alligators if they needed to
be relocated.

"If they were in my head, they'd hear how I
scream inwardly like a frightened school girl,"
was his answer.

And sometimes, he was indeed bitten. He never
made a fuss out of it. The most dangerous thing
that bit him was a vine snake that caused a bit of
swelling on his hand for a few days— even that,
he used as a demonstration.

He once humorously brandished Autumn before
the crowd, because she, still teething, had also
bitten him.

His scars added to the allure, even though he was
always honest about their origins when he was
asked. It didn't stop people from whispering about
them, or creating their own story of what had
happened to him. Perhaps one of those African
spitting cobras had sprayed him with its poison.

There were nights when he would arrive at
home, and he did not need to say it, but I saw that
he needed to sit out in the back garden and not
talk to another human being for some minutes
before he was ready to come inside for dinner. I
believe that if he did not marry and have children,

he'd have dropped off the face of the earth, just like Mr. Kelley.

During this time, I was at home (in Bristol, of course), but still very active. Ruth assisted me in my charity efforts now, and we were part of a tightly woven web across southern England, through which underprivileged young girls could receive temporary housing and education on female hygiene, completely free of charge. It had no name, but it was affiliated with the church I used to attend in London, along with Ryan Mulligan and his wife.

Grant Abernathy would find himself a wife on his foray in India. She was a native woman who introduced herself as Sarah Rivers. Michael had spent two years in India as a young boy, so he burned with envy while Grant sent him postcards, and took a liking to the new Mrs. Abernathy straight away. He even named a new aviary in honour of the bride and groom.

I never imagined Grant would be the sort to marry and be tied down. He was too spontaneous. Still, I thought that maybe a wife would temper him.

Sarah Rivers did not speak much, but seemed quite lovely, and she was a gracious hostess when we visited. I did find it strange that she would not wear shoes or stockings, even when it was cold, but she was free to do as she pleased in her own house. She'd certainly put a spell on Grant. He made her his muse right away, writing her as an ethereal princess in many compositions, even if they were never finished.

Was I jealous? No. Michael was no artist, but he carved the image of a dove into all of his woodwork— the bird of June. Some of his workers delighted in marking them on a map when they found them.

He also brought me rocks.

In addition to Grant and Sarah, Hannah Lavigne came once in a while to offer us consultations we didn't ask for, especially about our marriage, and asked us of our travels.

Well, aside from Michael's exhibitions… there were none.

"What! You've been here all this time? All these years?" she cried, right in poor Autumn's ear.

"Oh, no… you know, I used to travel through southern England for my nursing—"

"It doesn't signify! England is so small."

"Ah, well— maybe six or so years ago, we did go to New York—"

"Six years, five months, and about twenty days from departure," Michael interjected, as he remembered every date except his own birthday.

That day, it just so happened to be my twenty-seventh, which was the reason for Madame Lavigne's visit: to bring a beautiful and decadent fruit cake, and to remind me that I should have had more children by now, as my youth won't last forever. I was determined not to huff and puff, and was tired of being interrupted, so I said no more.

"That's nothing!" she said to Michael. "Get yourself to the continents— Europe and Asia! The Orient! That's culture! That's real history! There is a whole world beyond this little island."

Her delivery was not so favourable, as per usual, but there was an idea! In fact, I'd discussed it with Michael many times. He already had a list of the cities he'd wanted to travel to since he was a young boy, and we marked them on a map. There was a clear path. All we needed was spare cash, and for Autumn to be big enough for travel. We were not hurting for money, but every shilling we could spare was put towards the animals, and I respected that. And we had plenty of time.

But by the time Autumn was big enough to travel with us, Michael had more workers, more animals, and more training to do. Once, we did travel to Ireland, just the three of us. When he finally began to settle down, we then had Ashley.

Once or twice a year, we travelled without the children, leaving them in the care of my parents, or Mary Jones, but never very far, as we wanted to be close at hand if anything was amiss.

Until she was seven, Autumn did not go to school. I taught her reading and writing at home, and sometimes tutored the small children of Michael's workers, or the girls that visited— so she was plenty civilised even without it, *despite* Michael's influence.

He took her outside quite often, and let her pick up some of the creeping, crawling things— something he was harshly scrutinised for, as it would turn her into a tomboy.

Really, nothing he did as a father was good enough for many of our relatives, especially when it came to discipline. He never once raised a hand at her. He refused. I did not, either, but as the man of the house, he was expected to. The worst we ever did was tap a wandering hand that had been warned with words.

Michael thought that even whipping animals was barbaric. Aside from his own convictions, he believed that if Autumn was anything like him (which she most certainly was), then physical punishment would do no good. Being whipped only increased his tolerance for pain, and then it was just a minor inconvenience to suffer through until he could go back to being "naughty." Once it no longer worked, he was strapped to a chair in the corner, which was far more torturous: that is, until he was strong enough to break the straps, but by then, he'd shed his rebellious streak.

The only striking that had an effect on him was his hands, which he usually received for careless handwriting. Now, his penmanship is flawless.

As for me, if my daughter ever cringed at me the way I sometimes shrank away from my own mother, I'd never be able to rid myself of that shame.

When I was eight, and cut myself with her good scissors, my first instinct was not to go to her and tell her I'd been injured, but to hide the evidence and treat the cut myself. I was scolded for being afraid of her without reason, and for making a bloody mess of my linens, but she decided that my cut was a suitable punishment for disobedience, after she finished her lecture about my disregard for other people's property.

I had always been so dreadfully afraid of losing my temper at my children. That fear was more common than me actually being angry. I admit—

sometimes, I handled her quite roughly, and I shouted if I needed to get her attention, but not once did I strike her, and certainly did not berate or provoke her.

Michael's rule of thumb was that he would direct her in the way he wished he'd been at that age. He was usually more lenient than I. Scraping up her knees once in a while was a sort of self-correction.

I discussed it with my mother while visiting in her parlour, when Autumn was about two, and for a little while, we had a civil conversation.

"If she grows up with me hitting her any time she does something wrong, she'll start to think it is right for other people to mistreat her," I stated; Michael had said the same to me earlier, and I agreed. "Furthermore, the punishment should fit the crime, and dropping a cup does not equate to violence, does it?"

Mama nodded, but the next words to escape her lips were completely disagreeable, and she had the nerve to utter them with my child in her lap.

"But she should know from a young age that her words have consequences, and she needs to mind her elders."

"It would only make her fear me," I replied.

"She should fear you, just a little. Look how well you turned out!"

I remembered at that moment, when I'd sometimes been slapped across the face for interrupting, or speaking in an unsavoury tone, and what she'd just said to me delivered a sting so familiar that I reflexively touched my cheek.

"Why are you looking at me that way?" she asked. "What did I say?"

"Nothing," I reached over and took Autumn away from her. "I was just thinking."

"Hmph! Don't get like that. My hand may have moved on its own once or twice, but I never hurt you on purpose."

It was quite telling that she knew immediately what I was thinking of. I considered it a subconscious admission of guilt, which was the best I was going to get out of her.

But for her to act as if she had no control over her actions boiled my blood, and was an affront to me as a mother, as I was doing my very best to refrain from upbraiding her simply because my daughter could hear.

"Don't try to justify yourself," I spoke coolly. "You did not discipline me. You humiliated me, and robbed me of my dignity by making me the target of your frustrations."

"Please! I rarely left a mark on you— consider yourself lucky. You speak of me as if I were some tyrant. What I did is not even comparable to how my mother beat me!"

"Maybe so, but just once, could you admit to your shortcomings without making excuses?"

"I know I wasn't the perfect mother, but—"

"And I never wanted you to be. Just once, I wanted an admission of fault without *'but'* attached to it."

"Oh, I see!" she huffed. "Your husband can do no wrong, but you won't forgive your own mother who did everything for you, for one little outburst said in anger!"

Could we not discuss our problems without bringing a man into them? Worse still, Michael had nothing to do with this conversation, and then my patience was wrought to its limit.

I stood up.

"Leave *my* family out of this, and save your melodrama for somebody else. I'm not staying for the reprise"

"I suppose I don't know you as well as I thought I did!"

"No, you don't!"

"Well, if you're leaving like this, then don't come back to my house!"

I took Autumn, and I left as calmly as I could, though I was in tears by the time my mother could not see me. Half of me hoped she would follow me. I hated having no control, and sometimes the only way to reclaim it was to depart.

During my little visit, Michael was with my father in the next town, and found me walking down the empty road on his way to retrieve us.

"Pigeon!" he cried out, and he plucked Autumn out of my tired arms and raised her above his head, kissing all over her face to her screeching delight.

Then he tucked her under his arm like a sack of flour (her favourite way to be carried by him) and addressed me.

"You spoke with your mother?"

"Yes."

"Would you like to tell me about it?"

"Maybe later."

Autumn babbled endlessly in fragments of sentences about the creek and showed Michael all of the yellow leaves she had in her pockets, and then she was fast asleep by the time we arrived home late that night.

I put her down to sleep— she had just begun sleeping in her own little cradle all the time — and then I lay myself down next to Michael, who had turned in unusually early, and was reading by candlelight. He was not wearing a shirt, so I nestled into the soft underside of his arm. That was my favourite place to lay my head. He put the book down.

Then I could tell him about it.

A few weeks later, Ellen sent comfits and a cheerful letter, as if nothing had happened.

I am sorry that so many accounts of my mother are so bitter. It is not like that most or even half of the time— but unfortunately, those were the instances that have stuck out to me after all these years. It was hard to talk to people about it. Michael listened, but he did not fully understand. He could not, and it wasn't his fault.

From what I've witnessed, she is a doting and gentle grandmother, and I felt terrible for taking Autumn away from her; however, I could not stop myself from seeing her anger, and most shamefully, there was a sharp pang of envy and longing, remembering how tender she could be when I was small.

When Autumn became old enough to speak for herself, she could see her grandmother any time she pleased— but even now, old as I am, we are not in close contact, and it is all I can do to avoid stoking that fire. I always swear that I will never see her again, but I keep going back. She has mellowed out now, as she is an old lady, but she has no memory of such events; she is not even angry at me for bringing it up, because she does not know what I'm talking about.

But that is often the way of it. No matter how much effort you give, there will always be loose ends: some, you may even take to your grave, and that is alright. You may never have it all figured out.

As for my Papa, he has long since apologised for his indifference as a husband and father. He is almost the same as a grandfather: cool and uninvolved, but not unkind.

He held Autumn for the first time, and said, "Maybe I was not built for fatherhood after all, but I don't regret it— only my methods. You had a difficult time of it, and I was not much help at all. I am sorry that I could not be everything you needed me to be. I'm glad Michael is better at it."

And that was enough for me.

Michael had only sweet things to say about his mother, but she'd died when he was eight or nine. From what I heard, she led a sort of non-conforming lifestyle despite marrying into nobility— long retreats into the wilderness, running around with no shoes, wearing flowers in her hair at breakfast, and spending the whole day with her son. She was an untameable woman.

Unfortunately, she'd succumbed to terrible bruising after being thrown off of a horse that she was well-acquainted with— this knowledge only worsened my fear of those large beasts.

ANIMAL FEARS AND FUNCTIONS

For Michael, it was chickens— fowl in general,
really. For me, it was horses.

In his case, however, it was understandable.
When he was fourteen or fifteen, a rooster he'd
approached lunged at his face, leaving a pale
groove that narrowly missed his left eye. He told
me that any time he saw or heard chickens, he
had an uncontrollable urge to flinch back, as if
somebody had kicked sand in his eyes— he also
admits that this was all his fault for crouching
low to the ground and startling the bird, but the
fear remained. He once refused to leave through
the front door because a goose was on the other
side.

In my case, there was absolutely no reason. One
day, as a small girl, I wandered too far from
Grandfather Ronald's house and got a good look
at a big black stallion that was fenced up and
minding his own business. The coat did not shine.
It stood out like an ink spot against that sunny
spring day, and when it turned its massive head to
the side, I got an awful feeling in my stomach,
and ran back home without ever stopping to catch
my breath.

And that was that.

Soon after, while Mama and Papa were still living together, they brought home an old grey mare named Betty. She was so sweet and docile, and it was not her fault that the sight of her made me ill. When Papa placed me on her back just once, I wailed and wet myself.

He never put me on her again. James laughed at me for years to come. Though she terrified me, I was still sorry when she passed away.

But whereas Michael could hunt, handle, and even caress wild birds whenever the situation called for it, I could not tolerate any horse that wasn't under someone else's control.

Even though his mother had been killed by one, Michael wanted Autumn to become used to them as soon as possible— I thought it was madness. He should have been terrified of them, but he harboured no ill feelings towards the creatures: only a healthy respect for their power.

He was so very pleased to inherit Kelley's two horses. It was the first thing to lift his spirits when the old man disappeared. He named them Bismarck and Lorelei. I don't know where his penchant for giving animals German names came from.

At first, I was furious when I learned that he had intended to put Autumn on Bismarck. My own

terror overcame me, rational or irrational. I could
only see her breaking her neck or being trampled
to death.

Michael said, simply, "I will not let Autumn get
hurt. It *will not* happen."

He of all people would not have made such a
promise unless he was absolutely certain, and he
would not have bet Autumn's life on being
wrong. I knew that I could trust his judgement
with animals more than most people's, and I also
knew she was safe in his hands, so I allowed it,
but only if I could watch.

She was first spoken to in great length about the
nature of horses, and then Bismarck was
presented to her. She was beside herself with wild
glee, knowing she would finally learn to ride
Daddy's horse (though Michael himself did not
ride Bismarck, as he was smaller than Lorelei).

And right away, I knew I made the right choice. It
was magical to see her face light up, knowing she
wouldn't be burdened by the same petrifying fear
that I was afflicted with. Additionally, it was very
amusing to behold, because she was so little, it
looked as though she was riding a dragon.

Michael took Bismarck around the gardens, and
Autumn, little princess that she was, ate up the
attention of adoring onlookers. The dogs

followed, which of course made me nervous, as they were another animal I was a degree uneasy about, but I grew more comfortable with them, the more that Michael collected.

Most that he came across were abandoned or lost.

Ginger, the one that I named myself, was in particularly bad shape when he found her, and she was not with us for long.

He'd stumbled upon her wallowing in waste with her deceased litter in the outskirts of the city, when he had been summoned to help dispatch a pair of bats that had entered a storehouse. It was soon after Jeannine's passing, after he'd sworn he did not want another dog.

I wonder how many people had walked past her and decided it was not of their concern, or hadn't even given her any thought, not even thinking to put her out of her misery.

Not Michael, of course.

"Fate has brought us together!" he cried, digging her out of the filth and borrowing a wagon to cart her straight to a veterinary surgeon.

She had suffered a bad blow to the head and endured constant tremors as a result, and one of her hind legs was rotting. Against all advice, he

believed in her and would not put her down,
electing to have the offending limb amputated
and give her all the luxuries she had been denied
thus far.

He asked me to name her, and she was dubbed by
the colour of her freshly washed coat.

At first, the poor creature was deathly afraid of
Michael, but was too ill to try to fight him off.
She howled and shook and snapped her jaws at
him when he came close. Any large man scared
her, so I and some of the other ladies lent a hand
in tending to her until she learned to trust him.
We found her contently eating out of his hand
early one morning, though she never lost her
shyness of other men.

Then came several months of rehabilitation for
her. She managed to walk on three legs, and
Michael trained her to sink low to the ground
when her convulsions began.

Those got worse over time, and it probably could
not have been helped. As they began to happen
several times a day, and it became harder and
harder for her to recover, he saw the writing on
the wall. It was time to put an end to her
suffering.

He had been forced to put down animals several
times before, and often did so himself so that the

other workers did not have it on their conscience. Mr. Kelley, a former veterinarian, had taught him the most effective and painless methods of administering fatal drug dosages.

In the hours leading up to the act, he revered her as royalty. She feasted on an entire roast goose and licked the pan clean, and he played the piano for her for close to an hour. After being drugged, she slept in his lap until her heart stopped.

And again, he swore he did not want another pet.

Wolfgang and Seuss, he acquired at about the same time. Wolfgang was large and intended to be a guard dog, and the owners placed him right into Michael's hands because nobody in their house could handle him, and blamed it on poor breeding. Though he'd not yet reached his full size, he was powerful and awe-inspiring.

He was very sweet to people, but he was notorious for property damage. Most notably, somebody's pig had wandered into our yard and made a bluff charge at one of the children, and Wolf, a formidable Mastiff-type beast, launched himself on it straight away.

I had been hanging up wet clothes in my garden and was summoned by the commotion. Autumn, who was then about nine, tried and failed to call Wolfgang off.

This matter eventually went to civil court, as the pig farmer demanded that he be reimbursed for his lost property, whereas Michael maintained that as the pig had trespassed and both animals did what they were naturally going to do, nobody was at fault, and the matter should have been dropped.

I think it was the farmer's fault for not containing his livestock, but Michael eventually paid the man simply to be rid of him, and then agonised for weeks over the disturbance in his carefully managed budget.

Not fully appeased, he insisted that the dog be shot, and of course Michael would not hear it. He then threw more cash at the problem, and the farmer never returned, nor did we find any more wayward swine, so perhaps he'd used the money to build a better fence.

I know for a fact that Michael would have offered up his right arm for his animals.

Indeed, he did, because he once put himself between Jeannine and a feral dog she had tried to get at while they were out late at night. The attacker latched onto Michael's arm, and she fought his reining so fiercely that she nearly threw him onto the ground, as she, too, was large and incredibly powerful. To keep hold of her, he had no choice but to kick the other dog away.

Once he'd managed to tether Jeannine on the porch and calm her, he went back to look for the other dog, and found it was afflicted by rabies.

Michael had already been subjected to preventative shots at my insistence, but I coerced him into receiving another round after the exposure. The drug had adverse effects, and he was bedridden for two days, but it was inarguably better than the alternative, even if he was not known for handling illness very well.

I did not particularly love his late night walks, and this was why. I'm amazed and so very grateful that the disease has been nearly eradicated from the country. This is in part due to there being more control over animals entering our borders.

I am not keen on the importation of exotic animals. As you know, a large portion of the creatures in Mr. Kelley's ownership came from the cast-offs of that practice, which is fueled by greed and decadence. Kelley had been known for diverting stocks of these creatures by bidding high on a large lot, or even stealing them (this could not be proven in courts). Some were even willingly surrendered directly to us, by caretakers who were overwhelmed, did not enjoy some deformity that they had, or simply grew bored of them.

I suppose that as long as people with more money than sense keep buying and maiming animals, my children have work. Indeed, Autumn in particular has stayed on and continues caring for the animals. She was always a very bold child who loved to talk, and tries to be friends with everybody she meets. She is a charmer as a young woman, as well, and though married now, and having given me a gorgeous grandson, she has not lost her pluck.

And she is not so little, now. She has been bigger than me since she was fourteen, and Ashley, much earlier. I always knew my children would be large in stature.

I have not spoken much of the children. Autumn is often reading over my shoulder, and telling me, "This book is about you! Write about yourself!"

It is hard not to write about them. They have been my life for more than half of it.

THE FRUITS OF MY LABOUR

Oh, but I've hardly mentioned Ashley at all! He is now grown, and is so similar to Michael, especially about the ears and eyes (Ashley's are blue, but the shape is identical).

Autumn was a surprise, but Ashley, we had to work for.

I do not think it is good for women to have babies on top of each other, within a year, as many of them do, nor is it good for the children; animals do not have new litters until their current brood is independent, and we humans should at least wait until our young can walk and talk, if we can help it. That being said, I place no judgement on women who think they can do it

There are many reasons that somebody may want more children. It could be a sense of obligation, wanting a boy or a girl, loneliness, or even superstition.

We had no reason. We just did, by hook or by crook. It felt right.

And this feeling began about when Autumn was three years old. We believed we simply should have had another child by then, so we twiddled our thumbs for another year, and then we started to seek help.

I almost wish we hadn't. It was likely a complete waste of time, and there are very few things that I consider a genuine waste of time. I think that if God wanted us to have Ashley, it would have happened no matter what we did.

Female gynaecologists were not new, but they were rarer than they are now. For my physician, I specifically sought a woman with children, believing that she would know better than any man if I described what I experienced.

I was told to stop drinking coffee, stop eating heavily spiced foods, don't sit up in bed or jump out of it in the morning, and strain my abdominal muscles as little as possible— don't even cough if I could help it. I could not pick up my daughter unless it was "absolutely necessary." The physician said she was too old to be carried around, anyway. Michael was ordered to stop consuming alcohol and stop swimming.

"You think they're going to make a run for it when he hits the water?" I asked, much to Michael's flustered amusement and the lady doctor's distaste.

"We in the Church Of Jesus Christ Of Latter Day Saints abstain from strong drink, and we have many children," she declared.

"Do you not have three or four women assigned to every one man?" Michael blurted out faster than I could stop him. "I'm only concerned with this one."

"I'll have you know, good sir, that polygyny has not been recognised in ten years."

"That's fairly recent—"

"I'm sure there's merit to your advice!" I interrupted him. "Thank you, Madam!"

I had hoped that her prescription would be purely medicinal, not coloured by heresy. Nevertheless, we gave it a try, and I curtailed Michael's uncouth (albeit innocent) curiosities in order to stay in her good graces for the next consultation.

Holding back a cough was more strenuous than allowing it to happen. Stopping each other from having a little coffee or red wine after dinner made us irritable. We went to bed grumbling. Michael was greatly put off by me lying there like fried fish, anyway, but after all, I could not risk straining anything.

The physician I'd seen made me feel inadequate for struggling under her demands. I was "selfish," which was ludicrous, because Michael wasn't thrilled, either.

We heeded her advice, because we were desperate, and all it seemed to do was ruin our marriage.

Moreover, I was tired of Michael searching my clothes for traces of blood. How repulsive!

When none of the strange and exhausting instructions were any help, I was put on a strict regimen of herbal elixirs to put in my tea as a fertility aid. In three months, it only gave me these awful pains. She told me to be patient and wait for the medicine to work, but I insisted that there had to be something else to do.

Male doctors were no better. They were more scientific, but more condescending and dismissive of my background in nursing. Worse still, my physician insulted my husband, right in front of me.

Michael came with me on my first visit; he did not want a strange man touching me without supervision, and demanded to see all of his credentials going back to grammar school before he was comfortable enough to walk out for even a minute.

Once he was gone, the doctor commented, "A noble creature, you are, and truly knowing the heart of the Lord, that you cling to your husband in spite of his looks."

I was incensed enough to leave, right then and there, but restrained myself. Mostly.

"In spite of! *Not so!* I like the way he looks and would not have him any other way!"

"Ah? Is that so? My mistake, young lady."

Michael returned, absolutely perplexed at my unfriendly disposition, when I was so warm and eager moments ago.

"Perhaps she has not had breakfast," the physician offered.

"That would make anybody choleric!" Michael replied. "But I remember her eating before we left."

"I did eat breakfast!" I huffed. "Can we get on with it?"

"Ah! Poor creature. You are merely impatient, knowing motherhood awaits you," said the licensed fool.

I never told Michael what he said, because it would have surely hurt him.

I did not allow that charlatan to take a look until I felt there were no other options. It was the most mortifying experience of my life, and he found no structural abnormalities that may have inhibited childbearing— so it was all for nothing.

They said, "Maybe it just wasn't meant to happen," but I wasn't ready to accept that answer, and I knew it wasn't true!

Besides, Autumn had already caught little bits of our discussions, and was enamoured with the idea of being a big sister.

This time, I felt much more secure and content with the initial discovery. How did I tell Michael? I had to come up with something more original than knitting tiny socks or eating chalk.

But I was far too excited. I pulled out all of the clothes I'd saved from Autumn's infancy and sized them up, right in front of him, in his study. There was surely no way he could miss it.

It took him a minute to look up from his papers.

"Oh! You aren't already planning to give those away, are you?" he asked.

I don't know why that shattered my perfect mood, but it did.

"Are you being *intentionally thick?"* I puffed. "We're having another baby!"

He put his pen down.

"Oh! Well, I didn't want to ask again—" then he actually processed it. "Oh, really!"

"Yes, you fool."

His second reaction to such news was not as frenzied and panicked as the first— he was older, for one thing, and it was not a surprise, but a long-awaited outcome. He seemed more relieved than anything.

Well, he went downstairs, and about ten minutes later, Autumn was squealing and climbing into my lap, insisting she already had a name for her brother.

That's right. Everybody was on the same page.

It was fine that he told Autumn, but then his workers were trying to talk to me when I left the house the next morning, and a week later, Hannah Lavigne's carriage was clattering to a stop in front of our home.

I didn't scold him, because the damage had already been done, and he would soon be punished for his blunder.

Madame Lavigne's attention was diverted for a
good while, because she immediately descended
upon Autumn and spoiled her to her heart's
content.

Of course, the very first thing she said to me is
that it'd taken me "long enough" to have another
child, and I most definitely was not eating
enough, as I should have had at least four more
by then. She partially blamed the fact that I'd
nursed Autumn until she was three, which surely
must have delayed conception; I needed to have a
wet nurse, as Hannah had. In fact, there was no
excuse to nurse babies after they'd grown teeth!

I had no nurse for Autumn, and had no intention
of having one for Ashley if I was able to do it
myself.

Next, she turned on Michael and blamed him for
me not eating enough, not hiring more servants,
spoiling Autumn… he soon remembered that not
everyone needs to be told our business.

Ashley was easier to carry, but I suppose that's
because I knew what I was getting into; at least, I
thought I did. No two babies are the same.

I did not have harsh digestive issues, except
heavy spices made me nauseous, and the scent of
tomatoes was intolerable, as strong as fresh
blood. Michael would cook hot curry for Autumn

when she wanted it, and simply brought me curds and toast, which he knew I could eat with no ill effects.

Even when I'd caught a terrible cold, I would not eat it, though he insisted that it would "clean out" the sickness, as his mother gave it to him when he had a cough, and it would subside in two days. He once subjected the whole household to curry soup potent enough to take paint off of the walls when everyone except he were stricken with a seasonal flu. It certainly cleared the sinuses, but it was unpalatable.

Ashley sat low, the same as Autumn, and I put on much more weight, because I could eat a full breakfast. At my heaviest, I resembled one of Sir Rubens's women. This pleased Hannah Lavigne, but it was hard on my knees. She was quick to lend me pieces from her daughters' very extensive maternity wardrobes. They were much taller than I, so I needed to hem the skirts. Michael said he did not care what I weighed as long as he could carry me, but I have seen him lift a twenty-five stone anvil. I do not remember why he did it. Anyway, I cannot even form the image in my head of a twenty-five stone woman.

Each of my babies was very active in the womb, especially after I drank a lot. Michael said it was because they were natural swimmers, just like him.

Even at three years old, the children could swim
better than I could— he began teaching them as
soon as they could walk. Another foolish fear of
mine is water, even now. I never could swim very
well. Michael tried to teach me, or at least get me
to float, which he said I should have been better
at than him, because my body is soft.

I was not. According to him, I was too rigid and
needed to loosen up, or I'd drop like stone. Of
course, he kept on telling me that it could "save
my life" one day; I just never found the time to
master it. This perplexed him, as he thought it
was only the city folk who couldn't swim.

 I told him of my mother's apprehension about
children being around water.

"Well, I'd say that is all the more reason to learn
how to swim!" he insisted.

I'm glad that the children had a better chance of
saving themselves than I had of saving them, but
I did not think he needed to teach them so early.
He insisted he simply must do it before he died,
because I sure wouldn't. I hated how he always
spoke of dying!

I believe he wrestled with mortality for a long
time. Ever since he was a small boy, he was
surrounded by death. All of the men in his lineage

perished before fifty for four generations, like some kind of familial curse. His father had succumbed to a rare blood disease, making him an orphan at nineteen. He admitted to me that he did not feel he would live a long life, so he would just have to get as much done as he could.

He told me this in the wee hours of the morning, by a small fire as I nursed Autumn, who was maybe just shy of one year old. It was soon after Abraham had passed.

"How long have you felt that way?" I asked.

"It's tickled at my brain for a long time," he admitted. "The first instance I really felt I had to face death was when I became very ill with pneumonia— and then, after Autumn was born…"

He drew in a breath to steady himself, and his eyes had this mysterious shine to them.

"I was at both my parents' deathbeds; once when I was eight, and once again at nineteen. I knew months before that my father was dying, and still, I was not ready. I thought I would be. I thought I would be at peace when his suffering was finally over. And—"

He reached his hand out and tugged at Autumn's ear.

"She's so little! She's so little! I cannot leave this world peacefully while she needs me."

"You won't," I said firmly.

"You can't be certain of that."

"I am!" I insisted. "Nothing will happen to you: not for a long, long time."

He seemed settled by my words, but this sentiment returned yet again when Ashley was due to arrive.

As for his reception of the pregnancy and subsequent trials, at least he was not pulling his hair out, as he was before. With Autumn, he meant to wrap me up in wool and keep me cushioned away from the cold, scary world, but he had relaxed considerably this time. He now knew that breathing damp air or pricking my finger would not be the death of me, and since we were already well-equipped with Autumn's things stored away, he was not so pressed to prepare—but no less excited.

Even though Autumn had been around many young mothers before, there was a lot that she did not understand. No, she could not hear him. He didn't make any noise. No, he would not be born tomorrow. It's going to be a long time. Not next week. I cannot control it. No, he likely would not have the same birthday as her. November is what we're planning for. He's not coming out of my mouth. Babies can't form from the soil. He's in me because God put him there. It doesn't matter how He did it.

Regardless, she was always in my lap, with her hands on my belly.

She began knitting very young, because Aunt Lavigne taught her at four, afraid that Michael's influence was making her too boyish, and she needed to spend more time inside. Autumn happily took her knitting outside and made a charmingly ugly pair of mittens for her brother.

Laura was not my intended midwife that time. I'd fallen out of contact with her— not for unfriendly reasons. We slowly began to stop exchanging letters, as her life went in one direction, and mine went in another, and we were merely friendly inmates, not devoted companions. There are some relationships that you grow out of— and some you grow into.

Autumn overheard our discussions at the dining table and volunteered, not knowing what it entailed, but eager to help.

My chosen attendants were two ladies from church, Lucy and Beatrice. They stayed with us for a week, arriving two days before the delivery. Most of all, I was grateful that the hottest months of the year were behind me by the time I had gotten so big.

Ashley's birth was much easier, as well. He arrived on time. This time, I knew the feeling well the day before he arrived, so I was ready. I told everybody in the house, "He is coming tomorrow, I know it," and I wanted everything to be ready.

Michael had no sleep that night. He almost did not go to work the next day, but I insisted he carry on as if it were any other day until something happened.

The tremendous pressure on my back and strong urge to walk were the same. I spent the first hour pacing my barren garden on a delightfully chilly November mid morning, filled with tranquillity and wondrous anticipation as I knew I would not be rudely interrupted this time around. Autumn marched behind me. She was welcome company.

I had Mary Jones prepare a warm bath with soothing oils when I came inside, and told her to have somebody fetch Michael and tell him— and let him know that he did not need to leave work right away, because all was well.

He came within an hour, anyway, and he was all covered in dirt and leaves.

"I fell down," was all he said.

"It looks as though you need this bath more than I do," I answered.

"I'll make sure I look presentable. First impressions are important."

He sat with me, and kissed my hands and continuously asked me how I felt while I took my bath and had a cup of coffee, and he refilled my cup as many times as I wanted and put my hair in plaits. I think he was attempting to make amends for how he'd been steamrolled so easily the first time.

I finished the bath, and put on a clean gown. Autumn still wanted to do her grammar lessons that afternoon, and I obliged her, but we were both too anxious to sit still. Michael? No chance.

She earnestly begged for an occupation, believing she needed to assist me.

"I have a very important assignment for you!" I took her aside and told her. "You need to take care of Daddy for me. He'll surely tie himself up in knots."

He collected Autumn, and they kept each other
out of the way. I heard their chatter downstairs.
I confined myself when I felt ready to do so and
had prepared a room for myself beforehand.
There were large windows and a suitable chaise
longue where I could sit *whenever I felt inclined,
and no sooner.*

Lucy and Beatrice read and prayed with me, and
did not interfere more than was wanted. Though I
was not wearing much, I let the fire die down,
because labouring made me hot.

I paced in a dreamlike trance until the
contractions were powerful enough to bring me to
my knees, and then I waited for them to subside.
This repeated standing and sitting was harsh on
my legs, but it was an impulse I could not fight.
Sometimes, I amused myself by swaying to
imaginary music.

It took me some minutes to realise that I was not
imagining the music. Michael was playing the
piano again. It was immediately apparent when
Autumn started playing, too. My laughter brought
the spasms back.

This time, I was prepared for him to drop, and did
not feel that immeasurable mortal terror, because
I knew the end was near.

Though I did not suffer, the fruit of my labour was just as sweet.

Ashley was born in the evening— under a crescent moon. I was standing up. I think it was much easier that way, but it was not intentional. I had risen up once more, and I scarcely even had a moment to push, because he was more ready than I was.

"Ah, here he comes! Here he comes!" I gasped.

Beatrice meant to push me back down, but I was stronger than she was, and used her to instead hold myself up, and I just barely caught him with my own hands.

He was smaller than Autumn, and he had more hair. With such a grand entrance, I knew he would be a runner. The dying fire threw sparks as he opened his eyes. I demanded more coal so that I could clearly see his lovely face. I bathed him myself, and my touch soothed his cries. He instinctively snatched at my fingers, realising the terror of being alive.

"Oh, he's a pretty baby!" Lucy cried out.

I heard shrill chatter, and excited little feet tapping in the gallery. Somebody was impatient.

"Let them in," I instructed the ladies.

I didn't realise how fatigued I was until I reclined, but the moment I did, I trembled as though I'd been submerged in the Arctic Ocean. Since I did not intend to move from that spot, I arranged myself comfortably with my prize, quite pleased with myself, as I already had a name for him.

The name Ashley, which you know as Michael's middle name, is something of a family heirloom, given to every firstborn son in the Bennett family for many generations. Naturally, Michael's uncle Gabriel had it, and Samuel did not, but as Gabriel Bennett had no children, Michael inherited the name. It served as a reminder of their heritage, honouring the ancient ash trees of Scotland.

Michael expressed no such inclinations, though he was sure we would have a boy this time, and he surrendered the naming to me. I thought that it was perfectly suitable for a given name, and I wanted to encourage Michael to cling to his family traditions a little more.

"What good are traditions and wealth purely for the sake thereof?" he'd ask frequently, which surely would have gotten him ostracised and maybe even stoned in his former social circles.

Samuel was the name I considered giving Autumn when I thought she would have been a boy. In the end, both of them had names that lauded Earth's beauty, which Michael and I both appreciated.

Lucy let Michael and Autumn in. I presented Ashley Samuel Bennett— despite our agreement, Michael was unsure about it.

"Are you not Michael Ashley Bennett?" I asked. "It is familiar."

"I think he deserves a nicer name."

"It's a pretty name, and it's my turn."

"I suppose it is."

"Well, Autumn, what do you think?"

Mind you, Autumn was not still that whole exchange. She stood over Michael while he knelt at my knee, just about rattling to pieces as she panted and waved her hands about her face.

"He's the perfect baby! He's *perfect!*" she sang out and stamped her feet around her father, and Ashley pinched up his little brow trying to focus on all of these sounds.

"Autumn has spoken," I decided.

I was always pleased to place them in his arms, and the simple image of Michael receiving each of our babies with such tenderness is the purest joy. It is a smile that must be seen to be believed. Autumn beaming over his shoulder at her little brother made this scene particularly sweet. I wish he could have held our grandchildren.

I'd say it took me about the same stretch of time to fully recover, but I did not need to sleep so soon after the birth, and could stay awake to enjoy my family.

Ashley was not a very fussy baby. He awoke more frequently than Autumn, but he was easier to soothe.

Family came to visit and meet him, in addition to Michael eagerly showing him to everybody who was paid to be around him. Even Grant came, and Autumn was not at all pleased when he tried to hold him. Only Mammy and Daddy could hold Ashley; even if they allowed it, *she* did not!

I got enough sleep, but I was sleeping whenever I could, so I was not always awake when Autumn got up. Michael managed her before he went to work. Once Ashley started to eat food from the table, he could be handed to his father more often, and I could carve out equal time for both of my children.

Not that they were separated often. As soon as Ashley could walk, he followed Autumn everywhere— indeed, he began to wean himself just to be at her side all the time, and he brought me rocks, clovers, and snails from outside. To my dismay but eventually acceptance, it was also when Michael started handing him lizards and frogs (under very careful supervision).

He was not so engaged with the visitors in the garden, because he was a timid boy who kept to himself. Autumn, however, wanted to be put to work as soon as possible.

When she approached womanhood, this troubled Michael to some degree, because she feared no-one. Any male who spoke to her was met with extreme prejudice.

I remember one time, when a young fellow came to Autumn and marvelled at how she wore a rat snake as naturally as though it was a string of pearls. She delighted in the attention, and spoke freely to him, and he leaned closer and closer, almost flush with her face.

I went to relay my observations to Michael, but when I found him, he was already on his merry way down the pavement.

He told me that he simply sent the fellow on his way, but I did not hear what was said. Autumn told me years later.

Michael came from behind the gentleman, and said so modestly, "Good afternoon, young man!"

The lad turned and froze. Michael was probably a good seven inches taller than he.

"Good afternoon," he answered.

"You appear to be a strapping lad in good health, and from a nice family," Michael leaned himself just as close as that man had to Autumn. He then displaced the patch over his cloudy eye. "Let me have a better look at you. I say, how old are you, son?"

"Ei— sixteen, sir."

"Sixteen! A fine age, about the age I hire most of my workers. I remember being sixteen. I was a brute. I fought anything with a head on its shoulders. In my prime, I had a blow that could send a man flying! Imagine that!"

"I can't imagine, sir."

"And I see you've met my daughter! She is about ten, an equally fine age, wouldn't you say?"

"Tha— I suppose so," he shrank away from
Autumn. "I was only talking to her, Mister!" he
asserted. "Words don't hurt people."

"You're right, old boy!" Michael patted him on
the shoulder. "Words don't hurt people at all—
but daddies with pretty little girls— they hurt
people."

The boy opened his mouth—

"Check your words if you wish to walk away
from this exchange."

He tipped his hat and was on his way.

After that, he taught Autumn how to box, much
to Hannah Lavigne's dismay (fencing was so
much more ladylike).

"Real fights are not ladylike," he stated. "They're
ugly and dirty, and you don't wait your turn."

As for me, I did not argue.

He did not teach her how to fight fairly. He taught
her how to bite, gouge eyes, pull hair, and knock
the air out of somebody three times her size.
These, he taught her under one condition: never
to start fights, but if they're started, finish them.

He started Ashley's training as early as possible, still dreadfully fearful that he would soon become an invalid… or die.

"You will not die any time soon, I forbid you!" I told him, pointing to our map. "We have not even begun our travels."

"You will simply have to make enough memories for both of us."

"I'll do nothing of the sort, because you will come with me!"

His tone, previously light-hearted, became deathly serious.

"You simply must take care of everything if something happens to me, and the children are not old enough," he ordered me. "That is a possibility you cannot change."

I did not reply for a minute, because to acknowledge the prospect was a ghastly duty.

"Alma?"

"I will… you will need to show me how."

"Now?"

"No. Some other time. I'm tired."

I went to bed, and since I could not convince him to follow, he went to do God knows what.

People who cannot put down a task until it is completed naturally sound admirable and inspirational, but it is what you may call a double-edged sword. They are good providers and difficult lovers.

For Michael, it started with nights when he awoke after only an hour or two of sleep, and as he was too alert to drift off again, he said to himself, "I may as well get something done since I'm awake."

His body adjusted to it until he never had that first hour of sleep at all.

Soon, it was an all-consuming need. It was not a matter of immediate necessity, but a vision he had in his head that he could not banish until it was realised. He had made work his mistress. It was possible for him to leave the house at four o'clock and come inside past eleven— me having only been alerted to his presence when he roused me as he stirred in his sleep. The only evidence that he'd even eaten those days was the disappearance of food in the kitchen.

He often came to bed in a lot of pain. Many times, I had to knead the soreness out of his back and shoulders just so that he could fall asleep. Moreover, he was too exhausted to engage with me in any meaningful way. I missed our late night conversations.

This, I imagine, had to be the reason his knee had begun to fail him at such a young age, but he also refused to wear his brace, as it slowed him down and was hard to adjust, and there was just too much to be done in a day!

I knew he was doing something important, and since I did not want to hinder him, I tried to hold my tongue. He always promised that he would be working less as soon as he finished one more project, and then another took its place.

Ruth White's husband suggested the possibility that there was a real woman he was seeking out— to the shock of Ruth and the sheer outrage of Grant, who nearly smashed one of my good saucers.

I felt a sharp, stabbing pain at the idea, but I did not entertain the thought. I knew it was not true, because I felt that, as well. Besides, I could always go out and find him myself if I had to. He always told me where he'd be. If I was still asleep, he left little written notes.

A few times, he did not come inside and sit at the table for meals. We really got into it. He told me that he didn't mind if we started supper without him, but my case was for the family time that he was missing, when he was already out and about most of the day for six days in a week. In my anger, it was difficult to curtail accusations of neglect, because he was truly terrible at keeping time, and showed genuine remorse; he admitted fault, but it was not in him to grovel. I knew he wanted to be home and wanted to see us. I *knew*, but sometimes I felt differently.

And in my sour mood, I further injured us both when he would reach for me in bed, and despite wanting his warmth more than anything, I would spurn his touch and inwardly scold myself for it— he in turn would retreat to a far corner and go to sleep without making a fuss. I wished that he would… I did not want this to become my whole life.

One morning, I woke at around four o'clock, as he had just finished washing and dressing. There was a low light on his bedside table so that I could just barely make out his shape. I watched and waited for him to turn and face me, so that I could see the lamplight in his eyes.

"There's a problem," I said at last.

"Yes," he agreed.

Not an unfixable problem. A marriage is not a contract you sign only once. It is alive, and as it grows and changes, it cannot live on the same sustenance that kept it in the beginning, just as you cannot nurse a child forever.

He is not solely at fault, of course, because I was never very good at firmly stating my wishes until they became a dire need.

It ended up that I had to set up a curfew, and he needed to carry a watch at all times. Unless a life was in danger, he had to stop what he was doing and come home, and just get used to leaving things unfinished once in a while. Sometimes, I had to go and take him away from his task. His workers knew what they were doing by then, so productivity did not suffer. I allowed him ten hours in a day!

The routine that served us best for a long time was him working two shifts of five hours. He would usually start at seven, and come home a bit past noon. Then, he would eat, put one or both of the children down to take a nap so that I could have a cup of coffee in peace, or nap with them, and he would leave at two o'clock, and be back just in time for supper. When the children stopped taking naps (Autumn didn't stop until she was seven, because she loves her sleep) they would play or do lessons quietly for an hour, and this was good for everyone's sanity.

With time to spare as the children grew more and more independent, I tended to my own little gardens of exotic plants and good berries, and I brought home a pair of cats from a litter that the owners could not rear, and allowed Autumn to name them.

They were brothers. One had a creamy coat with dark patches on the face, legs, and tail; the other was all black, except for white sprouts on the feet and breast. She brought them to us when she made her decision.

"This one is Soot, because he looks as though he crawled out of a chimney, doesn't he?"

"And that one?" I pointed to the other.

"Suit."

She was truly Michael's child. She still is.

Those two cats are still living! Soot is blind and only has three teeth left, and Suit can probably hear, but doesn't want us to know.

Fortunately, Michael's dogs liked cats. The feeling was not initially returned. Suess was a lap dog that Michael got for Autumn and taught her how to train. She was afraid of her own shadow and was particular about her food, but she was an easy animal. She lived about ten years. I had never seen a dog that was terrified of cats.

Wolfgang quite liked them, despite his fearsome drive to hunt. He was a bit too excited by them, and wanted to engage in rougher play than they agreed to. A swipe on the nose dispatched him.

I was never good at dealing with Wolf.

COME BACK

When Michael died, I didn't have a choice. I could not bring myself to give Wolfgang away. I had much bigger things to tend to, anyway.

I remember everything, every little detail. It all clings to you.

That day, I went south to visit my father, and since Michael had "pressing" business to take to, he told me to go ahead of him, and that he would catch up. My father expected us at the train station at a very specific time, and I did not like to change things on short notice.

Michael awoke after I did for once, so I was able to make him a hot breakfast and set out tea the way he liked it. I did not eat anything. I never did right before I was going to travel.

He told me that Grant Abernathy would be coming to help him move some things in the house, as his knee was agitating him that day. I didn't think anything of it. My last words to him were scolding him for not wearing his brace, and his reply was to chuckle and kiss the tip of my nose.

I plainly see to this day: we arrive at the train station, and I get out of the carriage before the children, and he pecks at them and plays with their hair. He lifts Ashley up over his head and carries him, but Autumn rebuffs his grasp, as she's "grown." He affirms her declaration, kisses her once more, and then sends them off. If I had known better, I'd have gone back to speak with him once more. I'd have never left.

The children loved train rides. To me, they were merely a means to an end, but I could tolerate them. Nothing stood out to me that morning. My father met us when we arrived, and listened to Autumn talk.

By the time we passed the post office, we were rushed by a man waving a hot telegram in our faces. I had no reason to think that something terrible would happen— no ill feelings of any kind. I thought nothing of that telegram, but decided to read it right then and there, in case it was something pressing.

The message was simply as follows:

'BENNETT. COME BACK.'

Those three words dropped my heart into my feet. I left my belongings and the children with Papa and hopped straight back on the next train back towards Bristol. It took two hours longer to get back than it did to depart.

All the while, I told myself that it was nothing dire, or there would have been details. After all, surprising me in that way would be cruel. Perhaps there was simply something Michael couldn't do himself that couldn't wait. I held onto this conclusion for as long as I could, until I arrived at the front gardens. I had to pass through it to get to my house.

Why was everybody so solemn, and why did they stare at me?

Grant stopped me at the door. He stood at the threshold and didn't say a word. His expression was unlike anything I'd ever seen before. He looked so… lost.

"Oh, Mr. Abernathy! What's the matter?" I asked and tried to manoeuver past him, but he spread out.

"What happened? Has there been a collapse? A flood? Let me in!"

"Not yet," he replied, and his voice was very hoarse. "First, let me explain what you are about to see."

Just then, I realised Michael never came to greet me, nor did I see him anywhere outside.

I waited for bad news, but I never imagined the blow I was due to receive.

"Michael fell—" Grant began and stopped himself. "Michael had an accident. He's slee— He—"

He drew in a breath, and it poured out from his lips.

"He's dead. Michael's dead."

I laughed— I laughed!

"No he isn't!" I gasped wildly.

His expression did not change.

"He fell down the stairs. He died in an hour."

"Pardon? That isn't possible! How could that happen?"

Only old people and little children had those sorts of accidents. It just couldn't have happened, certainly not so quickly.

"I wish it wasn't possible. I've pinched myself raw trying to free myself from this nightmare."

I said nothing while I pieced together what he was saying.

Grant finally stepped aside, and pointed down the front hall, into the open parlour door.

"He's in there."

The following events, I remember as a bystander looking through a window, detached from my own flesh. Very slowly, as an automaton, I shuffle my heavy feet inside.

Yet another man blocks my passage. He introduces himself as a medical examiner.

"You are Mrs. Bennett?" he asks.

"I am," I reply in an airy whisper, with the lilt of a curious child.

"Mr. Michael Bennett passed away at about twelve-thirty."

So his accident was not even three hours after we'd left Bristol.

He offers to describe exactly what happened. I do not want to know.

He lets me pass. I don't want to go in.

Michael reclines on the couch with his arm draping over the side. The lamplight and setting

sun cast a deceptively ruddy glow over his skin,
but I'd seen many corpses in my time. There is no
mistaking: he is dead.

Even knowing this, I kneel quietly over his face,
as if he is asleep, and I move his hair away from
his cool brow. He does not stir. His jaw is bruised
and crooked. I touch where he was injured, and
he does not recoil. As his lips are slightly parted,
I see that his front teeth were chipped. They
wiped away the blood, but his trousers are wet.
How could they leave him in soiled clothes?

"All injuries are antemortem," the examiner
explained, standing behind me. "That means—"

"I know."

"A lawyer will be coming to speak with you," he
adds.

I had a strong distaste for law men, ever since
learning how they'd wronged my husband. I
anticipate being manipulated the same way.

Nevertheless, I nod and rise up, calm and serene.
He's still speaking. I don't understand any of what
he says. For me, it is still not possible. It's not
real. I expect to wake up soon, but I allow the
story to play out.

We must go upstairs to get documents in
Michael's study. I freeze at the bottom of the
stairs, wondering if I'd stepped where he bled.

The lawyer arrives, and I ask Grant to sit in on
our conversation, because he is more acquainted
with legal matters than I am. We pile a lot of
papers on a desk and discuss the immediate
actions that must be taken. I won't bore you to
death with those details. It was all very dull, and I
only listened to half of it. I made the process
harder for everybody: not on purpose. I could not
summon the resolve to listen readily. I was
fighting with all of my strength to simply remain
on Earth. With Grant acting as an interpreter of
sorts for both parties, it took twice as long as it
probably should have.

The property was left to me— all of it. I knew it
would be. He asked me to keep it until the
children were old enough and prepared to handle
it.

Grant stayed with me until ten o'clock, and then I
was left alone to decide what to do next.

I did not go and retrieve the children yet: not
while their father's body lay in the parlour. And,
quite frankly, I was not ready for them. I couldn't
even imagine how I would tell them, because I
couldn't believe it.

I must have gone to sleep, because I awoke. My
bed was empty, and he was still dead. Still on the
couch in the parlour, but he was wrapped up in a
sheet. There was a blue cast of the early morning
over the room, and I stared, motionless on the
threshold, until golden sunlight hit the windows.
They were coming to take him away, and they
asked what I wanted done with him.

This is really happening.

Michael did not believe in embalming; contrary
to the opinions of many, he even found it
disrespectful to the corpse (not to quite the same
extent as Mr. Kelley, who was opposed to even
autopsies and research). He believed bodies
needed to return to the soil as naturally as
possible. He asked if I was willing to accept such
a burial for myself, and when he explained it to
me, it made sense. He was content to be rolled in
burlap and thrown into the swamp. I respected his
wishes, mostly; I arranged for him to be buried in
the old Bennett family burial plot within a week,
as that was the longest they would keep the body
without embalming it.

Since it surely would not have violated Michael's
desires, I requested that his body be kept cold and
packed with salt until then. Treating his remains
as one would a fresh fish sounded undignified
when I voiced my request, but in case the

children wanted to see him, I didn't want him to be too upsetting to look at.

"And, please— please change his clothes," I entreated and laid out a nice mustard-brown day suit that he hadn't worn in ten years. If I could have stomached touching his cold flesh, I'd have done it myself.

"I'll see to it that it is done when he is no longer stiff," one of the men answered, and if I'd had anything in my system, I'd have vomited.

I sat beside him, just to remind myself that it would be the very last time I could do so. Pulled the sheet from his face, and I beheld his still and passionless features frozen in an endless sleep, and I felt nothing. It would not come to me until later.

After that, I prepared breakfast that I didn't eat, and then I went to go and get Autumn and Ashley. When I set out, I was accosted by a handful of young men asking me what to do that day, telling me which animals they'd tended to that morning.

They… wanted to take orders from me…

"Oh… well done. Good work. Do what you normally do!" was all I said, and then I scampered down the walkway and made my way into town, to the train station.

The train guard was perplexed to see me once again. I did not respond to him. My vision was too narrow. I didn't even see the familiar faces greeting me in the village where I grew up.

Papa intercepted me at the door. Nobody told him anything yet, but he already knew that something must have happened.

"I'm taking the children home," I told him.

"I see. Would you like to tell me what happened?"

" … not yet. I'll write when we get back to Bristol," was my reply, because the truth was that I still hadn't figured out how to say it with my mouth.

"I understand. You know, you can come back any time."

"Yes, I know."

The children could feel how tense I was. Looking at them made me feel that I needed to weep, but I was composed. They asked me what happened, where Daddy was, why he hadn't come yet… questions I was not ready to answer. I promised I would explain it all when we arrived home. It was

wrong of me to postpone such a necessary
revelation for so long, but that was my timid
nature. I tried to justify it by reasoning that they'd
handle it better in their home, where they knew it
was safe.

*Where they knew it was safe? Where their father
had just died? What if they could never sleep in
their beds again?*

At the doorstep, I finally found my voice.

"Something happened yesterday after we left," I
began. "Your father got hurt badly— well— he
died yesterday. On the stairs— he hurt himself on
the stairs, and he died."

I waited for them to absorb it. They stared, as if
they had not heard. Maybe they had chosen not
to.

I brought them inside.

"Are you hungry? I'll make anything you want."

"I'll make something for myself," Autumn went
into the kitchen. I knew she was going to make
carrot and butter sandwiches; that was her
favourite thing to eat, possibly only because of
the colours. Ashley ate them only because he did
everything his sister did.

I made tea and set out four cups in the parlour,
and I tried to forget that his body was on the
couch that morning. Autumn came in with a tray
of food and gazed at the fourth cup across from
mine. She offered a sandwich, and I realised that
the only sustenance to touch my lips since supper
two days ago was the milk in yesterday's coffee. I
ate the thinly sliced carrots and the bread and
butter separately, as I thought the combination
was horrid.

"Where is he?" she asked.

"Where is he— where's your father?"

"Yes. Where is he?'

"He is at a mortuary. They will bury him very
soon. His funeral is in six days. I must write
letters, and meet with somebody to make those
arrangements."

"Today?"

"No. Tomorrow. We don't have to do anything
toda—"

I heard clattering in another room, and suddenly I
could move again. I sprang to my feet and made a
wild dash into the hallway, searching every room.

"Ashley?" I rasped, and I barely heard it over my own heartbeat.

I found him in the study, playing with Michael's leg brace.

"What are you doing with that?" I asked.

"We need to bring Daddy his brace," he insisted with total sincerity and conviction. "He forgot his brace. He needs his brace!"

My composure crumbled immediately.

"Ashley… he doesn't need it— you know he never wore it unless you forced him to, anyway!" I chuckled in spite of myself. "He won't be coming back for it. You know that, right? He's not coming back. He is in heaven now."

"But can we go and see him?"

"We will see him in heaven," I assured him. "But that is a long way away. We'll just have to make a way on our own until then."

"How, Mammy?"

"We just will," I said, as I didn't have an answer. "Because we must. We will cultivate our own gardens and be content."

I know it must seem ghastly, that the day seemed
so normal. That is how it is. It comes to you very
slowly.

You wake up, and the bed is cold, because he's
not there. This is not so bad, because he often
wakes up before you, but you see that his side
was never disturbed. You begin to make
breakfast, and you never hear his footsteps
coming to the table. You make his tea just the
way he likes it, and turn to give it to him before
he goes back to work, and it lands untouched at
his seat. He is as near and natural as the floor
under your feet, and he's just not there.

You try to describe it, but the words won't come.
You wish you could talk to somebody who cares
and understands you better than anyone else,
but… well, you know.

When Helen Connor died in 1891, I made myself
a brand new mourning set, because… truthfully, I
don't know why. I made sets for the children
when one of Michael's cousins died. Autumn's
was just a bit too small. I thought she'd fully grow
out of it before she ever needed it again. Ashley
most certainly did. I hastily dyed a few shirts for
him.

I wore no jewellery except my rings, and
Michael's favourite watch. I fastened it to my
waist and adorned my high collar with one of

those silk scarves he always wore. Given the circumstances, I thought a bright splash of colour among all the black was in good taste: for his life.

His body was displayed to be seen by only the three of us, right before the ceremony actually began. The cold conditions he was kept in slowed decomposition. He did not look much different from a week ago, except that his skin was more severely discoloured, his cheeks had begun to sink, and his lips were pulling away. They replaced his damaged teeth with porcelain, even though I'd asked them to make no changes to his appearance.

Do you know the smell of a forgotten cut of flowers that has gone bad in its water on a hot summer afternoon? It is a distinctly sweet and yet sharply putrid odour. That is very similar to how a body smells at first. It was the beginning of spring, and yet it would be many months before I could enjoy flowers again.

I told the children that they did not need to see the body if they didn't want to. I had to force myself, because I didn't want my last recollection of him to be so dreary, but I had to be sure they had respected his wishes.

Autumn held Ashley's hand and put on a brave countenance for him, but when she drew her head out from behind me, she whimpered and hid her face in my cape. Ashley looked on with a silently troubled expression. Adults around him that day murmured that Death had "taken" his Daddy, and the poor boy asked me why and where, and how— since he was right there?

"That is not him," I explained to them both, hoping that it helped; even for me, it was hard to understand. "It is his body. He has gone where he doesn't need it anymore."

I brought a little picture of him in the watch, and told them that they could look at it if they wanted to see him. The scene was immortalised: an unused shot for the local newspaper, in which he had erupted into a ridiculous grin while a spider crawled over his eyepatch. He thought the photograph was spoiled, but it was one of my favourites, and I needed it then more than I needed air.

Grant wrote his obituary so that I didn't have to. I think that nobody could have done it better. It was an important and necessary duty for him, and unbearable for me.

My father's only comment was, "Well, I never imagined I would outlive him."

"Nor did I," said Mary Jones, who was then quite old, and would live another five years.

Mama was there, "For you, and the children." I
thanked her for coming, and that was it. She had
nothing to say about Michael, good or bad. She
offered to stay with me for a little while, and I
declined. After that, she became morose and
didn't speak to me.

Hannah Lavigne howled into a handkerchief,
crying out for her "little prince." Perhaps she
thought that the louder she was, the more she
appeared to care.

All that time, I had not wept. I remained solemn,
until a moth came down in broad daylight and
landed on my veil. Tears ran down to my chin and
dripped on that scarf, but still, I was silent. I
began to feel it all over the course of many days.

And I knew the children were always watching
me. They had to. It was unlike anything they'd
ever experienced before, and they depended on
me to know how to feel. They did not cry until I
cried.

They must have been reminded of Lilly.

She is not mentioned at all in Grant's book,
except in an excerpt containing the obituary. He
knew of her, of course, but he could not bring
himself to write about her. Even for him, it was
too much— and now, when she would be almost

eighteen, I still find it difficult to write about her for the very first time.

Lillian Adelaide Bennett is our third baby. We did originally want three children, maybe four, but Michael did not want any more at thirty-five, because with his failing knee, he was afraid of being too sickly to make a living before they were independent. Since Ashley was a long time coming even when we tried, we didn't think we'd have to worry about it.

I had lost two, maybe three pregnancies very early on before Ashley, and one after him. I only told Michael about the first one, and it greatly troubled him, as he was concerned about my health. I didn't tell him about the others, because I was worried he would not want to keep trying.

Michael's mother struggled for years to bring a baby to full term after him, and every attempt made her quite sickly (another fact concealed for years, and made known to him by Abraham, when both parents were deceased). The only one to make it was Berthe, who did not live even a year.

Lilly came to my attention in November of 1902, and I waited a little while to make sure that she would stay. I was pleased, myself, but nervous about telling Michael, though I knew I had to eventually. I wasn't feeling particularly clever, so

I simply made my announcement over tea one afternoon. Autumn and Ashley shouted and frolicked from the open window we faced. Other than that, we were alone.

He raised his eyebrows and chewed his lip for a minute.

"Are you sure?"

"I'm certain! I know how it feels."

He nodded and put his cup down, and parted his lips to speak, but only to call the children inside, as the sun had set. It seemed he needed time to ponder it, and the more he pondered, the more nervous I became.

"Are you upset?" I asked.

"No," he rubbed his wrinkled brow. "It's a lot— but I'm not upset."

"Is it alright?"

"Yes, it's alright— merely unexpected."

"Are you happy?"

Autumn and Ashley came tripping through the gallery, and he turned his attention to them, beckoning them to have tea.

I told them why their father was so quiet. Of course, Autumn was delighted. Ashley did not entirely know what it entailed, but he was excited because his sister was.

Michael did not speak of the matter when we went to bed. I knew he was not angry, but it was deeply troubling that I could not tell what he was thinking. Even so, I thought it best to leave him be and let him sort out his feelings. Eventually, we would have to face them. My heart raced steadily for about an hour before I could fall asleep, and naturally, he was gone by the time I woke, and would be back for breakfast.

"Yes, I am happy," he decided as I forked toast onto his plate.

It took Michael a while to warm up to that baby. He was eager to prepare and was always attentive to my health and my desires, but that familiar paternal fondness did not blossom until January— when he could finally feel her moving.

In February, she stopped.

My relief as Michael finally began to enjoy this child overshadowed a chronic brooding feeling that something was very wrong. I'd written it off as a product of Michael's initial unease, but it lingered on, and I first realised one morning that

she did not flutter and kick after my second cup
of coffee, as she always did.

Mama told me that all babies slow down as birth
approaches, but this was far too soon. I could not
think of much else even as I resumed my regular
routines, but I could not tell Michael, either. How
would I tell him? Would he diminish my distress
as hypochondria? Would he be even more
panicked than I was?

A few days later, I went to a physician to be
examined, despite my previous experiences. He
prodded at me for many minutes, and listened
intently. As I watched, his features pinched into
an awful grimace.

"I cannot find a heartbeat," he declared.

"What do you mean, you can't find it?" I
demanded. "It must be there! You didn't search
well enough!"

He shook his head.

"If it's there, it's very weak. It's possible that its
heart has stopped."

I wanted to shut my ears and hear no more of
what he was saying. He did not know what he
was talking about! This was a perfectly healthy
baby. Hearts don't stop for no reason.

"Madam, are you listening?" he asked, shaking
me from a sort of stupor.

"And what if it has?" I asked, and I hated asking,
because that gave a voice to the worst
possibilities.

"You will know if you experience pains in seven
to ten days," he said. "It should soon expel itself
if it has died, but if not—"

"She hasn't!" I cried out, as if his words scalded
me.

I went home, and still, I could not for the life of
me figure out how to tell my husband. For a little
while, I maintained a facade of cheery smiles and
frenzied nesting, and he saw straight through it.

"Well, of course I'm nervous," I replied. "A lot
can happen in only a handful of months."

Concealment was as bad as lying. I inwardly
condemned my actions, but found myself unable
to do any different.

On March 2, I had almost (almost) convinced
myself that all was well after all, and I even
thought I'd felt her stirring within me; I fancied
she'd awoken from a long slumber.

The pain came at ten o'clock, when I'd already prepared for bed. It was a real, sharp pain like no other. I tried to ignore it, but my body wouldn't allow it. As with my other labours, it summoned me to rise and walk. I wanted to, but I also did not, because I knew what it meant.

I wandered the house in just my robe and gauzy night clothes, numb to the cold and darkness. I could not do anything but call out within myself.

'Be not far from me; for trouble is near.'

Yet, I knew the trouble had already passed, and I was waiting to behold the destruction left in its wake.

I heard claws clattering in the hall, and knew Michael was coming inside with the dogs. A candle was lit, and it threw their shadows over the floor, long and pale. I stood and waited, still and silent as a mouse, though my flesh wanted to reject it.

I heard him feeding them scraps from the kitchen, and then the light drew closer.

He was delighted to behold my form until he brought the candle to my face.

"Has something happened?" he asked.

"She's coming very soon," was all I said.

"She— who—" it took him a moment to process what I'd told him. "You mean now? You must be mistaken! It's too early!"

We expected her in May at the soonest, June at the latest. Her birthday was supposed to be close to mine. This time, there was no doubt that this was a very early baby.

"She is, I know it. She's coming now."

He almost splattered the candle on the floor, trying to set it down.

"No—no— no? No, no, she's too early," he insisted, not knowing what I knew.

"It is so!" I replied, but I could not bring myself to be impatient with him. "She will be here before the sun rises, I'm certain."

"And who do I go and get at this hour?"

"Nobody. You will do just fine."

Even in the brassy candlelight, he turned pure white.

"Me? I don't know what to do."

"I do. Just be close at hand," I assured him, feeling as though I was leading him into a trap. If I was going to tell him, it had to be now.

And I was lying, because I knew what to do when delivering a *grown and living baby,* but this was new.

He built up a bright fire in his study, and made tea over it. All the while, he rambled endlessly about how small babies had survived in the past, and since spring was approaching, the odds were even greater. We would check on her every hour, and he would stay home for half a year. He spoke of Autumn's joy when she first held Ashley, and how he wanted the same for him. I said nothing, and drank nothing.

"Would you like some music?" he asked.

"No. Don't leave."

"You've thought of a name for her, yes?"

"No," the idea that she'd never had a name for as long as she'd lived was unbearable. "Perhaps something floral."

I stopped pacing. I wanted to walk, but I was too afraid. I seated myself in one of the stiff wooden chairs in the study.

"What changed?" Michael asked.

"Nothing. I'm tired."

Soon, the fire was almost out, but it didn't matter, because the sun would rise very soon.

"Maybe she's not coming, after all," he suggested.

"No, she is, I know it."

"You have not pushed even once."

"It isn't time yet."

"Does it hurt?"

"Yes," I admitted, but it wasn't bodily pain.

I'd held it off for as long as possible, but eventually, she had to see the outside world, no matter what happened next. I sent Michael to wake Mary Jones— just in case, I said.

It is so bitter, dearest reader, but it must be known and remembered. Read on carefully.

My sweet girl came with disturbingly small efforts. I caught her up and thrust her to my bosom, with my eyes fixed to the heavens. I did not look at her. I refused to make it real. She was warm, but the warmth was mine. The hands didn't grasp. She never made a sound.

Michael returned. He saw a wee thing in my hands, but the flash of rapture on his face was smothered in an instant.

"Why isn't she moving? Why isn't she breathing?" he placed his ear to the tiny little heart.

I shrank into the chair.

"Alma, she needs to be resuscitated!" he pulled me towards him instead of prying her from my hands.

I couldn't let him. I'd allowed him dead hopes for long enough. I nudged him away.

"Alma, help me! What are you doing?"

"It isn't necessary."

"What are you saying?" he shook me. "Look at her! Look at her!"

Michael's shouting was cut short, as he was then violently sick on the carpet, something I'd not seen in a very long time. I looked on, feeling like some beast, shielded from it all by a hastily erected shell of indifference.

He sobered, and rose back up and pawed at my hands.

"Alma, look at her!" he ordered me once more.

I brought her into the light. She was all black and blue. Her eyes and lips were so relaxed, as if she was asleep.

Yes, she was asleep. She would always be sleeping.

He was an emotionally forthright man, but very rarely did he cry. His cry is a peculiar one. He doesn't ever sob or bawl, instead venting his distress in a sort of low and stuttering moaning or hissing, like a mortally wounded animal.

He gnashed his teeth. I heard them crack, and he released this awful throaty snarl, as if he was being disembowelled.

I held her to my breast. She did not nurse, and never would. Why was I so calm?

"Isn't she beautiful?" I asked, stroking her white lashes.

"She is, she is!" he nodded and came close. "Let me have her, please."

I properly placed her in his arms, possibly for the very last time. Michael had his head to her bosom again, and searched for a heartbeat. He lifted his face and gazed at her, as if he searched for some answers in her features.

I thought if I never looked at her, it wouldn't hurt, but then I knew that if I didn't, I'd have regretted it for all my life. She was lovely, and carrying her was a blessing, as I knew that at least I had cared for her for as long as she lived.

"Lillian is such a pretty name," he said at last.

So she was Lillian Adelaide, my little dreamer, perfect in every way.

I took her and washed her, then wrapped her in the linens we prepared for her. We tended to her just the same as if she was a living baby— only it was apparent very soon that she was slipping through our fingers. Her skin was like soft wax, and blood settled in her limbs. She was quickly turning cold.

We put her in the cradle and watched her until the sun rose, knowing full well that it was all for our own sake, as she'd already left us. Of course, we knew she could not stay there.

No matter how we looked at the perfectly-formed hands and face, we could not determine what had happened to her.

Ultimately, she belonged to God. That was the only way I could justify Him taking her from us. Yes, she was set apart before she was born. Her heavenly Father had already received her.

I looked at the clock. It was approaching six. Autumn and Ashley would be awake very soon.

I looked at Michael and gasped at his incensed countenance.

"You knew it, didn't you?"

"What do you mean?" I asked.

"You stopped me, as if you already knew. You were so gloomy and sure of yourself, and you scarcely made a sound."

"I had an idea," I admitted.

He huffed and shot to his feet, looking around frantically as if searching for something to smash.

"And you didn't say anything?" he demanded, in a dangerously soft voice. "You just let it hit me?"

337

"Ah, I—" I tried to speak, but couldn't think of anything that would help.

"Why wouldn't you tell me?"

"Would it have made a difference?"

"It would have to me!" he cried, and his voice had a crackling lilt to it.

I raised a finger to hush him, as if he might wake her.

"Why? What could you do to stop it? Do you know how I—" I panted for breath, and the floodgates opened— the tears came as a continuous stream. His face was murky, but I tried to meet his eyes.

"Do you know how I suffered," I continued. "To think that I was a vessel of death? The dread— that I was waiting for a child that would never cry for me? And there was nothing I could do to stop it? I wanted to spare you."

"You did nothing of the sort," he insisted, thrusting an accusing finger under my nose. "You shut me out and left me in the dark. You lied to me."

"I did!" I was not afraid to admit my guilt. "And would you have been happy to know the truth?"

"I would have known! I could have prepared for what was to come."

"I knew, and I was not prepared!" I snapped. "It nearly killed me! I knew and I suffered alone."

"That was your choice."

It was, indeed. I could have sought him at any time.

"I was afraid," I answered.

"Of what?"

"I don't know!" I howled. *I DON'T KNOW!*

All that I'd repressed left my body in that feral shriek, and then I sank to the floor in my soiled gown and wailed into the bedding, clawing at anything I could reach.

I was so angry. Women all over the world did not want their children and discarded them without a second thought. God should have taken those babies, not mine. Why did He take her? I did everything I was supposed to, and it didn't matter.

I'm not entirely sure what happened in that interval, but when I came to my senses (or as close as I could come to them in that state), I was lying on the floor at the end of the bed, my hands hurt a lot, and my head pounded like a drum.

Michael was straddling me. He had my wrists fixed to the floor, and his cheek held to mine. It was soaked, and he trembled so badly, my teeth rattled.

I writhed underneath his weight.

"What are you doing?" I asked.

"I couldn't think of anything else to do," he answered. "You were hurting yourself."

I looked at my arms and hands. They were bruised and scratched. Michael had scratches on his hands and face. He often did, but these ones were fresh, and unmistakably the contour of human nails.

"Did I scratch you?"

He bent his head to examine his hands.

"I suppose you did."

I heard shuffling feet in another room.

"Mary is cleaning the study…" Michael explained.

"Autumn and Ashley are probably awake."

"They are, I heard them as well. I will explain to them," he said, but did not release me. "They should see her. Do you want them to?"

"Yes. Go and get them now."

He placed me upright and then left, and I quickly shed my clothes and threw on a clean robe. I knelt beside Lillian's cradle. She was exactly as we placed her there.

What did he tell them? That she went to sleep? No, Autumn would have known better, and Ashley would have asked when she was going to wake up.

They surely expected to see a plump and pink baby. I was afraid that seeing her would perhaps upset them, but it was important for them to understand.

I put on a warm and inviting face. Autumn came in ahead of Ashley, holding his little hand. Michael followed behind them.

I wept at the sight of them. They were beautiful.

"Come and see her," I beckoned softly. "This is your sister."

Ashley climbed into my lap. Michael stooped down and put Autumn on his knee.

Of course they wanted to hold her. Autumn tried to take a tiny finger, and she gasped and started when the flesh had been distorted. They understood that they were saying goodbye, and then I wrapped her all up in the linens, because she was becoming unrecognisable, and I wanted to preserve her pristine appearance in my memories.

Ashley did not cry. He likely didn't fully grasp the situation, and may have forgotten about her afterwards. Autumn shed a few tears, and then she sprang from Michael's knee and ran out of the room. He rose to follow her, but I stopped him. We waited a minute, and she returned with one of her little dolls. It was about the same size as Lillian.

She placed it in the cradle next to her sister and said, "I never play with it, anyway."

We buried her that morning. Autumn and Ashley did not want to be present. We did not mourn her in the traditional way, because we were afraid of confusing them, and drawing outside attention to ourselves that we didn't want. She was our precious little secret, not a sponged-away stain of the past, as Michael's sister was treated. When we

spoke of the children, her name was on the silent
end of our breath.

Soon after the birth, my breasts became very sore with milk that I could not offer my baby. It was acutely distressing, and seemed such a waste. I did not feel the same effects of birthing a child as I had with my first two. There was less trauma inflicted upon my body, and yet, there was a more profound feeling that I had been injured.

I would not touch Michael. I knew he needed it, but I could not offer it, and I felt cruel when he tried to lay his head on my shoulder, and I wouldn't allow it. He tried to take my hand once or twice, and I pulled it back. I leaned away from his attempts to kiss me. He did not try to force me, but I could see that he suffered. I did not even want him to look at me.

I was frozen. I thawed myself each morning, and fought with all of my strength to lift my dead limbs out of bed. I subsisted on obligation. I did everything that I was required to do as a mother, and no more. I had completely deserted my station as a wife.

As for Michael, he tried to be a husband, and I wouldn't let him. I expected him to fill that extra time with more work, but he didn't, and merely observed me from a distance.

He asked me about my charity work. I told him I would take it up later, and he took it upon himself to write to some of the women I corresponded with.

One day, he came to me after breakfast, with pen and paper in hand, and said simply:

"I know of a young woman who cannot nurse her child. It has been nearly two days since the birth, and she has not produced milk…"

"… And?"

He raised his brow, as if he'd already made his intentions perfectly clear.

"Well, would you be interested in nursing the child for her?"

I could not believe he would ask such a thing! It seemed so insulting to suggest that I be reminded of what I could not have. I must have really glared at him, because he shrank away from me and lowered his eyes.

"It is not my fault she cannot feed her child," I spat.

"It is not hers, either! It is nobody's fault, you know…" his voice wavered and trailed off. "And Lilly—"

"You did not want her anyway!" the words escaped my lips before I could check them. "I imagine you're relieved."

"How dare you!" he bellowed, thrusting the pen down against the table and smashing it. Ink pooled all over his papers.

The mess tempered him in an instant. He stared down at his stained hand and ruined papers as he heaved and panted.

I immediately regretted my foul words, and not just because I was startled.

"It is a time-sensitive issue," he mumbled. "Give an answer by the end of the week, that is all I want."

Michael cleaned up, insisted upon bandaging the injury himself, and avoided me for the rest of the day. He did not come to dinner, but put the children to bed and ate cold bread and butter in the kitchen.

He would surely have to come to bed eventually…

I found him on the carpet in the downstairs parlour, with his head on a cushion from the sofa. My candle must have roused him. He turned his head to look at me with his good eye, which was quite inflamed.

"Yes?" was all he asked.

"That doesn't look comfortable."

"I can sleep anywhere."

It was true. I'd seen him napping upright at his desk, in a ditch, in a half-dry creek…

"If you can, then come and sleep in your bed."

He closed his eyes again.

"I can sleep down here," I offered. "I'll fit on the sofa."

"That won't do. Go back to bed."

I obeyed. I did not have the resolve to wrestle with him.

I had not apologised yet, as I felt it needed to be a good apology, so I needed it to simmer for a while… and because I still felt slighted by his entreaty.

Having soon forgotten the feeling of being injured, I pondered his point of view. I thought he was making a callous request at my expense, but I

347

believe Michael mourned in a different way. He wanted so badly to preserve life, and may have seen Lilly in that woman's baby. He needed to make sense of it somehow; he needed something good to come out of it, meanwhile I resolved to drown in pity.

I was used to going to bed alone, since Michael often worked long hours. I fell asleep soon after putting my head down, and when I awoke in the night, I felt a familiar warmth.

He was asleep. I touched his face with only the tips of my fingers. Immediately, his eyes opened, and he leaned into the contact.

"Oh! Am I dreaming?" he asked in a stupor.

"I don't believe so."

He mumbled something and closed his eyes.

I didn't need to say anything dramatic.

"I'm sorry, Michael."

"For what?"

"For saying something so horrid."

"I know you didn't mean it."

"Doesn't matter. I said it, and I shouldn't have. Aren't you upset?"

"Yes, I'm upset!" he opened his eyes again. "It must be worse for you, though."

I said nothing. I withdrew my hand and turned away.

"You only eat once a day. Do you want somebody to cook for you?" he offered. "Do you perhaps want me to go and buy you some chocolate?"

"I don't want to eat anything."

"You're acting like a child!" he snapped, but then he stopped and drew in a long breath. "I know why you're doing it."

He reached over and grabbed my arm.

"You're so thin already. Have you not noticed? Do you mean to waste away and die?"

I didn't know what he was getting at, so I still didn't answer.

"Dying for somebody is easy," he continued. "You have to fight the part of you that wants to live, but you only have to do it once. All you have to do is die. Living for somebody is harder. Sometimes, just living for yourself is hard enough. There's a part of you that wants to die, and you have to fight it every day."

"I don't want to die!" I protested.

"And it doesn't seem that you want to live, either. A lot of people need you to live."

I tried to pull my arm away, but he pulled it back. Hard.

"I'm trying to help you, but I need you to help me!" he entreated. "We can't function like this— but we can't fail, either."

I had, of course, been punishing myself by refusing to be touched, and punishing him by extension, as we were so entwined, and I had truly meant to sink us both.

And when I could repress it no longer, I came close and kissed him. He gave a gasp— that's how long it'd been— and cautiously leaned into it.

Then the dam broke, and instead of painstakingly wringing out one tear as I'd done for many days, I really began to cry.

"Is that all?" Michael chuckled incredulously. "That's all it took?"

He kissed me repeatedly, and we both wept.

Getting out of bed wasn't any easier than it was the day before. I spread butter and jam on cold bread for breakfast, and we spoke aloud of our disappointment in how things turned out, but we agreed we were finished having children.

Ashley, being so little, was probably not pressed, but Autumn seemed relieved that her parents were starting to function normally.

"You can write to that woman and tell her to come here," I decided that afternoon, after continuing to ponder it all morning.

She came to our house and assisted in the housekeeping in exchange for my services.

At first, I did it because he asked me to. I resented the task I was given, and was determined not to grow fond of that child.

It was a bewildering series of highs and lows for me. I quickly realised how I'd missed the feeling of nursing, but then I was bitter because even then, I felt it'd been robbed from me. In fact, I tried to hate this woman. I just had to hate something.

Autumn came in and saw me nursing the boy one day.

"Whose baby is that?" she pointed, clearly confused.

"This is the new maid's baby," I explained, placing her rude little pointing finger down at her side. "His Mammy cannot nurse him, so I'm doing it for her."

She sat beside me and watched for a little while, and then she asked, "Could I hold him?"

"Sure, you can," I handed her the child.

She gazed down so fondly at him. I think it was good for her to hold him, since she'd spent many months anticipating a baby to rock to sleep.

She helped me that day. By seeing her hold him so naturally, as dearly as if he was her brother, I understood the act of charity I was carrying out, and how it eased my own suffering.

After that, I did it for the baby, and a little bit for me.

I slept in a spare room with the mother and child so that I could quickly answer his cries without disturbing anybody, but sometimes, I caught Michael standing outside the door, listening—with the same expression that he had when I found him curled up in Autumn or Ashley's bed many nights since Lillian was born. He told me that he needed to make sure their hearts were still beating, because sometimes, he wasn't sure if his was.

I had the boy for five months, and he grew fat and hearty, and was big enough to take cow's milk. After that, his mother left us, saying she could never repay me for my kindness, but the truth is, it was she who'd done a great service to me.

I also thought at first that it was disrespectful to Lillian, but I know she is such a kind and gentle soul, she surely would be pleased to know that I could save another life because of her.

Now she is with her father again— but forgive me for taking us so far off course. That was 1903.

After Michael's funeral, in 1905, we of course went home. The children slept in my bed. Many times, I was awoken by their nightmares. I could not make them stop.

The thing that surprised me the most was the silence. It was not tranquil, as it used to be. It was torturous.

Ashley followed me up and down the stairs all through the day. I didn't mind at first, because small children follow you everywhere, but it became excessive when he would stop what he was doing as though he were a machine and run to the staircase.

"Why are you following me like that?" I asked.

"I'll catch you, Mammy!" he insisted. "Don't worry, I'll take care of you."

"Ashley, you don't need to worry. Nothing will happen to me."

"Right! I'll watch you, and nothing will happen."

It is difficult to explain such things to a child. There's only so much they can understand, yet they pick up more of our feelings than we realise, such as the guilt of things we cannot control, and that's too much for them to reason with.

As he was then six, he was growing his independent streak and did not want to be picked up anymore, except in a playful way; recently, however, he was curling up in my lap like a kitten, or having me carry him to bed.

Cradling him as I did back when he was tiny was a sobering reminder that I would not be having any more children, and one day, I would pick him up for the last time.

Autumn had been going to school all this time, and she did not want to stop, but one day, she came home slamming her books down and ripping her coat off.

"What happened? Did you get into a fight?" I asked, knowing that it was in her blood.

"No, but I wanted to!" she answered and let me gently take the coat.

"Now, what prompted this? You are such a sweet little girl."

"I'm not little!" she protested.

"Alright, you are a sweet girl, usually," I huffed. "Now, what is your trouble?"

"Some other children told me that Daddy is in hell!"

"Did they? Whatever for?" her words shocked me as much as they probably did her.

"They told me that because he didn't go to church every Sunday, he's an atheist and he's in hell."

I didn't know how to respond, so I hung up her coat and busied myself fixing her hair while she fumed.

"Is he in hell?"

"No," I answered firmly, even though there was just the faintest bit of doubt in my heart. "Daddy is not in hell. I think he worshipped in his own way."

"He did not rest on Sunday. He didn't keep the sabbath."

"I think he did! Rest looks different for everyone. Don't you like knitting, and do it to relax?"

"Yes I do."

"Well, knitting would be restful for you, but I hate it!" I chuckled. "My rest would look like something else, just as his looked like the trials of Hercules."

She laughed, too. She laughed so hard, she began to cry.

I thought when they were born that I could give them everything they needed, but they needed their Daddy, and he was far beyond my reach, and there was nobody to blame.

Except him.

He rushed his entire life, believing that he would die very soon, and he sealed his own fate. Grant thinks that Wolfgang tripped him on the stairs. I don't blame a dog that Michael hardly trained for doing what it was naturally going to do. Michael, on the other hand, was going up and down the stairs and doing a lot of heavy lifting without his knee brace, and without direct supervision.

I suppose this, too, is something he was naturally going to do.

In those days, the idea of death was strangely comforting: a guilty pleasure to ponder the end of my troubles, but I knew that I certainly could not afford to die any time soon.

And what if I did?

Having never been faced with a deadly illness or grievous injury, and never owning much, I hadn't once thought to write a will. I always thought that Michael would outlive me, simply because he is so much more resilient than I, and thus I would never have to handle his effects in his stead.

And the children… what would happen to them? I never entertained the thought of them being raised by somebody else, until then. Most likely, they would be sent to one of my parents, possibly one of my aunts, maybe James, *maybe* even Ida.

Lord forgive me, but none of those options appealed to me. My parents were getting old, and should they have been the next to pass away,

Autumn and Ashley might have been passed around like a hookah pipe in a harem.

The aunts were unacceptable. James had a hard enough time taking care of himself. Ida didn't want children of her own, so she certainly wouldn't want mine.

That left Madame Lavigne, Ruth, and Grant.

Madame Lavigne would surely cherish my children, though her influence is questionable, as her eldest daughter died of an opium overdose, one daughter has nearly a dozen children with five different men, and her youngest son has been arrested at least six times. That was a one-in-three rate of failure. We had even once offered to take the child of Michael's deceased cousin so that his aunt wouldn't have as much on her plate, but she wanted her house to always be full. As a widow, I understand now, but I was not so keen on my children becoming decorations in her home.

Ruth had been working with orphans all of this time, and had adopted three of her own. She loves all human beings and is generally a much better sport than I, so I know that she would take them in and give them the best that she could.

Grant would most certainly take them if they had nobody else, and they are the most familiar with him out of those three, though by his own admission, he doesn't know the first thing about raising children, and never wanted them.

I wrote to all of them about these concerns that weighed heavily on my mind in those days, but the women only sent back nonsense reassurance.

Grant came in person on my birthday to respond to my letter. I did not feel up to the task of partaking in any festivities. He brought me a pudding that his wife made, and I thanked him and set it to one side. We both knew that no matter how much she tried to pretend she was born in England, her English cooking was terrible.

He embraced and kissed the children, and they went out to play together while the adults had tea.

"So, thirty-six? Why, you look half that age! I wish the years had been so kind to me," he nervously tried to flatter me as he elected to refill my cup. "And how do you feel?"

That was a big question. I did not feel thirty-six. I felt eight and eighty at the same time. I preferred the latter. Oh, to be so near to the grave…

"I feel well," was all I said.

He checked his cup on its way to his lips.

"How do you truly feel?"

"What! Don't condescend me. I told you how it is. You don't trust me?"

He sighed.

"Alma... I trust you with my whole heart under most circumstances, but I fear you are not your entire self right this minute."

Of course I was not... half of me was buried and could not be retrieved. The other half was asking me too many questions, crowding my bed, and kicking me while I slept.

I looked down at my tea, and beside it, that chipped cup that I had filled once again. I wanted to dash it onto the floor.

Now that Autumn and Ashley could not see and hear, it all poured out of me.

"He's an *idiot*," I set my teeth. "I warned him— I warned him! How could he be so careless? How could he do it to us?"

Grant trembled and set his cup on the table.

"You don't mean that!" he cried.

"Don't tell me what's what! You know nothing!" I snarled, my voice becoming increasingly shrill with every breath. "I could not even see him in his final moments! I could not even have that! He took it from me! He took it from the children!"

I collapsed on myself, just like one of those fallen queens in Greek tragedy, but when I gasped and wailed and gagged on my own tongue, it was not so elegant.

"Michael!" I shrieked, as nothing else was in my head. "He's *dead,* Grant, *Michael's dead!*"

Grant cradled my face in his hands and kissed my brow, but he did not look at me. He did not say anything for many minutes, and I continued to screech, too distraught to be self-conscious.

"I killed him," he murmured, and that shook me out of my death throes.

"What do you mean? No, you didn't."

"I did!" he protested. "I shook him so hard. I shook his broken neck. He might have lived if I was gentle with him. I killed him, Alma."

"No! Hush! Don't say it!" I ordered. "There's nothing you could have done differently. It was not survivable. You are not to blame."

Now it was his turn to weep, except he chuckled softly, with a solemn expression, true to a man of theatre.

"You're the only one who knows," I told him gently. "Only you and God."

"What? What do I know?"

"His final moments— his final words. I'm ready to hear them. Do you remember?"

"I don't think I could possibly forget."

"Tell me— tell me, please."

He folded his hands over his quivering mouth and heaved a great big sigh, and then he told me. They were not the same as what Grant wrote. They are our secret that my children may share if they want to— long after I'm dead.

According to Michael, his father's final request was to live with no regrets, and he thought this was an unfair burden to place upon his son when he knew that all men stumble. It caused him to flee from his mistakes when he was young.

"What do you think he regretted?" I asked after a long pause.

Grant furrowed his brow. It seemed this was a difficult question.

"You needn't answer if you can't."

"No, no," he shook his head. "I must."

I allowed him to contemplate it for a little while.

"I think he regretted working so much."

"No! Surely not!"

"More specifically, I believe he regretted being away from home. He actually told me once before— he lamented the time he'd missed, and there wasn't any way to take it back, except to do better."

"He never was good at balance."

"And that is why we got on so well!"

"And why he fell down the stairs."

We had a real laugh for the first time that day.

Well, as you know, our lives went on without him. There was nothing else we could do.

I needed to take immediate action in securing the finances and maintenance of Michael's garden. I

didn't know anything, and required the help of
many people.

To add insult to injury, Dolores Gaye left us
shortly after the funeral, because she had since
found her work "too uncomfortable." I had no
such luxury.

Mary Jones stayed on and helped with the house
as well as she could— not that she really had
much else to do, as an old woman with no
relatives.

The budgeting, events, and construction projects
were written out years in advance, so I had to do
my part in bringing his ideas into fruition. This
man had done (almost) anything I asked of him
for nearly sixteen years. I felt that this was the
least I could do.

I continued to set up all of the charity events he
had planned, but just as the old patrons had to
grow accustomed to Mr. Kelley's absence, they
had to adjust to Michael's untimely departure.
This both drove people away and brought in new
ones. I did not possess his charms, and very
rarely did I touch the animals. Some of them
pitied the poor young widow— some of them did
a little more than pity me. Even while I still wore
black, they promised an enormous sum of money
if only I would entertain an old bachelor, or a
lonely widower whose plight I surely understood.

After all, thirty-six was young enough to remarry… or be a treasured mistress.

I told them exactly what they could do with their money, and never heard from them again.

Autumn was a far better representative. Ashley was too shy and soft-spoken, and frankly far too young.

Aside from the animals, which I never took much part in caring for, I didn't imagine that his occupation was so taxing. I should have considered it, because all he complained about was the paperwork, and I was smothered under its weight. I wished he was there. I wished he'd explained it all to me. I wished I'd asked while I still could. I hired many accountants and solicitors, but I think they just couldn't have explained it as well as he could.

While he was alive, he fought for months to make sure his will was iron-clad, and that the property in its entirety would end up in my hands.

"Well, thanks for *nothing!*" I shouted into the abyss.

I could not sell it. He made me swear that I would not, and that was sensible, because it was secure employment for generations to come. We both understood, anyway, that the children would inherit it when Autumn turned twenty-one.

That was eight years into the future, so I had to manage it as best as I could, and prepare her for it.

When it was too much, I whispered again and again into the darkness of his big study, *'Be not far from me; for trouble is near; for there is none to help.'*

And no-one helped. I had to help myself. After all, you do not help a caterpillar by cutting it from its cocoon.

Michael really loved lepidoptery. Did you know that the caterpillar inside of its cocoon is destroyed in the process of becoming a mature moth? He told me this during our first spring as husband and wife. I like to remind myself of this when it feels as though my entire life is falling apart, which happens quite often.

On some days, I was still angry with him for all that he'd left me to do on my own, but it wasn't his fault.

Well, yes it was, in a way.

I asked him why he was so careless on that day.

He didn't answer.

Once in a while, Grant came and sat with me.

"Awake and working at four o'clock? I see you've truly taken up Michael's sword."

"I wish I could fall upon it," I answered. "I've had six cups of coffee. He never touched it. I cannot wait until I replace Dolores. Where did he find the energy?"

"I believe he fed from the sunlight, as plants do."

"You don't need to keep me company. I can stay awake on my own."

"No, no, I couldn't fall asleep if I tried. It seems I can only sleep the whole day away, or I can't even shut my eyes. Besides, you're wonderful company."

"Mrs. Abernathy?"

"Ah, well… she doesn't really talk to me much anymore."

"Have you had new work placed in front of you?"

"Unfortunately, it's been very slow."

I dearly love Grant, but I must admit, he never reached very far in his acting career. It is reported that he was unreliable, temperamental, and had too many clashes with his employers and colleagues (I've not witnessed this myself, and he was never anything but polite to me and my family).

Moreover, he lost interest in projects and ideas at the drop of a hat. One day, he was writing the greatest story that would ever grace the stage, and the next day, it went into the fire.

Soon, his name was infamous in that sphere, and nobody wanted to work with him, no matter how handsome and dramatic he was. He took whatever work he could, sometimes offering himself as a muse for designers, which he deemed "degrading, but easy money," as he thought standing in one place for several minutes at a time was a waste of his talents. Sometimes, he wrote for the magazines, because as difficult as he was, he was known to be a sharp dresser.

He returned to full-time writing in 1908— wrote Michael's book, and I believe it was the first full novel he ever saw through from start to finish. He did not want his eccentric image to deter people from picking it up, so he used a different name. Since multiple people together (Grant, Michael, and myself) created it, he penned a pseudonym that suggested the three of us, and gave me permission to use it. Once the public had learned of the true author, his reputation was restored somewhat.

But evidently, it too late.

In 1910, Sarah Rivers returned to India. She was hoping to make a name for herself in England, and separated from Grant in order to preserve her own image, as she was associated with his difficult personality. According to him, the straw that broke the camel's back was her portrayal in his book, though I saw nothing offensive about it. She was barely present.

In those days, he came and went from the house as he pleased, mainly to consult me about his new book, and he was a great help with Ashley in particular.

Naturally, he came over late at night to languish over the dissolution of his marriage.

"I wish I'd written her as she truly was—" he growled, spilling his eleventh glass of whiskey on her final letter. "A harpy! A damned beast!"

He grieved for many years! One thing that the two of us had in common were sleepless nights. He often stumbled upon my doorstep late in the evening or early in the morning, regardless of the implications to onlookers, and I poured liquor for him and coffee for me while we took turns bemoaning what we'd lost. Many times, I held him while he wept at my feet. Sometimes he cursed the day of her birth— sometimes he wanted to crawl from Germany to India on his hands and knees and beg her to return to him.

"I never was close to my parents— I thought I had an unbreakable bond with my darling Sita— oh, my Sita, my love!" (That was her real name, that only Grant knew until then). "Even her feet were perfect— she didn't like to wear shoes or stockings in the house; her toes were smooth as polished stones, and her nails were always immaculate."

I cleared my throat and tucked my feet under my skirts.

"What of your closeness with your parents?" I did not want to discuss toes all night.

"I love you!" he blurted out. "You, and Autumn, and Ashley— even George," (that will be Autumn's husband). "You are as precious to me as my own flesh. You are all I have. And Michael… Good God… I miss Michael."

"Even after all this time?"

"Always."

I first loved him because of how he loved Michael and my children, but I soon grew to adore all of him. We have a friendship that transcends associations, as we have more in common than either of us realised.

"What are your dreams?" he asked one day, and I was not sure what he meant.

"My dreams? They can be quite nice, but sometimes they're troubling indeed."

"No, no! I mean, what are your aspirations that you've not yet realised? Anything from mastering needlepoint to going to the moon, I'd like to know them. You've heard me speak endlessly of mine."

I pondered it a moment. I thought of our map— you know the one. "I want to travel. I want to see everything Michael wished he could behold himself, and bring it back here."

"Then you shall travel as far as your heart desires," he leaned towards me over the table. "Come with me, Miss Alma. I will do anything to make it real— we will fulfil Michael's wishes together. We'll bring the little ones."

The "little ones" were bigger than both of us.

He had that manic sort of glint in his eyes again. I think Sita's departure was dredging up old habits of his. Would he see this transaction through?

I sat on it for several weeks and continuously checked our funds, and then I consented.

In six months, we went through Germany, France, Belgium, Italy, and Egypt. I took it all in, wrote it down, drew it up, and kept those memories in a locked trunk. I recorded all of the unique flora and fauna that captivated me. Michael would have been able to navigate better than I, as he knew some of the languages.

And not even a year after we'd returned to England, The War had begun. That gave Grant more to write about, at least.

But then he asked again, as soon as we returned home.

"Tell me again— what are your dreams?"

"I've already told you! What were we doing, running all over the continent?"

"I think you told me Michael's. What are yours?"

"What game are you trying to play?"

"No games, Alma… you have given of yourself for so long… I don't think that is a bad thing. But you have paid your dues to Michael. What do *you* want?"

"I have everything that I want."

But the truth was, I didn't know. I certainly felt content, but the truth was, I'd spent most of my life attached to somebody else and their wishes. I don't regret it, but I cannot deny that I'd buried a lot of myself under that sense of duty. Soon, my children would leave home, and I would have no choice but to serve myself.

A week later, I started simple.

"I've never been to a hairdresser before. I want to get my hair made up," I decided.

I did it by myself, and I did it on the other side of the Island, where nobody knew me. Instead of *Michael Bennett's widow,* I was simply Alma, and wore that title for a little while. The former was a title I wore with honour and privilege, but the latter was an exciting clean slate that I wore for just a few days.

"Who are you getting preened so nicely for?" the hairdresser asked.

"Myself," I answered.

I got a trim, and intricately arranged oiled ringlets that I wore for a week. I'd not gone anywhere on my own in a very long time, so I stayed in the city until the curls fell out.

Thus began the process of rebuilding myself once more.

I went back to London to see what had changed: very little. There were motorcars on the streets here and there, but the pavement was not much cleaner for it. I walked past my old dwelling and gazed at it from afar. Three children ran out. I ached to know the fate of my former inmates. Since I could not, I spoke to the children.

"Pardon me!" I called to them, and they turned. "Who lives with you?"

"We live with Grandmother Rose!" the smallest little girl answered. "And Mama, and Uncle Danny, and Aunt Nora, and our cat—"

"Margaret!" the tallest girl pulled at her tattered coat. "Stop talking to that old lady! We can't be late for school again!"

Old? I was only forty-five! It was perhaps my old-fashioned attire that aged me.

I walked through all of London that I felt safe venturing into by myself. Nobody questioned me or knew my face. I went to Mrs. Green's inn. She was not there anymore, but the coffee was better. Men did not bother me.

Inwardly, I was glad when I gave my name to people, and they did not know me. Being recognised was exhausting.

Michael held onto modest local fame in his life: more as a novelty than an educator, much to his dismay. Even when the strange circumstances around his sudden death made him a household name, nothing really changed. It brought a great deal of traffic to the zoological garden, but these guests had no interest in the animals. Folks began to read about his past and his associations, and speculations on what they believed to have truly happened circulated as fast and steady as blood in a warm body. People approached me and my family while we walked down the street or enjoyed our coffee in a salon, playing the part of friendly strangers meeting by chance as they tried to subtly pry into our lives.

Most fantastical of all was the rumour that Grant Abernathy had murdered him, and that was not helped by his one drunken confession to the fictitious crime at half past three o'clock on a Friday morning. The authorities paid no mind to it, and escorted him home.

This only brought more attention to the case. Completely random and unknown men sent anonymous letters claiming to have slain him; occasionally these accounts included declarations of love to me or my daughter.

And that is all why Autumn asked for Grant to write about him: because she wanted England to know that her Daddy was "a real person, one of the greatest, not some ghostly folk character."

As you surely know, human beings cannot be pleased. Michael's name was elevated, and so were ours, but some dragged Autumn's through the muck. Her vibrant personality, taste for high fashion, and presence in local magazines, aided by Grant, caused people to accuse her of using his death for her own status.

She said, "I would burn every scrap of paper with my name and my likeness printed on it if I could have my Daddy back," and that was that.

The little princess grew big and powerful, and she now stomps around in rubber boots and trousers just like the young men do, but she also likes to wear lipstick and colour her brows. She has her Daddy's presence about her, and men twenty years her senior obey her.

She is every bit Michael's little girl even now, but Ashley is uncanny. Everybody else says that he more closely resembles me, but I think he only got my colouring laid upon his father's shape. You would only have to change the nose and the teeth.

Many people meeting him as an adult comment that they imagined he would be taller, but he is about five feet and ten inches tall, only small compared to Michael, since almost everyone is. Reluctantly, I allowed him to take charge of Wolf when he was eight years old, and the boy and his dog were inseparable for the last six years of his life. Since then, Ashley has not had any new pets, as he began travelling quite a bit. He was not as involved with the garden as Autumn and George, and he had taken to learning how to fly when he was seventeen.

Autumn's husband, George Feldman, was born on January 4, 1893, a mere four months apart from her. He first came to us in 1913 as a recruit in the zoological garden, and he was a piece of work—stubborn as a mule. Ashley liked him immediately.

And George did like Ashley, but my, he took such a shine to Autumn, right away. He didn't say it, but we knew. He was talking to Ashley, and as he turned to look behind him when he heard clopping hooves, he saw Autumn passing on her horse.

"Oh, that is my sister!" Ashley nodded to her, but the fool had already wandered off, as if possessed. He followed close behind, trying to catch a second glance at her face. Ashley and I watched with amusement and a little bit of fear and held our breath. Autumn's horse Cherry did not startle easily, but he was not used to being touched from behind and did not recognise that voice.

And George yelled out, "Hallo there, Madam!" and struck his flank.

Cherry nearly threw her off. George's attempts to soothe him were fruitless, maybe even detrimental, and he then stared in shock as Autumn struggled to keep control.

Perhaps we should have stopped him, but we honestly did not think he would try something so stupid.

She turned with fists clenched, and demanded to know the "idiot who tried to kill" her.

"That would be me, dear lady," he meekly stepped forward, with his hat in his hands.

Her face softened immediately, but after apologising profusely, he ran off. She chased him down on Cherry, determined to speak to him.

From then on, they had their own little thing going for about five years, which is a very long courtship if you ask me. I'd asked him numerous times when he would propose to her, as he clearly meant to marry her. He always told me that he couldn't think of how to do it.

She proposed to him! It was quite a spectacle—seeing her in trousers and wellingtons, all covered in mud, sleeves rolled up showing her muscular arms, and he looked at her as though she was the prettiest little flower he'd ever picked.

They were betrothed for eight months, but everything was placed on hold when Ashley went to war.

He was initially tempted to volunteer, but I talked him out of it, because I am selfish and simply would not tolerate losing one more child. I had struggled many years to procure just two living, after all. Moreover, having a repentant military father, and being a bit of a contrarian, I was more resistant to propaganda than most.

Ashley was not first pick to be drafted when he came of age in 1916, as he is my only son. George Feldman was exempt due to having flat

feet and an abnormal spine, but as soon as he
applied for a marriage licence as a foreigner, he
was listed as family, and Ashley was targeted.

They knew that he had flown aeroplanes before,
so they made him a pilot with hardly any training.

I remained so very wickedly selfish. As the death
tolls continued to rise, I found myself
praying, *'God, not my son, not MY son,'* and I
believed nobody was as earnest as I was.

Autumn took the news even worse than I did,
huffing and snarling, and stamping her feet at her
grown age.

"I'm the firstborn, *I am!*" she insisted, tossing
around papers as fat, juicy raindrop tears poured
down her face. "I'm not going to outlive both of
them, *I won't!*"

I didn't have the heart to tell her that Michael had
outlived every last one of his siblings…

She volunteered as an ambulance driver, half
hoping and half dreading that she would intercept
him.

That meant that I spent much of the time alone
with George. I harboured some resentment
towards him for applying for a marriage license

before the war ended, but we can laugh about it now.

God brought my boy home after only five months, after he had a brush with death when an engine exploded. The impact had broken three ribs, and shrapnel narrowly missed his heart. He spent two months in a hospital, temporarily blinded by flash burns. The war would officially end soon after.

Autumn and George married on October 14, 1918, on the sunniest of afternoons. In the midst of war and ruin, we had peace and unity upon us— it almost seemed undeserved. Ashley gave her away, and Grant escorted me to my seat and sat at my left side. In the chair to my right, there was a solitary candle. Her "something old" was one of her father's watches; her "something borrowed," was a set of my favourite pins. Her stockings were blue, as a part of her absurd humour. The rest was "new."

She made herself up so elegantly, and of course, her dress was yellow. It was specially hand-sewn by the two of us, and some of the Lavignes. She put daisies and big dandelions in her hair, and donned dazzling lavender kids. Instead of a standard veil, a golden lace cape fluttered behind her, sweeping over the floor. And underneath it all, I catch a glimpse of those muddy boots!

Four ladies prepared the reception breakfast
George proposed a toast to Autumn's "lovely"
mother, and her father that he never got to meet.

Currently, they live with Hannah Lavigne. The
last of her brood finally moved away, and she was
eager to fill her empty nest with her darling pet
Autumn; it's likely that she's still holding onto her
hopes of making her a real lady.

Autumn is not as involved with the garden as she
used to be. She approached me and sheepishly
explained that she would be moving back to the
home she was born in and would pour most of her
time into her marriage and her children. I don't
know why she was so meek with this delivery. I
was not injured in the slightest; really, I was quite
pleased, and I'd hate for her to feel obligated to
stay. My only condition was that she wrote me
every week and visited frequently, and she does
so to this day.

Ashley went straight back to work in the garden,
but he has been really struggling ever since his
return. He does not like the sound of loud
machinery, and I think that losing Autumn as a
business partner causes him some stress. He has
recently met an American girl that he writes
letters to, and I hope things get better for him.

As for me, I feed these old cats, draw some of the
things I see outside, and I wash Ashley's muddy

clothes. He, too, has the habit of bringing me rocks. In the morning, he spends some time in the kitchen with me and learns how to cook, and we have coffee out back before he leaves for work. I tease him about bringing a woman home so that I can finally have my mornings to myself, but secretly, I like that he's here.

Though he really does need a wife eventually. He is almost twenty-three, and I will soon be fifty-five, and am slowing down. I do not want to be too frail to run around with all of my grandchildren. He does not go out as much as he used to, saying he doesn't like all of the noise in town, but lately, he has been writing a lot of letters ever since he took a trip with George and Autumn.

Having so much spare time to myself for the first time in almost thirty years, I do all of the little art pieces I had been putting out of sight for so long. I had been saving cut hair all this time, and I did meticulous work to make a small cameo of it. My hair, Michael's, and that of my two eldest (Lilly only had white fuzz) twined lightest to darkest make a beautiful nature scene. Autumn knows that she will have to allow me a few strands from her children's heads.

Michael, Autumn brought us a grandson in December of 1919. Ashley was home by then. I held him for you, because I know you are holding

Lillian in heaven, and I took him into the gardens, and let the sun shine on his little face.

Papa died in early 1920. After an apoplectic attack which greatly diminished his strength, he lived with a caretaker for the last three years of his life. The last I saw him, I placed his great grandson in his arms. They were so weak, I had to hold them up, and his eyes were so bleary that he could just barely decipher shapes and colours.

"He's wonderful," was all he had the strength to say.

I think he held out just long enough to meet him.

Mama attended his funeral, "for me and the children," of course, but under her veil, I saw that her features trembled.

I saw James. He wished me well and spoke to Autumn, Ashley, and George. I wept at the sight of it, but at least I no longer wished for a better youth— only because I cannot be sure how things would turn out if not for my adversity.

Loss is simply a life-long journey. Some days will be easier than others. Some days, maybe even years later, it will hit you with the force of a train, and you will be picking up pieces of yourself once again.

I used to think all the time of the things Michael would never have. He'd never send the children to college. He'd never see Ashley become a pilot or serve in the war. He'd never meet Autumn's love and approve him personally, nor would he put the Bennett family bridal jewellery on her himself and walk her down the aisle. He'd never hold his grandchildren— maybe even great grandchildren. He wouldn't pass gently in his sleep on a quiet Saturday morning. He wouldn't travel the world just as he wanted to. It would never be his.

At least, that was how I used to think, but they are ours— the two of us planted and cultivated that garden together, and it is his even in death, because though he took so much of me when he left, he left behind just as much of himself, and we are one whole. I went from scorning God for taking him so soon to thanking him for giving him to us for as long as we had him.

It is easy in the moments of raw and profound agony to dress our wounds in dirty rags, shouting, "This is too cruel for me to endure! Why must somebody like this be taken from me so soon?" However, the cleansing salve we seek is gratitude, else our sores fester and we waste away.

After all, it is not often that you meet that sort of person, and for us to be so entwined was by the grace of God.

And if I knew that we would only have him for a fleeting moment, that my children would spend more of their lives without a father than with one, would I have chosen him again?

Every time.

I would come to my young self in my dreams and say, "Indeed, the times ahead, they are good. They are better than we had ever dreamed before."

You don't sit at a grave to feel somebody's presence. The body is not what is left of him. I feel his presence when I walk alone through the gardens— everything he built with his hands, and the weathering of his old shoes. He is in the children's grins when they laugh so hard that they show all of their teeth. They are so much of him, and still so much of themselves.

I know that the Great War saw many young widows and bereaved mothers joining me in my special hell, more than I can comprehend. I know that they are numerous, and if you are among my readers, I see you, and my heart bleeds for you.

I believe I have been blessed in ways that few people will experience. However my time will end, be it swift upon me or a long while coming, it is an ending to a full, rich life. I want the same for you.

Thank you, dearest reader, for keeping me company.

Alma Temperance Bennett